THE BATTLE OF CARHAM

By

H A CULLEY

Book two about the Earls of Northumbria

Published by

Orchard House Publishing

First Kindle Edition 2019

This novel is a work of fiction. The names, characters and events portrayed in it, which sticking as closely to the recorded history of the time and featuring a number of historical figures, are largely the product of the author's imagination.

TABLE OF CONTENTS

Author's Note

This book is set in a period when Northumbria encompassed a large part of Northern England. In addition to today's Northumberland, Bernicia covered the Borders Region and Lothian in Scotland as well as County Durham, Tyne and Wear and Cleveland in England. Deira, the southern part of Northumbria, corresponded roughly to the three counties that make up modern Yorkshire.

In the last book of the series '*The Kings of Northumbria*' I said in the historical note that Uhtred the Bold died at the Battle of Carham and, indeed, several sources reflect this account of his death. However, further research on my part leads me to believe that Uhtred was killed two years before the battle by Thurbrand the Hold, possibly on the orders of King Cnut (also spelt Canute). As a blood feud evidently followed his murder this makes it the more likely of the two versions of Uhtred's death.

In past books about the Anglo-Saxon period I have used the ancient names for places, where known, to add authenticity to the story. However several reviewers have said that this is confusing, especially when the reader has also had to cope with the unfamiliar names of the characters. I have therefore used the modern names for places with two notable exceptions. I have retained the Anglo-Saxon name for Bamburgh – Bebbanburg - as that will be more familiar to readers who like this period, and I have used the Saxon name for what is now Yorkshire - Deira. As this would have been divided up into a number of administrative shires at this time, to call it Yorkshire would be confusing.

I have also used Aldred instead of Ealdred for Uhtred's eldest son. This is to save confusion when so many characters have names beginning Ea.

I have used the term knights for the Norman mounted warriors but the word itself first appeared in common usage in the late eleventh century. It derives from the German knecht, meaning servant, bondsman or vassal and cniht meaning boy or servant in Old English. Gradually the meaning changed to household retainer and then to military follower of a king or lord.

I felt it would be wrong to use the word for Aldred's mounted warriors and the Anglo-Saxons didn't have knights. I have therefore opted for the word 'milites' which is a Latin term and preceded knight as the term for a horse warrior.

The idea of using heavy cavalry had been introduced into Europe by Charlemagne in the eight century. The French and the Normans developed the concept until these mounted warriors became minor nobility, partially because only the upper class could afford the horses, armour, weapons and servants required to maintain themselves as milites.

Heavy cavalrymen needed attendants and the Franks, later the French and the Normans, employed boys and youths of noble birth in this role. At the same time they learned to become mounted warriors themselves. The Medieval term squire derives from the French word escuier, which derives from the Latin scutifer (shield bearer). An alternative word in Latin was armiger (armour bearer) and this is the term I have opted to use.

At the time that this novel begins Northumbria, or what remained of the ancient northern kingdom, was divided into two; Deira in the south centred on York; and Bernicia between the River Tees and the Firth of Forth. Although absorbed by Bernicia in the seventh century, the northern part of Bernicia between the River Tweed and the Firth of Forth was still known as Lothian.

The inhabitants of Lothian were mainly descended from the Goddodin, a tribe of Britons who had more in common with the Welsh and the people of Strathclyde than they did with their conquerors – the Angles from Bernicia. Over the centuries three peoples – the Picts, the Scots of Dalraida and eventually the Britons of Strathclyde –united to become the Kingdom of Alba. However, again to save confusion, I have used the modern name of Scotland and the Scots for the inhabitants.

Although the first King of the English, Æthelstan, had subjugated the Danes of Yorvik – the Danish name for York – and brought them under his rule, they had retained their Viking identity and their relationship with a king who lived in Wessex was a fragile one. Since Æthelstan's time the differences between the Danes and the Angles – the occupants of Deira before the time of the Danelaw – had been somewhat eroded by the passing of the years, inter-marriage and conversion to Christianity; nevertheless Deira stood out as a largely Danish ghetto in the midst of an Anglo-Saxon England. Although people of Danish descent lived in other parts of England as well, they were in the minority.

Since the demise of Northumbria as a separate kingdom it had been split in two, the Danes ruling the former Saxon Kingdom of Deira, centred on York, in the south and the hereditary lords of Bebbanburg governing Bernicia (including Lothian) in the north. However, Lothian became disputed territory between Scotland and England in the second half of the tenth and early eleventh centuries. Views are mixed on whether the Battle of Carham was the decisive battle that sealed the fate of Lothian. Some maintain that it was de facto a part of Scotland before that, but certainly the region was never claimed by England after that event.

Æthelred (King of the English from 978 to 1013 and again from 1014 until his death in 1016) had re-united Northumbria under Earl Uhtred the Bold but, shortly after Cnut invaded England, Uhtred was ambushed and killed. Once more Northumbria was split in two. Uhtred was succeeded in Bernicia by his brother Eadwulf Cudel and the Norwegian, Erik of Hlathir, became Earl of York (i.e. Deira). It isn't clear whether Erik was in fact Earl of Northumbria with Eadwulf as his junior or whether there were two quite distinct earldoms.

List of Earls of Northumbria & Bernicia

Northumbria

Uhtred the Bold	1006 - 1016
Erik Håkonsson	1016 – 1023
Siward Bjornsson	1023(?) – 1055
Tostig Godwinson	1055 – 1065
Morcar	1065 – 1066
Copsi	1066
Osulf	1067
Gospatric	1067 – 1068
Robert de Comines	1068 – 1069 *[Norman]*
Gospatric (restored)	1070 -1072
Waltheof	1072 – 1075 *[last Anglo-Saxon earl]*

Bernicia

Eadwulf Cudel	1016 – 1020
Aldred	1020 – 1038
Eadulf	1038 – 1041
Under Northumbria	*1041 – 1065*
Osulf	1065 – 1067
Under Northumbria	*1067 onwards*

NOTE: Names in bold are members of the Bebbanburg dynasty

List of Characters

In alphabetical order, historical characters are shown in bold:

Ælfflæd - Uhtred's posthumous daughter, later wife of Sigurd, Earl of Northumbria

Ælfgifu – Daughter of King Æthelred and Emma of Normandy, Uhtred's third wife

Aldhun – Bishop of Durham

Aldred – Uhtred's eldest son

Aodghan – Eadwulf's body servant and Sigfreda's lover

Beda – Elder son of Leofwine, Ealdorman of Durham

Bjorn – A Danish noble, father of Siward who was later Earl of Northumbria

Ceadda – Captain of Aldred's warriors

Ceolfrith – Son of Ulfric, Thane of Norham

Cnut – King of England, later also King of Denmark and Norway

Colby – One of Aldred's scouts

Eadulf – Uhtred's second son

Eadwulf – Earl of Bernicia, nicknamed Cudel (cuttlefish – an invertebrate) because he lacked backbone

Ealdgyth – Uhtred's elder daughter, later married Maldred of Dunbar, brother of King Duncan of Scotland

Edgar – An agent in Findlay's service

Edith – Aldred's daughter

Emma – His sister. Former wife of Æthelred, King of England who died in 1016; later Cnut's queen

Erik Håkonsson – Earl of Northumbria

Findlay mac Ruairi - Mormaer of Moray

Fiske – A Norse boy, body servant to Eadulf

Gillecomgan - Máel Coluim's younger brother, who succeeded him as mormaer

Gosric - Ealdorman of Selkirkshire in Lothian

Gunwald – Illegitimate son of Cnut; fostered by Bjorn

Gytha – Cnut's sister; married to Erik Håkonsson

Hacca – Ealdorman of Edinburgh, later Earl of Lothian

Iuwine – Ealdorman of Berwickshire in Lothian

Kætilbiǫrn – A wealthy goldsmith in York

Kjetil and Hakon – Captured Norse ship's boys, later warriors in Aldred's warband

Leofwine –Ealdorman of Durham

Macbeth – His son, later King of Scots

Máel Coluim mac Máel Brigti – Findlay of Moray's nephew, later Mormaer of Moray

Malcolm - Nicknamed Forranach (the destroyer), King of Scots

Oeric – The son of a tenant farmer who later became one of Aldred's warband

Osric – A novice at Melrose Monastery

Owain ap Dyfnwal – Nicknamed the Bald, King of Strathclyde

Regnwald – One of King Cnut's senior housecarls

Richard - Duke of Normandy

Sigfrida – Aldred's half-sister and Eadwulf's wife

Synne – A street urchin in York, later Aldred's wife

Thurbrand – A wealthy Danish Jarl who conspired with Eadwulf to kill Uhtred

Uuen – Body servant to Aldred

Wictred – One of Aldred's warriors

Wulfstan Lupus – Archbishop of York and Bishop of Worcester

Prologue

April 1000 to June 1003

Uuen stood up to stretch his aching back. He was eight years old and, along with the other children in the village, he was busy picking weeds from the fields of oats and barley. He looked around him, at the cold blue of the sea below the hillside where he was working, at the other children, and then back towards the Pictish settlement which was home.

Suddenly he stiffened in alarm. Three Norse longships had appeared over the horizon from the north and were rowing towards the beach below where he stood.

'Vikings!' he yelled to warn the others and then he was off, sprinting towards the gates in the palisade that surrounded the village to warn his mother.

As he sprinted through the gates he ran into the headman, a man called Durst, coming the other way to see what all the shouting was about. He grabbed Uuen by the collar of his filthy flea ridden homespun tunic and brought his face close to the boy's.

'What's all this shouting about? Why have you stopped work in the fields? You'd better have a good excuse…'

'Vikings, Durst, three longships heading for the beach down there.'

Durst stood there, indecisive for a moment. He was tempted to go and see if Uuen was telling the truth. If he was, he needed to organise the men to defend the settlement and get the women and children away into the low hills to the south. On the other hand he didn't trust small children to tell the truth. This could be a ploy to make him look stupid. If so, it wouldn't be the first time.

Uuen had never forgiven Durst for killing his father, the previous headman, and he tried to undermine him whenever he could. Durst had beaten the boy nearly to death the last time and it had taken him months to recover. However, judging by the desperate look in Uuen's eyes, Durst thought that he was telling the truth this time. It was confirmed when he saw that all the others who'd been weeding were running towards him. He let go of Uuen's tunic.

'Go and spread the word for the men to arm themselves and for the women and children to head into the hills. You know the drill.'

Uuen nodded and ran through the jumble of huts yelling his message on his way to the hovel where he lived with his mother, three brothers and two sisters. His brothers were all older than him and they grabbed their weapons and headed for the gates, including the youngest, Brac, who was only just twelve. Uuen was about to join them but his mother hustled him and his sisters out of the hut and they headed for the small gate in the southern section of the palisade. However, the boy did manage to grab a hunting spear on his way out.

Once out in the open he led his family along a stream bed which concealed them from view until he judged that they were safe. Other families trailed along behind them and Uuen felt important as if he was the leader now. There were other boys his age and a little older behind him but he ignored that. An hour later they reached the source of the stream and the ground became very boggy.

He led everyone up onto the higher ground. From there he could look back towards the settlement in the distance. He cursed in fury as he saw the black smoke rising into the still air. The Vikings must have captured the place, pillaged it and were now burning it to the ground. He worried that his three brothers were either dead or captives.

He had foolishly assumed that, as they were now a good three miles away, they would be safe, but, as he turned back with tears in his eyes to continue on his way to the valley where they kept the livestock, safe from thieves and raiders, he saw a group of men coming over the moorland towards him.

Vikings! They had a captive with them and Uuen realised with shame that it was his brother, Brac. He must be leading them to the hidden valley. As they hadn't had to bother about keeping out of sight, they had reached the same place in half the time. He was furious with Brac for betraying his people and, without conscious thought, he drew back his arm and threw his hunting spear as hard as he could towards his brother.

It was a long shot – almost fifty yards – but anger lent him strength. The spear flew up in a curve and came down to hit Brac. Uuen was barely conscious of his mother screaming 'no' at him as Brac fell backwards and lay still with the spear sticking up from the centre of his chest.

The Vikings stopped for an instant, then started to move towards the group of women and children emerging from the stream bed. The rest of the Picts ran away from the Vikings but Uuen stood rooted to the spot. He'd been livid with Brac for his treachery, but he'd never meant to kill him. Now he was filled with remorse. As the Vikings came towards him he found he didn't care enough to try and run; he waited there, head hanging in shame, for them to reach him and kill him.

But they didn't. The Norse leader was Sigurd the Stout, Jarl of Orkney, and he had been impressed by Uuen's throw. Instead of slitting the boy's throat he decided to keep him as a thrall.

Sigurd had had enough of traipsing over the rough moorland for one day and so he let his men do the chasing whilst he headed back to his ships, leading Uuen by a rope halter around his neck.

Uuen later learned that the Vikings, weighed down by their heavy byrnies - a short sleeved coat made of chain mail which came down to the upper thigh - had only managed to capture a few of the older women and younger children. The rest, including his own family, had escaped. The old women were raped and killed and the children joined Uuen in the bottom of the longships to be taken back to Orkney.

ϮϮϮ

Three years later Uuen was called from his usual work looking after Sigurd's pigs by one of the jarl's sons and taken to the hall where he was stripped of all his clothes. The blacksmith came and removed the iron collar from around his neck – the mark of a thrall – and he wondered if he was being set free.

Some attempt was made to clean him up but he fought so violently with the women who tried to give him a bath that they settled for washing him with a wet cloth as best they could. The new clothes he was given were finer than anything the boy had ever seen and he found wearing shoes strange after spending most of his life going barefoot, even in winter.

'You are to play a role soon,' Sigurd told him. 'You are to pretend to be my son. Do you understand?'

Uuen didn't but he was scared of Sigurd so he nodded. During his time as a thrall he had learned to speak Norse more or less fluently, but with a slight accent. The jarl didn't think it mattered because the man he was trying to fool wouldn't know any different. The man's Norse was a lot worse than the boy's.

Apart from the time when he'd been brought to Thurso as a captive, tied up in the bilges of a longship, Uuen had never spent any time at sea. This time it was quite different. He was allowed to go where he wanted on the ship, provided he didn't get in the way. He enjoyed looking at the passing scenery a couple of miles away as they sailed down the coast and he relished the movement of the longship as it powered through the waves. The chafe marks left by the iron collar had healed and now only a few red marks betrayed the fact that he was a thrall.

The next morning Sigurd's longship, together with the rest of the fleet, sailed into a shallow bay and they beached the ships. Uuen couldn't see any signs of habitation but the jarl and his men headed inland, leaving the shipmaster and three ship's boys to guard him. They went and sat on the beach with the boys from the other longships, talking and laughing together, whilst the ship masters sat separately playing some gambling game. One of the men yelled across at the boys and three reluctantly left the group and walked up to the top of the dunes overlooking the beach to keep a lookout.

Uuen didn't know what to do. He was the same age as the youngest of the Norse boys but he was a Pict and thrall, so they treated him with contempt. He wandered off down the beach and everyone continued to ignore him. After he'd gone a few hundred yards he looked back but no one was watching him. He got excited when he realised that he might be able to make a run for it and find his own people.

Just at that moment one of the Norse boys noticed that he had wandered off. He stood up and yelled something at Uuen. He was too far away to make out what the boy was saying but he had a pretty good idea that he was telling him to get back to the ships.

He glanced up at the dunes that lined the beach, trying to reach a decision. He wasn't a fool and he realised that, if there were any Picts living nearby the Norse Vikings would have meted out same treatment to them as they had done to his village. Even if he had managed to evade the inevitable pursuit and find some of his own people, they would probably have only taken him in as a slave, in which case he would be no better off than he was now. Besides he was intrigued by his new clothes, his release from the thrall's collar and his presence on this raid.

He turned just as several boys started to walk towards him and headed back in their direction. The oldest boy cuffed him around the head when he reached them and thrust his dagger in Uuen's face.

'Wander off like that again and I'll cut off your tiny little balls, you hear me, pig boy?'

'I hear you,' Uuen mumbled contritely, but inside he yearned to take the other boy's dagger and slit his throat with it.

He went and sat on the sand away from the two groups of Vikings and waited for the raiders to come back with their loot and captives.

There wasn't much of either, which had put Sigurd in a bad mood. The settlement they'd pillaged had been poor and the people, including the women and the boys, had put up a fierce fight. He'd lost a dozen men and had killed everyone except for four young girls in revenge, even the babies and infants.

That night the four girls, the eldest of whom couldn't have been more than thirteen, were raped repeatedly by the drunken Vikings and in the morning their dead, ravaged bodies were left on the beach for the seagulls to feast on. Uuen was sick over the side as they sailed away, and it wasn't due to the motion of the sea.

'It's a waste of time raiding these Scots villages,' the eldest of the jarl's sons said to his father once the sail was hoisted and the oars shipped. 'We lost a dozen men and for what? A handful of copper coins, a ham and a night of pleasure.'

'I gave my oath that I wouldn't kill or take captives from the Northumbrian places we raid.'

'Who's to know? Just say that they're Scots. We need more thralls and the men won't be happy if we don't take some young girls back with us.'

His father nodded.

'Very well, we'll sail straight down to Northumbria and start raiding the places that Uhtred has told us about.'

†††

After a month of raiding the Vikings left the ships once more, but this time they took Uuen with them. By now the longships were full of plunder and captives. The fact that some of the places raided were monasteries or churches didn't seem to bother the Norsemen, despite the fact that they were all supposed to be Christians. But then Uuen was a Christian too and that hadn't helped him. He was pleased, however, that Sigurd had given him a small silver crucifix, taken from their plunder, to wear around his neck.

All signs of the marks left by the thrall's collar had now disappeared and he almost felt like a free man as he walked side by side with Sigurd, the jarl's hand on his shoulder, towards the long line of warriors standing facing them.

A few men on horseback rode forward from the shield wall facing the Vikings and Sigurd and Uuen walked to meet them, followed by Sigurd's sons and several of his chieftains.

'I'm Uhtred, son of Waltheof, Earl of Bernicia. I represent the people of Deira, many of whom you have pillaged and made captive. Who are you?' the leader of the horsemen asked in Norse.

'Sigurd, Jarl of the Orkneys, the Shetlands, Caithness, Sunderland and the Scottish Isles. I go where I like and take plunder from those weaker than me. How are you going to stop me? With that rabble? Most scratch in the dirt for a living and have no more idea of how to fight than my son here has about how to read Latin.'

The other man looked at Uuen dubiously. This lad was wearing a fine blue woollen tunic with silver embroidery at the hems and the neck but it was too large for him, his face was filthy and his hair was lank and matted. Norsemen and Danes were much more diligent about personal hygiene than this boy. Their hair, in particular, was kept clean and well groomed. Uhtred guessed that this boy was a thrall who had been dressed up to look the part.

Uhtred stared at the boy, who refused to meet his eye, looking down as if ashamed at the deception he had been forced to take part in. Any Norse boy, especially the son of a man as powerful as Sigurd, would have stared back with defiance, and like as not hatred.

Another horseman, a thane called Ulfric, rode up to speak to Uhtred and said loudly in English, a language that luckily none of the Norsemen understood.

'That boy is no more Sigurd's child than I am a sheep's dropping.'

'I know; but if I challenge him he'll have no option but to fight. I want to end this without bloodshed, if I can.'

Ulfric smelt a rat. Uhtred hadn't said that with conviction. Ulfric didn't know exactly what was going on but he guessed that this was all a charade. Uhtred dismounted and walked forward to the edge of the river where he and Sigurd wouldn't have to shout at each other. Sigurd came to meet him, waving his men back but bringing the boy with him.

'If you let us depart in peace with our plunder then I swear not to harm your lands further. I'll leave my son with you as hostage. Reject my terms and you'll all die.'

'You'll swear by your gods to keep faith?'

'I'm a Christian, not a pagan,' Sigurd replied, affronted. 'I'll swear on the Holy Bible.'

'Very well. One of my men will ride over and collect your son, then the Archbishop of York will come across to you to administer the oath. But first you have to release all the captives you've taken.'

'They are all Scots,' Sigurd said blandly.

Uhtred doubted that very much. Some might be as no doubt the Vikings had done a little raiding on their way south along the coast, but most would be from Deira. However, Uhtred decided that it would be foolish to openly call him a liar.

'Nevertheless you will release them. I have a treaty with the King of Scots.'

That gave Sigurd pause for thought. He might decide to defy Uhtred, but Kenneth was trying to recover Caithness and Sunderland. If the armies of Northumbria went north to help him it was probable that together they could defeat the Norsemen. However, taking the Northumbrians all the way up to northern tip of Britain was as likely as snow on a hot day in August. The fyrd, in particular, wouldn't would want to leave their homes to fight so far away. Nevertheless, Sigurd decided that he couldn't be certain of that.

'Very well, we will release them and send them across to you. Let's get on with this.'

And it was as simple as that. Although the banks were slippery, horses managed to climb the soft mud, albeit with difficulty. Ulfric rode across with Archbishop Wulfstan and he administered the oath, then they returned with Sigurd's pretend son on the back of Ulfric's horse. The boy smelled like a latrine, which confirmed his suspicion that the boy was no Norse princeling.

The captives were released and Sigurd and his men departed without another word being said. Uhtred heard later that he had raided the coast north of the Forth and no doubt replenished their supply of thralls to make up for those he had been forced to leave behind.

Ulfric was puzzled by the whole business. Only later did Uhtred confess that he and Sigurd had conspired to bring about the confrontation between them. Ulfric could understand the reason for the subterfuge. The Danes and Anglo-Saxons of Deira, the southern half of Northumbria, had been at each other's throats following the massacre in Wessex the previous year. Uhtred's ploy had succeeded in uniting them to face a common enemy in the shape of the Norsemen. It had been an extremely risky ploy but it had worked.

Uuen fought like a tiger when Uhtred's men stripped him and washed his filthy body and hair in the River Ouse, but he was allowed to keep his thick woollen tunic and leggings, rich though they were and far too good for a servant. He was grateful for that and, when Uhtred gave him a choice: become a swineherd again or serve the earl as his body servant, the boy had the sense to choose the latter.

Chapter One – Flight to Normandy

April 1017

Aldred, Uhtred's eldest son, stood on the walkway behind the palisade that surrounded the fortress of Bebbanburg and gloomily watched the waves crash onto the rocks below him. The overcast sky, which gave the North Sea its leaden appearance, echoed his mood. Grief for his father's untimely death was matched by a fierce desire for revenge on the assassins - Thurbrand, a Danish noble and favourite of King Cnut, and his uncle, Eadwulf. However, another emotion troubled the twenty year old: fear.

When Uuen, his father's body servant, and Wictred, the only survivor of Utred's warband, had returned to Bebbanburg to tell Aldred and his step-mother, Ælfgifu, about the ambush and death of Uhtred, both had assumed that Cnut would allow Aldred to inherit Uhtred's lands and his earldom of Northumbria. However, word soon reached them that the Dane Erik Håkonsson was to become the new Earl of Northumbria.

Aldred had remained quietly at Bebbanburg and had become the de facto lord of Bernicia, that part of Northumbria north of the River Tyne, and had been accepted by the ealdormen and thanes of the region. Erik had made no move to exert his authority north of the Tyne and Aldred was lulled into a false sense of security, but under the surface he worried about his uncertain status.

His concern proved well-founded. It was nearly a year after his father's death that he heard that Cnut had appointed Eadwulf as Earl of Bernicia and lord of Bebbanburg. He was devastated.

'Why has Cnut waited so long to reward a man guilty of fratricide,' he asked Ælfgifu bitterly.

The two of them were seated at the high table with his half-brother, the nine year old Eadulf. The boy was scared by Aldred's vehemence and regarded him warily. He had never seen him so angry.

'I suspect that Cnut was afraid of Uhtred's power in the north,' she explained calmly. 'Don't forget that his position on the throne was precarious a year ago. I've no doubt that he wanted my husband dead but he couldn't afford to be seen as responsible.'

'So the Danish cur used Thurbrand and Eadwulf to do the dirty deed for him.'

'Be careful what you say, Aldred, even here in your own hall.'

'Why? What more can Cnut do to us?'

'If he heard what you just said he could accuse you of treason and execute not just you, but your family as well.'

That sobered Aldred up somewhat. In addition to Eadulf, he had two sisters; the children of Uhtred and Ælfgifu. Ealdgyth was now two and Ælfflaed was seven months old, having been born after Uhtred's death.

Ceadda, the captain of Aldred's housecarls, who was also sitting at the high table, spoke for the first time.

'It might be prudent to send out scouts, lord. We don't want to be caught here unawares when Eadwulf arrives.'

'We can hold this fortress against the king himself if necessary,' Eadulf boasted before his brother could reply.

'That may be true,' Aldred said thoughtfully, 'but what does that achieve. I need to think about our options.'

Aldred didn't have long for contemplation. Two days later one of the scouts rode in to say that Eadwulf and sixty men were about two days march away.

'We must leave, Aldred,' Ælfgifu insisted.

'Leave? Yes, but where for?'

'Normandy. My family is there as the guests of my uncle, Duke Richard.'

Emma, Ælfgifu's mother, had taken refuge there with her surviving sons when Cnut had conquered England and seized the crown. She had been the wife of the Saxon king, Æthelred, and her two sons were the last of the Royal House of Wessex. She knew that

Cnut wouldn't leave any potential challengers for his throne alive if he could help it.

Aldred looked out over the storm tossed North Sea and despaired. There was a small warship, called a birlinn, at the sheltered jetty in Budle Bay below the castle but it would be madness to try and cross to the continent in this weather. Then he looked to the north. The sea between Budle Bay and the Holy Island of Lindisfarne was full of white capped waves, but it was far less wild than the North Sea itself.

'We'll sail across to Lindisfarne and shelter there until it's safe to venture across the sea to Normandy,' he said with decision. 'We'll need a crew; I'll go and talk to Ceadda and the housecarls.'

†††

The birlinn waited three days in the lee of the ruins of the deserted monastery on Lindisfarne for the storm to abate. Only thirty housecarls had elected to accompany Aldred into exile and, as the birlinn had sixteen oars a side, both Aldred and his body servant, Uuen, had to take their place at the oars when necessary.

Normally ship's boys handled the sail, brought water and food to the rowers and kept the ship clean. However only one wanted to leave their families for an uncertain future abroad. Therefore Eadulf and his own body servant, a thirteen year old Norse boy called Fiske, joined him. In essence their duties were to handle the sail, keep lookout, clean the ship and keep the rowers fed and watered. They managed but their inexperience with the sail showed.

'Fiske,' the steersman called, 'up the mast with you and keep your eyes peeled for any sign of another sail.'

The boy nodded and scrambled up the ratlines tied between the shrouds that supported the mast. Once at the top, he sat on the yardarm from which the sail was hung with one arm around the topmost part of the mast. It wasn't exactly a comfortable perch, but nothing about a birlinn was designed for comfort.

Eadulf had watched him with trepidation. Fiske had climbed up with ease but Eadulf realised that doing so on a ship would be difficult and dangerous. He was no stranger to climbing but the rock on which Bebbanburg was built didn't move about as if it was demented.

Eadulf replaced Fiske as lookout just after everyone had eaten and his heart was in his mouth until he reached the yardarm. Just as he swung his leg over it the ship lurched and he nearly let go. He steadied himself and hung onto the top of the mast for dear life until he got used to the motion.

Fiske had watched him nervously. He liked his young master and had no wish to see him crash to the deck or fall overboard. Once Eadulf was safely in position the Norse lad tucked into what was left of the smoked fish, bread and cheese that was the staple diet afloat.

Just when Alfred thought that their voyage into exile was going to be incident free Eadulf gave a shout.

'Sail in sight, no wait, there's two of them. No, three.'

'Which direction?' the steersman called back, looking around, but from the deck the strange sails were still over the horizon.

'Over there,' Eadulf replied pointing to the north east.

'Vikings,' Aldred muttered and the steersman nodded.

'Most likely,' he confirmed.

'Can we outrun them?'

'They are longer at the waterline than us so they can sail faster and they are on the best point of sail.'

Aldred looked puzzled so the steersman explained.

'They are sailing on a beam reach so that wind strikes the ship sideways on. The sail is braced at forty five degrees to the direction they're travelling so most of the wind's force is used to drive the ship along. We are sailing close to the wind and so much of the wind is spilled from our sail. Think of it as twelve strong men pushing a cart compared to a dozen boys. Which cart will travel faster?'

'So they'll be much faster than us?'

'I fear so. The only good news is that it will be dark in two hours.'

'Can we stay in the lead for that long?'

'Not on our present course, no. We need to turn onto the same course they are on, then we may have a chance of keeping them astern until night falls. In the dark we can turn back onto our original course and lose them, hopefully.'

The ship's boys raced to adjust the sail for the new course and they began to pick up speed.

The three longships hadn't spotted the birlinn at first, or so it seemed. Perhaps their lookouts were stationed at the prow instead of up the mast. However, just after the three craft became visible from the deck of the birlinn a faint line of splashes appeared at either side of the ships. The crews were rowing to try and increase their speed.

'Their leader's an idiot; he'll just tire his crews out for the sake of perhaps an extra knot or so,' Ceadda said contemtously

He should have been captain of the birlinn as he was an experienced seafarer as well as a seasoned warrior but he deferred to Aldred and called him 'lord'. The truth was that Aldred was now a landless fugitive and lord of nothing. However, as Uhtred's eldest son the men regarded him as his father's rightful successor, not the despised Eadwulf.

The pursuing longships grew ever nearer until they were less than a mile behind the Northumbrians. They had long ago given up rowing, but now the oars were unshipped again and they began to close a little faster. They were soon close enough for Aldred to see the white surf at the bows of the oncoming longships.

At long last dusk approached as the sun sunk towards the western horizon. A few minutes later Eadulf saw a jagged line appear across the base of the setting sun.

'Land ahead,' he called down excitedly.

'Where is it?' Aldred asked Ceadda, who conferred with the steersman.

'By my calculations we should be somewhere near the mouth of the Tyne.'

That was hardly good news. The River Tyne was the dividing line between Bernicia, where Eadwulf was the earl and Deira, ruled by the Dane Erik Håkonsson. One wanted them dead and the other would doubtless hand them over to King Cnut.

As Ælfgifu was the niece of the Duke of Normandy she would probably be ransomed, along with her daughters, but Cnut would have little interest in her two stepsons. They would probably be killed or sent back to their uncle. Their fate would be sealed either way.

In the fading light Eadulf could just make out a strip of yellow beyond the white of the breaking surf from his perch aloft.

'Beach dead ahead,'

'How far,' his brother called up.

'Perhaps three hundred yards away, maybe less.'

'Right, down with you, and quick as you can.'

As soon as the boy reached the deck the ships' boys rushed to get the sail down whilst the rowers frantically slid their oars out through the holes in the gunwale. They backed their blades to slow the ship and managed to reduce speed just enough so that the thump when the keel grounded in the soft sand wasn't too severe.

The leading longship wasn't so fortunate. They had less warning of the approaching beach from the lookout, who was in the bows and didn't see the beach in the twilight until it was too late. The prow hit the sand so hard that the mast came crashing down, enveloping the crew in the sail. Many of them were thrown violently from their feet and broke limbs, ribs and a few even suffered smashed skulls.

Aldred saw his chance and, cramming his helmet onto his head and picking up his shield, he leaped over the side calling for his warriors to follow him. The other two longships had more warning but, instead of beaching to help their stricken colleagues, they backed off and stayed a hundred yards offshore.

The Northumbrians had an easy fight of it. Most of the Vikings had been trapped under the sail and those who managed to stagger away from the wrecked ship were in no fit state to fight. It was the work of minutes for Aldred's men to overcome them. A short time later they had killed nearly every member of the crew, including the injured. Aldred hated to kill helpless men but he couldn't guard prisoners when he was faced by two more longships full of Vikings. However, he made two exceptions.

Just as the last of the Vikings were dispatched, two frightened boys crawled out from under the sail and Ceadda went to kill them. However, Aldred yelled for him to take them prisoner instead.

'We need more ship's boys,' he called. 'If they will serve me as such they can live; if not, then you can kill them.'

He'd spoken in Danish so that the boys would understand. They were probably Norse but the two languages were similar enough for them to get the gist of his offer. They accepted and were taken across to the birlinn where they were tied up and left for Uuen, Fiske and Eadulf to guard.

By this time the two captains of the other longships had recovered from their surprise at the fate of their fellow Vikings and were now rowing their ships slowly towards the beach.

'Form shield wall,' Aldred called and his men rushed to form up in a line two deep near to where the longships would come ashore.

The Northumbrians had two big advantages; although they were outnumbered by over two to one, Vikings didn't wear armour at sea because of the certainty of drowning if you fell overboard and, secondly, ten of Aldred's men were trained archers. They took up a position immediately in front of the shield wall and nocked their arrows.

There was enough illumination from the new moon to see by but not enough to pick out individual targets. The Vikings leapt down from the two longships as soon as they grounded and Aldred's archers let fly, killing and wounding several of them. No sooner had they sent the first arrow away than they nocked a second one to their bowstring. A third was in the air before the second one struck home, and then the archers withdrew and exchanged their bows for spears and shields.

The Vikings should have waited for everyone to disembark before making a concerted attack but the killing of the other crew and the havoc wreaked by the archers had enraged them. They roared and charged the Northumbrians individually which was a grave error.

Aldred stood in the front rank with Ceadda on his right and another veteran warrior called Fecca on his left. Fecca meant low-born, appropriate in his circumstances because he was the bastard son of a thane and a slave. As a child he'd beaten every boy in his village and, instead of remaining a servant, his father had trained him as a warrior from the age of thirteen. There were few who could best him in single combat.

A giant of a man wielding a two-handed axe made for Aldred but he was only supported on one side by a Viking with a spear and shield. Ceadda chopped the end off the spear and Aldred pulled down the man's shield to expose the top half of his body. Ceadda thrust his sword into the Viking's chest and the man dropped to the ground.

Meanwhile, Fecca took the blow from the giant's axe on his shield. It was heavier than most shields, being reinforced with iron strips criss-crossing the lime wood board. Nevertheless, the axe cut through the wood but became lodged there. Fecca pulled his shield towards him and, whilst the giant was off balance, he thrust his sword through the giant's neck and up into his brain. He too fell dead in front of the shield wall.

In doing so he tripped up the next Norseman to attack him and Aldred cut at his thigh below the rim of the man's shield. His leg collapsed and Fecca's sword sliced into his neck, half severing it from his torso. In the brief pause that followed Fecca stuck his sword into the ground so that he could pull the axe from his shield.

The same fights had occurred all the way along the shield wall and, although two Northumbrians had been killed and several wounded, the Vikings had lost four times as many.

They withdrew back to the line of surf breaking onto the beach to form up and Aldred readied himself for a fresh onslaught. This time he expected the Vikings to be properly organised and for it to be shield wall versus shield wall. Despite their losses, the Norsemen still outnumbered Aldred's men by nearly two to one and he was far from sanguine about the eventual outcome.

ↁↁↁ

Aldred waited but nothing happened. The Vikings seemed to be arguing amongst themselves.

'What are they doing?' Aldred asked Ceadda.

'They've lost a lot of men, which is serious for whoever is in command of the raiders. He's expected to return with lots of plunder and slaves and not to lose anyone in the process. To do so harms his reputation and he'll have difficulty in finding crews the next time he wants to go raiding. However, they've lost so many to our blades that most of them will want revenge.'

'We should charge them whilst they're disorganised,' Fecca suggested.

'Ceadda?' Aldred asked.

'Might work. It gives us the initiative rather that standing here waiting for them to do something.'

'Good. Ready men. Charge.'

The shield wall swept forward. The fallen bodies in front of them caused the line to lose cohesion so Aldred slowed down to allow it to reform. The Vikings were taken unawares, still standing around arguing in small groups. When they realised what was happening they moved back into line but they were too slow. The Northumbrian shield wall hit them and cut down a dozen or more before they were able to respond effectively. Even then they were at a disadvantage as the Northumbrians' charge had forced them back into the sea.

'Hold,' a commanding voice said in Norse. 'We wish to negotiate.'

Gradually the fighting ceased and Aldred's housecarls withdrew a few yards.

'Let us depart and we will let you live,' a large man with a long grey beard called out as he stepped forward in front of his men.

Aldred also stepped forward.

'Do you speak Danish?'

'Enough. Who are you?'

'Aldred Uhtredson.'

'Uhtred? Uhtred of Bebbanburg?'

'The same.'

'He was a fine warrior and the way he was killed by those Danish scum is beneath contempt.'

'Not all were Danes. My uncle, his brother, was amongst the ambushers.'

'Then you have a blood debt to settle with Eadwulf Cudel as well as with Thurbrand.'

Cudel meant cuttlefish and he was so called because cuttlefish have no backbone.

Aldred couldn't help thinking that the Viking leader was remarkably well informed and said so.

'Our skalds travel everywhere. It's how we know what is happening beyond our fjords.'

'I may have a blood feud with my father's killers but I also have a grudge against you. You attacked us.'

'We're Vikings,' he said as if that explained everything.

Aldred thought for a few minutes and Ceadda whispered something in his ear.

'Very well. We'll agree a truce. You can take your dead but you leave behind their weapons and any valuables and coins they have on them.'

'No, they must go to their wives and sons,' the man said shaking his head.

'What about the unmarried warriors?'

'Very well, we will give you their weapons and what they have on them. Are you happy with that?'

'Yes, that seems fair.'

Some of the Norse warriors grumbled at the deal that had been struck but eventually they agreed and Aldred's men stood aside, wary in case there was any trouble, whilst the Vikings sorted through the dead and their possessions. The dead were loaded onto the two longships for burial at sea and then they were gone.

They left half a dozen swords, a few daggers, five spears and three axes behind on the beach, together with a quantity of silver arm rings and hack silver. It didn't really compensate Aldred for the losses they'd suffered but the men were happy enough after he'd distributed it. Half went to him and the rest was divided more or less equally amongst the warriors, with the weapons going to those who needed them most.

They stayed on the beach that night and pushed the birlinn back into the sea as dawn broke the next day.

ϮϮϮ

The two Norse boys they'd captured turned out to be twelve and thirteen. They were called Kjetl and Hakon and, when they discovered that Fiske was also Norse, their belligerent attitude softened. He told them that they'd be well treated and that Aldred was a good lord to serve.

Now they had a full complement of ship's boys the sail handling improved considerably. However, they were under strength after the men they had lost in the fight with the Vikings so not every oar could be manned when they had to row. They set a south easterly course to take the birlinn back out into the North Sea.

By dusk that evening the birlinn was passing Flamborough Head about ten miles to the west of them. They held the same course through the night; the wind shifted around to the north east which necessitated a change to the mainsail as they were now running on a beam reach on the larboard tack. The difference that having the two experienced Norse ship's boys was immediately apparent in the much slicker way they hauled the sail around and tied the ropes off. It also meant that the boys only had to do a stint as lookout for two hours in eight.

The wind had died by the time that the sun rose again the following morning and so the oars were run out and the rowers set to with a will to take them further on their way. Hakon was on lookout duty when the set of sails were spotted. By now the wind had started to pick up again and Aldred was on the point of getting the boys to raise the sail once more.

The ships were too far away to make out what they were but there was at least ten of them so they were probably trading knarrs who depended on the wind for propulsion. Their crews were too small for them to be rowed anywhere, except to manoeuvre them in harbour.

However, to be on the safe side he waited until they disappeared over the horizon before ordering the sail hoisted. The wind was now coming from the north-west so that they could run before it. The disadvantage, apart from the fact it was a slow point of sailing, was that the ship corkscrewed through the waves making quite a few feel sick.

An hour before nightfall Kjetl called down from the masthead that there was land on the starboard bow.

'That will be East Anglia,' Osric said confidently. 'It bulges out far into the North Sea. Now we can start to head south-south-west towards the easternmost point of Kent.'

The wind had veered more to the north and so they were now on a broad reach and the motion became easier as the ship heeled over more.

At dawn the next day they saw several sails off to the west and more heading towards them from the east and the south.

'They are all heading for or leaving London,' the helmsmen said. 'It's too busy here for pirates.'

'Do we stay on this course?' Aldred asked him.

'Yes, until we're past the next land we see, which will be the easternmost point of Kent. Then we turn south-west into the

English Channel and head for Normandy. Another twenty four hours and we should have reached Caen.'

He spoke too soon.

Chapter Two – The Mêlée at Caen

Late April 1017

Throughout that night the strength of the wind increased. It backed to the north-west so that they were now on a broad reach with the wind on the starboard quarter. In the middle of the night Osric told Aldred that they needed to take a couple of reefs in the sail.

'What happens if we don't?'

'Then you risk tearing the mast out of her or else capsizing.'

'Very well, two reefs it is.'

He gave the necessary order but it was a difficult operation to carry out in the dark. Without the two experienced ship's boys it would have probably been impossible. The sail had to be lowered and, whilst it flapped violently in the gale force wind, they had to gather the bottom few feet in and tie the reefing points together all across the width of it.

'Better make it three,' Aldred shouted above the sound of the wind as it strengthened further.

Once the reefing points had been tied the rowers had to bring the ship's head into the wind so that they could raise the sail again using the windlass. Even so it was impossible to raise it all the way. Once it was up and they came back on course, a dangerous manoeuvre in itself, before flying along with the mast creaking ominously. The waves were now much larger and they hit the stern quarter, lifting it, then they corkscrewed as it passed under the keel and dumped the bows in the trough before the next wave hit them.

There was a real danger of being washed overboard and Aldred went and tied his step mother, her attendants and his siblings, even the baby, to something solid. The wind went on increasing and half an hour later the boys, helped by two of the warriors, lowered the sail and, with difficulty, stowed it wrapped around the yardarm in the two cradles on the deck. After that they ran on bare poles.

Aldred knew that they were being driven towards the Frankish coast opposite the Kentish port of Dover but there was little they could do about it. It was safer to run before the wind that try and row beam on to the mountainous waves. They would capsize within minutes.

Then the mast broke half way up and deck was enveloped by the wreckage. Aldred and those of his men with axes cut the cordage free and heaved the top half of the mast over the side. However, it was still attached to the ship by two lengths of hemp rope. The broken mast acted as a sea anchor and the birlinn started to turn broadside on because of the drag on one side.

The ship heeled over alarmingly but, just as Aldred thought it was going all the way over, Ceadda and another warrior called Wictred managed to cut through the two ropes and the ship sprang upright again.

Aldred sent Fiske into the bows to watch for waves breaking on rocks offshore or on a beach. As the sun lightened the leaden sky he was grateful to see that no land was yet in sight. However the horizon was no more than four miles away from where he was standing on the deck and so they could still be dangerously close to land.

The wind had moderated during the night and he estimated that it was now blowing at about thirty knots. It was pushing the hull of the birlinn along at some five knots and the swell on the sea was still significant after the storm, however the oarsmen could overcome that and still make a knot or two away from the coast when they got close. Being shipwrecked was no longer his fear.

His main concern now was landing on a hostile shore, coupled with the fact that several planks along the hull had sprung loose and they were taking in water. The crew were bailing enough to keep the ship from sinking but they couldn't make Caen, or anywhere else in Normandy, without making repairs. They also needed to jury rig a replacement mast so that they could hoist the sail.

Aldred knew little of this part of the coast but Ælfgifu told him that they were likely to land in the lands ruled by Baldwin, Count of Boulogne, who was an ally of Richard of Normandy. However, they could be further north off the coast of Flanders. Its count was likely to be less friendly.

An hour later Kjetl cried a warning from the bows that he could see land dead ahead. The wind was still driving them onshore but, with the oarsmen backing away they managed to slow their approach so that the ship beached on the soft sand, if not gently, then at least without causing damage. They ran ropes and anchors ashore so they could haul the ship further up the beach as the tide came in. Once it went out again they could start the repair work.

Aldred sent four of his warriors inland to watch out for anyone approaching. Although this part of the Continent was peaceful at the moment, you could never be too careful. It was mid-afternoon by the time that the sea had retreated sufficiently for them to inspect the damage below the waterline as well as above it. Thankfully the planking was complete and undamaged, it was just a matter of hammering home new nails in several places.

After that they would need to caulk the seams between both the hull and deck planks to make it watertight. For that they would need oiled wool to make a temporary repair until they could obtain oakum, which was made by soaking hemp fibres in pitch. Ceadda and a few warriors set off inland in search of a farmstead which might be able to sell them what they needed. The rest went with Osric to find a suitable pine tree to serve as a new mast.

By the time the tide came in again they had felled the tree and trimmed it to make the mast. In the morning they would remove the old stump and step the new one in place before rigging it with the spare cordage they carried on board. However, the group sent to obtain oil and wool still hadn't returned.

'You could unpick the old rope and use the fibres instead if wool, I suppose,' Osric suggested. 'Ideally you should use pitch but oil might do.'

Aldred shook his head. 'Wool absorbs the oil, would hemp do the same?'

'Possibly not; you really need pitch, but it might suffice to keep the water out until we reach Caen. After all, we can bale if necessary.'

'Let's see what Ceadda comes back with.'

It was noon the next day before he reappeared. By then the tide had receded sufficiently to complete work on the new mast so all that they now needed was to caulk the gaps and re-launch the birlinn. However, when Ceadda and his men returned they weren't alone.

†††

Ælfgifu stood between Aldred and Eadulf as the oarsmen rowed around the long right hand bend in the River Orne and Caen came into sight. The town was dominated by a plateau on which stood the hall of Duke Richard. The hall itself and numerous other buildings were surrounded by a tall timber palisade.

When Ceadda had returned to the beached ship he had brought pitch, cotton and oakum with him in a cart and was escorted by several mounted warriors serving Count Baldwin. They were there to collect payment and, although the price was exorbitant, Ælfgifu told Aldred to pay it. She had brought the coffers of silver that Uhtred had left at Bebbanburg with her and, although there was a small fortune in the chests, it wouldn't last long as she'd have to pay her men in addition to renting accommodation for them. She hoped that her brother would house and feed her and her family but she couldn't expect him to do the same for the warriors.

It had taken two days to re-caulk the birlinn, a process which involved driving cotton and oakum into the wedge-shaped seam between planks with a caulking mallet and a caulking iron. Then they had to cover the new caulking with a putty, in the case of hull seams, or for the deck seams, with melted pine pitch. It was a laborious and filthy process and everyone was glad when it was finished. At the next high tide they re-floated her and set sail down the coast.

Aldred breathed a sigh of relief when they made it to Caen without further incident. The town was the main base of the Normandy dukes, although Rouen was beginning to compete with it. Caen was more central within the duchy but Rouen lay on the River Seine which led to Paris. This had been a relatively insignificant place until the last century when the Capetian kings of France developed it into an important commercial and religious centre. For the past sixty years it had also been the administrative centre of France.

As soon as they docked a man strutted pompously along the jetty accompanied by two men wearing padded gambesons and helmets. Each carried a spear and wore a sword on their hips but neither looked as if they would be much good in a proper fight. One was a youth with a few wisps of straggling hair on his chin and the other was elderly and fat.

He addressed Irwyn, thinking that he was the captain of the birlinn, in a language that no one on board understood. The man tutted impatiently and switched to Latin, which thankfully Aldred had learned when he was being educated by monks. The version the man, who turned out to be the deputy port reeve, spoke was adulterated with Frankish and Gallic words but Aldred got the gist of what he was saying.

'He wants to know our business here and to pay a fee of two silver solt for every night we plan to stay,' he explained to Ælfgifu.

'Tell him that I'm the niece of Duke Richard and he won't get a denarius out of me, let alone a solt.'

Aldred grinned and told the reeve what his step-mother had said

'Is the Duke here? Has my mother, the Lady Emma arrived yet?' she added.

The man's attitude did a volt face and he became obsequious.

'I'm sorry, my lady. Both the duke and his sister are in Rouen for the funeral of the duchess.'

'Oh! I'm sorry. When did Judith of Brittany die?'

'A week ago, my lady.'

'Do you know when the duke and Lady Emma will return?'

'I'm sorry my lady, but the chamberlain up in the castle might know.'

Castle was an unfamiliar word to Aldred but he assumed it was the French equivalent for a fortress.

'I'll go up and find out. Ceadda you stay here with my family and guard the ship. I'll take five men and Uuen with me.'

The rocky outcrop on which the duke's hall was built reminded Aldred in some ways of Bebbanburg. The plateau covered an area of over five hectares but only part of this large space was enclosed by a palisade; the rest served as an area where an army could camp when necessary.

The two sentries at the main gate challenged them and one called inside for the guard commander whilst Aldred waited impatiently. Once more he was addressed in a tongue he didn't understand so he asked if the sentry spoke Latin. Evidently he didn't but the officer who appeared a few minutes later did.

'What do you want?' he asked belligerently, annoyed at being dragged from his cot in the guardhouse.

'My name is Aldred of Bebbanburg; I'm the great nephew of Duke Richard,' he began.

It was stretching the truth slightly as the duke's niece was only his step mother. 'I need to see the chamberlain to find out whether the duke and my grandmother, the Lady Emma, will return shortly or whether we should go to Rouen.'

The man studied Aldred carefully. He wore an expensive tunic and cloak and the sword at his waist had a ruby mounted as the pommel. He nodded.

'You may enter, domine, but your men must stay here. You'll find the chamberlain in the great hall over there.'

He pointed to a large two storey wooden building in the middle of the compound. There was an external staircase leading to the first floor which Aldred correctly assumed housed the main hall and the duke's living quarters. The under croft would house the steward, clerks and other administrators than managed the duchy.

As there were no windows it was very dark inside the under croft, despite numerous candles. Aldred presumed that this was to make the hall more defensible if the outer palisade fell. He thought that the scribes must harm their eyesight working in such conditions but, as his eyes adjusted to the gloom, he found that he could see much better.

'Can I help you, lord?' one of the clerks asked in impeccable Latin.

'Yes, I'm looking for the chamberlain.'

'He's over there talking to the steward,' the man said, pointing further into the under croft.

The chamberlain must have noticed the new arrival because he broke off what he was saying and came towards Aldred.

'Are you looking for me? I'm Âdam de Liseux, Duke Richard's chamberlain in Caen.'

'Yes, I'm Aldred of Bebbanburg. I've just arrived with my step mother, the lady Ælfgifu, daughter of the late King Æthelred and Emma of Normandy.'

'And you seek sanctuary from the Dane, Cnut?' Âdam de Liseux surmised correctly.

'My lady seeks to be-reunited with her mother and my warriors and I hope to serve the duke,' Aldred said.

'Mmm,' the chamberlain said thoughtfully. 'It isn't my area of course, but the duke has been building up his contingent of mounted warriors; he doesn't need more foot soldiers.'

'Good. My warriors are all trained to fight on horseback.'

The chamberlain looked surprised; he had thought that Anglo-Saxons always fought on foot.

'The duke is expected back with the Lady Emma in a week or so.'

'Then it makes sense for us to remain here until then. Can you find accommodation for us?'

'How many?' the chamberlain asked dubiously.

'In my family? Apart from my step mother and me, there are three children and four servants. There are also twenty seven in my crew.'

'I'll see what I can do about quarters for the Lady Ælfgifu and the children but you and your men will have to camp on the plateau outside the palisade. There is a well and the constable can doubtless find leather tents for you, but you'll have to ask him yourself.'

'Very well. Where will I find him?'

'He is outside Caen exercising his knights at the moment. I'll find someone to take you to see him. You did say you could ride?'

'Since I was six.'

The chamberlain said something in the local language to one of the servants and the two men exchanged a sly smile. Aldred thought nothing of it but he had cause to remember it later. He sent a message down to the ship, telling Ceadda to draw up a rota for an on board watch and to ask Ælfgifu to bring the children and the servants up to see the chamberlain.

Taking Wictred with him as he was one of his best riders he made his way to the stables behind the chamberlain's servant. The man spoke to the head groom and the two turned to look at the two Northumbrians before sniggering together.

Shortly afterwards two grooms brought out two saddled horses for Aldred and Wictred to ride together with a rouncey for the servant as he was acting as their guide. The horses were much larger than the usual riding horses used in England; both were stallions and one stood at perhaps fifteen hands whilst the other wasn't much smaller. Each was trying to bite the other and the grooms had difficulty controlling them.

Aldred grinned. Obviously the chamberlain had thought that he was boasting when he said that his men were trained to fight on horseback. These were warhorses, destriers, which he'd heard of but never seen.

He swung up into the saddle and immediately pulled back on the reins to control the horse. It tried to bite him and jerked around trying to unseat him but Aldred gripped it tightly with his knees and, as soon as it realised that his rider knew his business, it accepted him and, apart from snorting his annoyance, he quietened down. Wictred was equally successful in subduing his destrier.

The look on the faces of the grooms and the servant were priceless. They had obviously expected the horses to either dump the two foreigners on the ground or bolt with them feebly trying to stop them.

'Well, come on,' Aldred said in Latin to the servant. 'I haven't got all day. Take me to the constable.'

'Yes, domine,' the chastened servant said and kicked his much smaller horse into a canter.

†††

'Who gave you those horses?' the constable asked with a frown when Aldred had introduced himself and explained what he wanted.

'The chamberlain.'

'The man's a fool. It's obvious to anyone with a grain of sense that you know how to ride as well as any of my knights; indeed there are many who would have difficulty with those two stallions. They are the best two warhorses in the duke's stables. The question is, can you fight on them.'

Aldred watched as the twenty young men in chain mail hauberks and helmets practiced charging a shield wall composed of straw men but the spears protruding from beside the shields were real enough. The knights were charging until they were mere feet away from the wicked iron points of the spears and then wheeled away, thrusting their own spears, which were longer than those of the pretend foot soldiers, into the straw bodies and heads as they went.

Aldred looked at Wictred who grinned back and nodded.

'Here, go and collect a couple of spears and show me what you can do.'

'Those spears are longer than we are used to,' Aldred replied. 'If it's all the same to you, we'll just use our swords but shields would be useful.'

The constable shrugged and watched as the two men lined up with the Norman knights. The shields they were given weren't the round ones they were used to but of an elongated kite design. This protected the knight from foot to shoulder but they weren't as manoeuvrable as round shields.

The on-looking Normans watched in amazement as the two Northumbrians used both shield and sword to knock away the two spears facing them at their chosen point of attack in the shield wall and then the two calmly proceeded to backhand their swords and slice off the straw heads complete with helmets. If they had been real men their heads would have been left rolling in the mud.

'Well done,' the constable said grudgingly when the two returned to his side. 'Are all your men as good as that?'

'Not all, but then are all your knights of a uniform standard?'

'Fair point. Very well, I'll send instructions for your men to draw the tents they need and tomorrow we'll put them all through their paces. Perhaps a mêlée against these knights? Shall we wager twenty silver solts on the outcome?'

'I'm not familiar with the rules for a mêlée.'

'Well, put simply, your aim is to smash into my mounted knights in massed formation with the aim of unhorsing as many as you can and breaking their ranks. This is usually followed up by individual combats. Once unhorsed the knight must withdraw from the fray, preferably extricating himself without being trodden to death. Swords are blunted as are the spears. The winner is the side with men still mounted when all their opponents are afoot.'

'I see. Even with blunted weapons I assume that there are casualties and even deaths?'

'Of course, otherwise its value as a preparation for war would be minimal.'

'I understand. Until, tomorrow then.'

☨☨☨

The concept of using heavy cavalry on the Continent had been developed some two hundred years previously by Charlemagne as a means of moving quickly during the Emperor's wide-ranging campaigns of conquest. The Frankish horsemen increasingly remained mounted to fight on the battlefield as true cavalry rather than mounted infantry, aided by the introduction of the stirrup to give the rider a more stable platform from which to fight.

Aldred was accustomed to using his own horsemen as light, rather than heavy, cavalry and the horses they rode were smaller and consequently more nimble. He knew that if he tried to emulate the Normans' tactics he would lose and so he planned to fight the way his men were used to doing, which would hopefully take the knights by surprise.

The twenty horseman selected by each side lined up in two rows facing each other a thousand yards apart. On the signal given by the constable they started to walk their horses towards each other. The mounts chosen by the Northumbrians were the lighter rounceys, being closest to the type they were used to. This caused much derision amongst their opponents who expected an easy victory.

As they changed to a trot and then a canter Aldred held up his spear and then lowered it in a pre-arranged signal. The wings of the line slowed their pace followed by those inside them so as they changed pace to a gallop they had formed a wedge.

Aldred held his blunted lance with the end wrapped in padded leather in front of him with Ceadda by his side but, instead of aiming for the approaching riders, they aimed at the heads of their destriers. The horses had been well trained to avoid enemy weapons and just before contact they moved to one side, opening a gap in the hitherto solid line.

As they did so the other destriers were also forced sideways and Aldred and Ceadda rode towards the gap, moving their lances' point of aim from the horse to the rider as they did so. The Normans were struggling to bring their horses back into line and so their attention wasn't as concentrated on the Northumbrians as it might have been. Consequently Aldred and Ceadda were able to strike the middle two knights cleanly and they flew off the rear of their horses, landing on the hard earth with a resounding thump.

The rest of the Northumbrian wedge flew through the gap pushing the Normans further out as they did so. Four more of them were unhorsed for the loss of only two of Aldred's men.

Once the wedge was through the second Norman line the two halves split and wheeled around. Because the rounceys were so much more agile than the heavy destriers, the Northumbrians were able to turn them and come up behind the Normans just as they were trying to reorganise.

The Northumbrians sent eight more of their opponents tumbling into the dust for the loss of one more man before the combat changed into a free for all. By then only six Normans remained mounted against seventeen. It should have been an unequal contest as both sides threw away their unwieldy spears and drew their blunted swords. However, now the heavy destriers came into their own, easily barging the rounceys out of the way and nipping them so that the lighter horses shied away from getting too close to them.

Aldred and his warriors only managed to unseat one more Norman for the loss of four of his own men before he decided a change of tactics was necessary. He called his men away and they raced away, hotly pursued by the five remaining Normans. Aldred called a command and his men split into two and turned outwards so that they could charge into the flank of the Normans.

They caught them off guard and managed to get in amongst the Normans before they could react. Five minutes later Aldred hit the helmet of the last Norman a resounding blow with his sword. Even blunted it dented the man's helmet and he crashed to the ground unconscious.

The contest was over and, despite quite a few broken bones, bruised ribs and sore heads, the Northumbrians were euphoric about their triumph. The constable handed over the purse of silver to Aldred with a grimace.

'Your strategic was, shall we say, innovative, young man.'

'That's how battles are won, domine.'

The constable laughed.

'I shall certainly recommend that Duke Richard employs you and your men after that demonstration of your prowess.'

However, it wasn't the Duke of Normandy that Aldred was destined to serve.

Chapter Three – Return to England

July 1017

Duke Richard and his sister returned to Caen ten days later and Emma immediately took Ælfgifu and Aldred's siblings under her wing. Duke Richard didn't send for Aldred immediately and he began to worry about the future for him and his men.

In May emissaries had arrived from Cnut and at the end of the month a treaty was concluded between him and Richard of Normandy. To the surprise of many he sealed the alliance by agreeing that Emma should marry Cnut. Not only did this give the Dane an important ally on the continent but, by marrying King Æthelred's wife, it added to his legitimacy as King of England.

As soon as the English delegation had left Richard sent for Aldred.

'My constable has recommended that I engage you and your warband as knights but, to be honest, I have no need of more knights at the moment.'

Aldred's heart sank. If the Normans couldn't offer them employment he would have to become mercenaries or adventurers in Italy where a number of landless knights had already gone to seek their fortunes.

'However,' Richard continued, 'My sister will need a suitable escort when she becomes Queen of England. It's not that I don't trust Cnut but I would be happier knowing that she had someone related to her to protect her.'

And so Aldred and his men had been engaged, not as the duke's household knights, but as Lady Emma's bodyguards. A few weeks later Aldred and his men were back aboard his birlinn heading for England. However, this time the destination wasn't Northumbria, but London.

By tradition the wives of the kings of Wessex, and later England, had been called lady, not queen, and had never been crowned. However, Cnut had agreed with Duke Richard that Emma should be his queen. As his coronation was scheduled for that July Emma and her entourage sailed from Caen at the beginning of the month in order to be in London in time.

In addition to the knarrs that carried Emma, her entourage, servants and the horses, the convoy was guarded by Aldred's birlinn and three Danish longships sent by Cnut. Unlike Ælfgifu and Aldred's crossing of the North Sea three months previously, this time the weather was benign and the voyage was uneventful.

The wharfs at the Port of London would be crowded with merchantmen, so it had been decided that Emma should land at a place called Tilbury in Essex. There was little there apart from a few hovels and a jetty which was used by a ferry. All around the land was marsh on which sheep grazed; consequently the ferry was mainly used for the cross-river transport of the animals and their wool for sale in Kent. The ferry was therefore large and so was the jetty where it docked.

When Emma's small fleet arrived the ferry was over on the south shore and so two ships could unload at the same time. It still took over an hour to complete and by that time a carriage and several wagons had arrived together with an escort of a hundred mounted housecarls led by a Dane called Regnwald. The man infuriated Aldred as soon as he opened his mouth.

'Tell this Norman oaf that we'll take over now as we are the king's escort for the Lady Emma. He can return to Normandy with King Cnut's thanks,' Regnwald told the priest riding by his side in Danish.

The priest stated to translate this into Latin but Aldred cut him off.

'Don't bother,' he replied in Latin. 'I heard what he said. Tell the ignorant fool that I am no Norman but I am the captain of the Lady Emma's bodyguards and that I was appointed as such by Duke Richard. To try to dismiss me is an insult to him; is that what he intends?'

He saw Emma and Ælfgifu, both of whom spoke Latin, trying to supress their smirks.

'What did the oaf say?' Regnwald asked impatiently.

'He, er. He speaks Danish, lord,' the priest said uncomfortably. 'He was appointed by the Duke of Normandy to guard the Lady Emma and, er, only the duke can dismiss him from that duty.'

Regnwald looked discomfited for a moment, then tried to bluster.

'I meant no offence, whoever you are, but the king had given me the duty of guarding his future queen, not you.'

'My name is Aldred Uhtredson and I doubt very much if Cnut wishes to insult my great uncle, the duke, after going to so much trouble to make him his ally.'

'I know nothing about that, but I know my duty!'

'What's the problem, Aldred,' the Lady Emma asked in English. 'I for one am getting somewhat impatient standing here whilst you debate with this man.'

Evidently Regnwald understood enough English to get the gist of this and he flushed with annoyance.

'Very well. You may walk behind the carriage whilst we ride ahead of it.'

'That's not acceptable, Regnwald,' Emma said in a tone that brooked no argument. 'You should have brought horses for my escort; as you haven't some of your men can give them up to Aldred and my guards.'

The man glared at her in astonishment when Aldred translated this into Danish and for a moment Aldred thought that he was about to refuse. In the end he nodded curtly and told forty of his men to dismount. They were the youngest of the warriors and they sat on their mounts like sacks of potatoes. It was clear that they only rode to get from one place to another and Aldred guessed that having to make their own way back to London would be preferable to getting saddle sore in any case.

The way they grinned at one another probably meant that they would take the opportunity to stop at every tavern on the way; something they would be even happier about, however angry their captain was.

Aldred knew that he had made an enemy and in retrospect he knew that he could have handled the encounter better, but the man was arrogant and he'd got under Aldred's skin.

†††

Nothing had been said until after the marriage and the coronation and up to that point Aldred's men had continued to guard Emma's chambers. Now she had moved into the bedchamber adjoining the king's it was a different matter and he was told brusquely by Cnut's chamberlain that his men were no longer required to do guard duty.

He and his men had kicked their heels in the mean hovel that they'd been allocated as accommodation for a week until the summons came. When he entered the king's hall he knew from the downcast look on Lady Emma's face and the smirk on Regnwald's that the king had decided to side with Regnwald.

'Thank you for your service to the queen,' Cnut said insincerely. 'But there is no longer a role for you. My housecarls are quite capable of protecting her, as they do me.'

He reached over and patted Emma's arm in a proprietorial, rather than an affectionate, manner.

'I'm told that Duke Richard doesn't need your services either. As you are a Northumbrian you are to travel north and report to your earl in York. He may be able to find you employment; if not perhaps you should throw yourself on your uncle's mercies.'

He was about to dismiss Aldred when Regnwald came forward and whispered in his ear.

'Ah yes, I'm afraid that I can't provide horses for you; you will have to get used to travelling on foot it seems.'

Aldred bowed stiffly and walked out of the hall with his head held high. He was damned if he would let the sniggering Danes that filled the hall see how furious he was.

Cnut had presumably forgotten, or perhaps never knew, that he had a birlinn waiting at Tilbury. He had left the ships boys, the helmsman and three warriors to guard it just in case it was needed. The only other option would have been to sell it but he had a faint suspicion when they'd landed that it might still prove of use.

It was twenty five miles back to Tilbury but just before they set out Fiske, his brother Eadulf's body servant, came to find him. Eadulf was staying with Ælfgifu and his half-sisters in Queen Emma's household for now and Fiske came with a message from his step mother.

'Be careful when you leave London, lord,' the boy told him. 'Regnwald has sent men to kill you on the road.'

'Do you know any more details?'

'No, Lady Ælfgifu just heard gossip that Regnwald has vowed that you would never reach York alive.'

Aldred smiled to himself as he thanked Fiske and gave him a silver penny. If the Dane thought that he would be heading north and had set an ambush he was wasting his time; Tilbury lay due east of London.

He realised that Regnwald wasn't such a fool as he thought when Wictred appeared out of the trees beside the muddy road that they were on. Aldred had told him and another warrior to shadow them to check that they weren't being followed. He had also sent two men ahead to make sure they weren't walking into a trap.

'Ten men on horseback are on the same road but they aren't hurrying. They've got two men riding ahead staying in contact with you but keeping out of sight. When you stopped to fill your water flasks at that stream back there the main group hid in the undergrowth until you continued.

'They didn't see you?'

'No, lord. They may be a lot better than most Danes at stalking but they're not that good.'

'Why only a dozen in all?' Ceadda asked, puzzled. 'They don't stand a chance against nearly forty of us.'

'Oh, I don't think that they are looking for a fight,' Aldred replied. 'I suspect that they're hired killers not warriors. They'll try to assassinate me when we stop for the night.'

'What do you intend to do?'

'Kill the killers,' Aldred said grimly.

He wouldn't say anymore and both Ceadda and Wictred assumed that he had a plan. He didn't; at least not yet.

That night they reached a farmstead just as rain started to fall and Aldred gave the owner a few copper coins so that they could sleep in his barn. The thatch was worn and it leaked in places but it was better than camping out in the open. He posted two sentries in an obvious position outside the barn door and they settled down for the night. However, four of his men had slipped away into the undergrowth under cover of the gloom and the rain just as the rest had entered the barn.

The four had divested themselves of the hauberks and Norman style helmets that had been a present to every man from Duke Richard. It was the only payment they had received for guarding his sister but they provided much better protection than their byrnies and were consequently worth quite a lot. The byrnies had been sold to an armourer in Caen for him to break up and re-use the chain mail.

The four had also left behind swords, shields, spears and axes. They would only need daggers and seaxes, a short sword with a single-edged blade, for the work they had to do that night.

Oswin, who was in charge of the four, picked a tree with a good view of the road, not because he could see very far in the murk, but because he could hear better from its lower branches. His men hid in the shadows at the base. They waited patiently, moving slowly and cautiously to ease cramped muscles from time to time. Just when Oswin thought that they were on a fool's errand he heard the snap of a twig breaking underfoot.

He dropped a small pebble onto the head of one of his men waiting below to alert them without making a sound and the group tensed. A minute later they could just make out ten men moving stealthily along the road, then turning off towards the barn. Presumably the other two had been left with their horses.

Aldred's instructions had been quite clear. No one was to be left alive to report back to Regnwald. Let him fret when he heard nothing. One of Oswin's men made his way silently back along the track to find the horses and deal with their handlers; the others stalked the assassins.

The two rearmost never knew what happened. By the time they realised that a hand had been clamped over their mouths their throats had been slit. The bodies were quietly lowered to the ground and Oswin and his two companions padded after the next few in the column as they neared the edge of the wood. A minute later three more of the hired mercenaries were dead but one had managed to bite the hand over his mouth and uttered a brief warning before he died.

Oswin and his men had more sense than to fight three against five once they'd been discovered and they quickly disappeared into the darkness. Evidently the leader decided that it was pointless continuing with his mission now that they had been discovered. Losing half his men must have been unnerving in any case.

Casting caution to the wind, the five would-be killers ran back to where they'd left their horses, only to discover the two left behind dead on the ground and no sign of their mounts.

A knife flew out of the darkness under the trees and struck one of the men in the centre of his chest. A moment later a horseman erupted out of the wood at the side of the road and cut down another of the mercenaries before disappearing across the road into the trees on the other side. The remaining three, now out of their wits with panic, fled back up the road towards London.

Oswin congratulated his men as they mounted three of the horses tied up just off the road and all four galloped off after the fleeing assassins. The mud muffled the sound of the approaching horses until it was too late for the three to bolt into the undergrowth and it was a matter of moments for Oswin's men to cut them down. One was screaming in agony from a shoulder wound; the other two had been killed cleanly. A second later the screams stopped suddenly as Oswin dismounted and cut the man's throat.

By dawn the twelve bodies had been stripped of all clothing and weapons and the heads severed from the torsos to make identification difficult. The severed torsos and the heads were then thrown into the Thames at separate places to be washed downstream, and hopefully out to sea.

Chapter Four – The Mormaer of Moray

Summer 1017

Findlay mac Ruairi, Mormaer of Moray, stared at the army of Malcolm Forranach, King of Scots. His twelve year old son, Macbeth, sitting on his horse beside him, muttered something, overawed at the size of king's forces.

'Did you say something, boy,' his father said sternly, not moving his head, his eyes fixed on his enemies.

'They are too strong for us father,' the boy said, expecting a blow from Findlay for his temerity.

'That's bloody obvious. There is a time to fight and a time to negotiate; now is not the time to fight.'

Findlay spurred his horse towards the bottom of the valley between the two armies with his son at his side, followed by his senior thanes and chieftains. They sat there for five minutes and, just as Findlay had come to the conclusion that the king didn't want to negotiate and he'd have to fight him after all, Malcolm rode down to meet him with a slightly larger entourage.

'You made a mistake when you challenged me for the throne, Findlay,' Malcolm began without preamble.

'Is that what men in the lowlands are saying now, Malcolm? Well, as with all things uttered by them, it is far from the truth.'

'Is that so? Well, perhaps you would like to tell me your version of this truth before I have your head part company with your body.'

'You always were over hasty to jump to conclusions, Malcolm. You want the truth? Very well. You have been so busy with your desire to eliminate your supposed enemies and with pushing your border to the south that you have forgotten about the north of your kingdom. You did nothing to stop Sigurd the Stout and his Norse turds from seizing everywhere north of the Moray Firth; aye, and much of the old Scots Kingdom of Dalriada too. If it wasn't for my warriors and me you'd have probably have also lost Moray. Now I have defeated them and killed Sigurd. Your northern borders are safe thanks to me; you owe me, Malcolm.'

'You'd do well to watch your words when you speak to me. I'm not one of your naked-arsed barbarian chieftains,' the king hissed at him, trying to control his temper, and failing.

'You may be the Ard Ri, the high king, but I am one of the ri, or king if you prefer, as well as your son-in-law so I'll speak to you how I damn well please. It was my fellow ri in the north who elected me to lead them to fight the Norse. There was never any suggestion that I should be the Ard Ri. You want to get your facts right before you start chucking accusations about.'

Macbeth kicked his horse close to his father and put a warning hand on the irate man's arm. Findlay glared at him and was about to knock his hand away, but instead he nodded his thanks.

'Forgive me, lord king. Perhaps the pride in both of us has overridden our innate common sense. We both have enough enemies without fighting each other.'

Malcolm bit back the angry retort he was about to utter and, although he visibly had difficulty in controlling himself, eventually he spoke in a much calmer tone.

'Very well. I accept your apology, but you will never to speak to me in such a fashion again if you value your life. Your words saved you just in time. I was about to replace you as Mormaer of Moray, but I've decided that you may remain in post on one condition.'

Findlay was about say that Malcolm could try to replace him if he dared when he remembered that he had only acceded to the title by killing his predecessor, who'd been one of his many cousins. There were plenty in his own family who would be only too happy to depose him and rule in his place, once they had Malcolm's backing.

'What condition?' Findlay asked suspiciously, restraining himself with difficulty from glowering at his sovereign.

'I'm preparing an army to invade Northumbria and conquer Lothian once and for all. For too long the Angles who live there have paid lip service to me whilst looking to Bebbanburg and York as their real lords.'

'You mean to raid the province around Edinburgh?' Findlay asked puzzled.

'No, this will be no raid. I will impose my will, not only on Edinburgh but on the whole of Lothian north of the River Tweed. But that will only be the start. Eventually I intend to rule everywhere north of the Tees.'

Privately Findlay thought that Malcolm was fooling himself if he thought he could conquer the whole of Bernicia without provoking a backlash from England. Lothian had been placed under Scots rule once or twice in the past but it had never lasted long. True, it was a long way from London and Cnut might not be too concerned if Malcolm seized Lothian, but he would be forced to react if Malcolm tried to take half of Northumbria, or else he would lose face amongst his nobles.

'And where do I come into this grand strategy of yours, lord king?'

'You will bring all the warriors and highlanders you have assembled here south to the muster point when you are summoned next year and you will help me to defeat the Northumbrians once and for all.'

He made as if to turn away but stopped.

'Oh, and just to make sure you don't betray me you will surrender your son to me as hostage. If you fail to arrive, or arrive with too few men, I will send you Macbeth's head in a basket, and don't think I won't just because he's my daughter's son.'

ϮϮϮ

'I want you to travel to Northumbria for me,'

'Yes, lord.'

The man Findlay was speaking to was called Edgar. He had been born in York but he had fled from there when he was fourteen after he had killed another boy in a fight over a girl. The dead boy was the son of a rich goldsmith whereas Edgar had no father and his mother was a whore. He knew that he would be hanged if he stayed and so he'd fled north of the Firth of Forth into Scotland.

He had earned a living as a thief for a while and then had joined a gang which specialised in extracting money through coercion. Eventually the town reeve had acted and raided the tavern where the gang drank. Most were killed but Edgar had escaped and had fled northwards once again.

This time he'd ended up in Moray at a time when Findlay was recruiting mercenaries to bolster his own warriors in his fight against the Norse in Caithness. Edgar had never been taught to fight like a warrior but Findlay quickly found out that he had other skills. Now he wanted him to travel back to the land of his birth where he was still wanted for killing the goldsmith's son. However, that had been six years ago and he hoped that people would have forgotten about him.

'Find out what sort of people the two earls are, particularly Eadwulf of Bebbanburg. How effective a war leader is he? I also want to know if Erik Håkonsson, the Earl of Northumbria, is likely to join Eadwulf in defending Lothian. I need to know their likely fighting strength too.'

As he later said to his wife, 'I want to know what I'm getting into by supporting Malcolm. If it is likely to end up with the sort of defeat he suffered at Durham twelve years ago I don't want to be involved.'

'What about our son?'

'If Malcolm loses badly then Macbeth may be killed anyway. Let's just see what Edgar comes back with.'

'If he comes back. You put too much trust in a man who would sell his own mother for a purse of silver.'

ϮϮϮ

Edgar decided to head for York first. He had sailed before and managed to find work as a deck hand on a knarr heading there with a cargo of sheepskins and salted beef. The voyage was uneventful and, although he'd signed on for a year, he disappeared into the hovels, taverns and brothels around the dock area whilst he was unloading the cargo.

He had changed a lot over the time he'd been away. Then he'd been a scrawny, undersized beardless boy; now he was tall, broader than most across the shoulder and had a bushy brown beard that covered much of his face. He doubted his own mother would recognise him now and he decided to put that to the test.

He stood outside the building that served as a brothel and watched men entering and leaving. It seemed it hadn't changed its role, but whether his mother still worked there was another matter. She had had him when she was fifteen so she'd be in her mid-thirties now. That was old for a whore. Well, there was only one way to find out.

The inside of the building was like a hall with a fire pit and tables in the centre where customers sat and drank whilst they waited for the girl of their choice to become available. Down each side of the building there were half a dozen curtained off alcoves. The noise of couples copulating came from within most of them and Edgar wondered whether the sound of one of the girls faking pleasure came from his mother.

An older woman had her back to him as she chatted with one of the men waiting. She must have sensed his presence because she turned and gave him a fake smile of welcome. Edgar realised with a start that the woman, who appeared to be in charge, was his mother. She looked much older and she had lost her looks but it was definitely her.

'Your first time, my love?'

'You think I'm a virgin?' Edgar asked with amusement.

A flash of annoyance crossed her face before she resumed the fake smile.

'No, I meant at the House of Freya.'

Freya was the Norse goddess of love, fertility, beauty, and fine material possessions. There wasn't much sign of the latter in the mean establishment and he knew that whores took a powder to prevent pregnancy. The last thing they wanted was a child to look after and most men didn't fancy rutting with a pregnant whore.

It wasn't his first time, either in the brothel or lying with a girl. When he lived there with his mother one of the other whores there had taken a fancy to him when he was barely thirteen and had introduced him to the delights of fornication. Once he'd tasted its delights he had to have more and set out to make a series of conquests in the town. The son of KætilbiQrn the goldsmith was in love with a girl who Edgar had managed to get pregnant and he had come looking for Edgar with murder in mind. Unfortunately for him, he was the one who ended up dead.

'No, it's not but I'm not after a girl this time. Can we go somewhere to talk? I'll make it worth your while.'

His mother glanced at the money pouch at his waist and nodded, leading him to the rear of the brothel where she had a private chamber.

'Now what do you want to know?'

'You don't recognise me, do you?'

'No,' she started to say, peering closely at his face. 'Edgar? Is it you?'

He nodded, smiling.

'What are you doing here? Are you mad? KætilbiQrn is still offering a reward for your head. He's even sent agents all over Northumbria trying to find you.'

'It's been six years. Surely he's given up by now?'

'Not him. You killed his only son. What could possibly have induced you to come back?'

'I need information.'

'And that's worth risking your life?

'Even you had trouble recognising me.'

'Yes, but you've come here. KætilbiǫrN will have someone watching this place day and night.'

'I checked the outside carefully before I came in. I didn't see anyone loitering.'

'What about small boys? They play unnoticed in a corner and then run off to tell their master when a strange face appears.'

'Oh shit! Yes, there were two playing knuckle bones. Meet me in two hours' time in the tavern opposite the west door of the Minster. I'll get rid of those boys in the meantime.'

When Edgar left he went in the opposite direction to the Minster. One of the boys got up and followed him. If he hadn't been expecting it he would have missed his shadow. The boy was probably eleven or twelve years old but so undernourished that his frame was almost skeletal. He was like many another urchin on the streets of York and most people wouldn't have paid any attention to him.

Edgar stopped at a pie stall and glanced around him as he ate it. The boy was nowhere in sight. Edgar had to acknowledge that he was good. He strolled on, half-eaten pie in hand and then turned into a narrow alleyway between two mean looking wooden houses. He stopped and flattened himself against one of the walls in the shadows.

He waited and a minute later his stalker turned into the alley, flattening himself against the opposite wall and looking down the alley. For an instant he wasn't aware of Edgar's presence opposite him but he must have heard the man's breathing. Quick as a flash he darted for the exit to the narrow passage, but he wasn't quick enough. Edgar's fist landed on the side of his head and the other side of the lad's head banged into the timber wall of the house. He dropped like a stone.

Edgar felt for a pulse and was relieved when he found one. He wanted to stop him following him but he didn't want to kill him. However, he had a problem. When the boy woke up he would run and tell Kætilbiǫrn what had happened. It didn't take a genius to work out that no one else would have been worried about being followed and therefore there was a good chance that the man was Edgar.

He couldn't leave York without finding out the information he'd been sent to discover, but if he stayed he risked being run to earth. The boy had to disappear. It would be suspicious but at least that would give him a little more time.

He went and hired a handcart and put the unconscious boy in it with a load of sacking over him. Ten minutes later he stopped outside a tavern near the docks and, checking that the boy was still out cold, he went inside. The man he sought wasn't there so he tried another tavern and this time struck lucky.

'I'm sorry I disappeared,' he told the captain of the ship he'd arrived on, 'but I had important business in York.'

'You're a deserter; I'll have you flogged for breaking your contract,' the man replied getting up and going for the dagger at his waist.

'Or you can sit down again and listen to the proposition I have for you,' Edgar said, pushing his own dagger into the man's ample midriff.

The man hesitated for a minute and then nodded.

'Wise decision. I have a replacement; he's only a boy but at least you won't have to pay him.'

They went outside and Edgar pulled back the sacking to reveal the boy, who was just coming to his senses.

'What the ..' he started to say before Edgar thrust his dagger into his neck, drawing a bead of blood.

'Shut up and come with us,'

The boy was disorientated and terrified. He nodded dumbly. A few minutes later he was being carried up the gangplank onto the knarr.

'I'll keep him locked up until we sail.'

Edgar nodded and, realising that most of the two hours had already passed, he hastened to return to hired cart and make his way to the north of the town where the Minster lay.

His mother was there before him and wasn't very pleased by his tardiness.

'It took longer to get rid of the boy tailing me than I thought,' Edgar explained.

'If you killed him KætilbiǫQrn will suspect that you've returned,' she said in agitation.

'No, no one is going to find his body. He's been taken aboard a knarr to serve as a ship's boy.'

'Good, but his disappearance will still arouse suspicions.'

'I'm sure that he's not the first urchin to vanish, it should buy me enough time to get what I want. I plan to be out of here by this time tomorrow.'

'Good. You're my son, but your presence threatens my wellbeing as well.'

They were standing in the shadows between the wall of a tavern and a house owned by a merchant.

'Very well, I'll be brief. I need to know all you can tell me about Earl Erik.'

'Erik Håkonsson,' she asked in surprise. 'Why?'

'Because my lord wants to know how he is likely to react if the Scots invade Lothian.'

'Lothian?' she repeated the name as if it was foreign country. 'Why would he be worried about Lothian? The Danes have never been too concerned about the land north of the Tees; from what I hear it's too much like the barren wasteland they left behind instead of the rolling pastures of the south.'

'So you don't think Erik would rush to defend Lothian if the Scots attacked?'

'From the gossip in the brothel, no. In fact there is a rumour circulating that a Scotsman landed from a ship a few weeks ago and went to see the earl. They were carrying a small coffer when they arrived, but left without it, or so the rumourmongers say.'

'So it's possible that Malcolm has bribed him to keep his nose out of Bernicia,' Edgar mused. 'Interesting.'

'Thanks mother, you've been a great help.'
'Are you leaving now?'
'Yes, you've told me what I needed to know.'

ᛏᛏᛏ

Edgar was surprised when his mother had cried when he left her. He'd always thought that he was an encumbrance to the whore she'd been when he was boy but perhaps absence made the heart fonder. However, he didn't feel anything for her and he left her crying without a second thought.

A little later he was back on board the knarr paying the captain for passage back to Scotland. This time he didn't need to enlist as a deck hand as he hadn't needed any of the silver that Findlay had given him for bribes after all.

The boy he'd kidnapped gave him filthy looks every time their paths crossed but Edgar knew that life as a sailor would be better for him in the long run than trying to survive as an urchin in York.

Chapter Five – York

Late Summer 1017

'Where will we go?' Ceadda asked as they approached Tilbury the next day.

'Our options seem pretty limited,' Aldred replied glumly. 'We can't go back to Normandy. I doubt that Erik Håkonsson will need the service of two score Northumbrian warriors. But if we don't find a new lord I've got a problem; my silver won't last forever.'

'You're still the Thane of Duns of course,' Ceadda said thoughtfully.

'I suppose that's true as it belonged to my father; strictly speaking Norham and Carham are also mine, although others look after them. However, Duns is in Lothian and the other two are just south of the Tweed in Bernicia proper. As soon as word reaches my uncle that I'm back he'll think I'm about to challenge him for Bebbanburg and the earldom.'

'Then reassure him that you're not.'

'He'll ask me to swear fealty to him; I just can't do that. He was part of the plot to kill my father and I can never forgive him for that.'

'You shouldn't have to. You'll have to take an oath to your ealdorman, of course, but Iuwine was never involved in the plot.'

Iuwine was the Ealdorman of Berwickshire. Ealdormen had originally been magistrates appointed by the king to administer a shire but as time went by the position had tended to become hereditary and the power of ealdormen had grown. Some answered directly to the king but others reported to an earl who governed a region, such as Bernicia.

Aldred reached the birlinn he'd left at Tilbury without further incident and they set sail for the mouth of the Thames within an hour of arrival. The first two days of their voyage north was uneventful but on the third day the wind died and they had to resort to rowing. Hakon was on lookout and, without a spar to sit on as the sail wasn't hoisted, he stood in the prow. Suddenly he called out that there was a sail on the horizon.

'It looks as if it's a knarr coming out of the Ouse estuary so it's probably come from York,' Ceadda said.

'If so, they will probably have news of what's happening in Northumbria. Let's see how close we can get without them spotting us,' Aldred said, well aware that any merchantman would view a warship with suspicion and avoid it if possible.

The wind was light and variable and the knarr had no other means of propulsion. It did have six oars but they were only useful for manoeuvring in port. To use them out on the open sea would have been futile. It had therefore been easy for Hakon to spot it from three or four miles away whereas the birlinn, with no sail, wouldn't be obvious until they got much closer.

When they were spotted the crew of the knarr sprang into action, arming themselves and lining the sides, which were much higher than those of the birlinn. However the crew of the knarr numbered no more than a dozen and none were trained fighters. The crew of the birlinn were warriors and outnumbered the other crew by a considerable margin.

'Heave to,' Aldred called across. 'We mean you no harm. I assume you come from York? I just want to know the latest news. Heave to and I will come across with half a dozen of my men, no more.'

'Who are you? You display no flag or device on a sail.'

'We aren't pirates if that's what you think. My name is Aldred, son of Uhtred of Bebbanburg.'

'Then you are welcome. We'll drop our sail so that you can come alongside.'

Edgar had been listening to this exchange with increasing alarm. If Aldred found out that he was a Scottish agent his chances of surviving were slim indeed. However, there was little he could do except stay in the background until the Northumbrians left.

It was therefore unfortunate that, as soon as Aldred and his men climbed aboard, the urchin that Edgar had brought aboard in York ran up to him and pointed him out, saying that there was a reward of twenty pounds of gold being offered for him in York.

Edgar moved forward with a dagger in his hand to silence the boy but Ceadda was too quick for him. He pulled out his own dagger and thrust the point into Edgar's forearm causing him to drop the weapon and cry out in pain.

'Bring the man and the boy aboard,' Aldred told Ceadda and followed his men back down onto his own ship. He watched the merchant ship slowly pull away in the light air and then told his crew to head for the mouth of the River Ouse.

ttt

Whilst Uuen attended to Edgar's wound Aldred took the boy to the stern where he would only be overheard by the steersman. He studied the lad, who returned his scrutiny with a defiant glare. He judged the boy to be about twelve or so but it was difficult to be sure. He was undernourished and had probably been so for most of his life, which would have hindered his growth. He was grubby and the rags he wore were filthy.

'What's your name boy?' he asked quietly.

'What's it to you?' he replied.

Aldred looked out to sea for a moment and let the pause lengthen until the boy shuffled his feet uneasily.

'You will answer my questions fully and honestly and I might just reconsider my current impulse to toss you over the side and leave you to drown,' he said with an unpleasant smile.

Aldred had no intention of carrying out his threat. Oh, he might have tossed him over the side but only after tying him to a rope so that he could be hauled back aboard after a dousing in the sea, but the boy wasn't to know that.

'Synne,' he replied softly.

'Synne?' Aldred repeated, puzzled. Synne was a girl's name which meant cheerful. 'You're a girl?'

Synne nodded.

'I see. How old are you Synne?'

'I'm not sure, I think I'm about twelve or thirteen.'

'And what exactly were you doing as a ship's boy on that knarr? And how do you know that there's a reward being offered for that man in York?'

'Because I and some of the boys in our gang were paid to watch one of the brothels and look out for strangers. Every one we spotted we followed and found out who they were and what they were doing in York.'

'Why?'

'Because someone rich has offered a reward for the son of the brothel owner.'

'What had he done?'

'Killed this rich man's only son, or so we were told.'

'And the reward is twenty pounds of gold? How do you know?'

'Because Tedman told us he'd pay ten silver pennies to the lads who found this man Edgar.'

'Tedman's your leader?' Aldred guessed.

'Not really, he's a petty thief who uses us sometimes.'

'Good. Now, provided you're telling me the truth I'll find out who the man offering the reward is and you'll get your ten silver pennies, if you want them that is.'

'Why wouldn't I?'

'Well, you can return to your life in York as a scavenger dependent on the likes of Tedman the thief if you so wish, or you can enter my service as a serving girl in my hall.'

That is provided I can reach Duns safely and persuade my uncle to leave me in peace, Aldred thought to himself.

'Serving girl? Do I get fed and somewhere safe to sleep?'

'And clean clothes befitting your sex and you get paid, not much but a few copper pennies a month.'

'Sound alright,' she said, a grin lighting up her grimy face.

'Sounds alright, lord,' Aldred corrected her.

'Yes, lord. Please, lord.'

Aldred laughed.

'But first you need to get clean. When you've done that I'll I get one of the boys to lend you a spare tunic. When we get to York I'll buy you some clothes more suitable for a girl.'

'Clean, you mean wash?'

Synne looked horrified

'Yes, you can use a barrel to preserve your modesty if you like, but you will clean your body all over, and Uuen will have to cut off your hair to get rid of the lice. Don't worry it'll grow again.'

'I'm not worried about boys seeing my body, but wash with water! Do I have to?'

'Yes, I can smell you from here, even with the wind blowing away from you.'

†††

Aldred found a berth in York and paid the port reeve for one night's stay. Then he, Ceadda, Synne and ten of his warriors set off with Edgar to find Tedman. Twelve armed men marching through the narrow streets of York was bound to arouse unwanted interest and so they travelled in three separate groups: Aldred, Synne, Edgar and two men leading, followed by the other two groups at discreet distances.

Synne led Aldred to a tavern near the docks where she said that Tedman could usually be found every evening. It didn't look very prepossessing from the outside and Aldred guessed that the clientele weren't the sort to let him haul Tedman outside without a fight, so he decided on a more subtle approach.

Whilst his men took up positions opposite the two doors he handed his sword, hauberk and leather gambeson, helmet and arming cap to Ceadda and went in alone dressed in just his drabbest tunic with only a dagger at his belt. Once inside he let his eyes adjust to the gloom before making his way to the plank of wood suspended on two barrels that served as a bar.

The room was full of men; perhaps thirty in all. Most seemed to be there with the sole intention of getting drunk but a number of small groups sat at tables engrossed in earnest conversation. He suspected that what they were discussing was far from honest. None wore swords as far as he could see, but there were several cudgels in evidence as well as a knife or dagger at most belts. There was little or no ventilation and the room stank of sweat, vomit and stale beer.

Aldred pushed a silver penny across the improvised bar and asked for a pint of ale. He took a sip and it tasted even worse than he'd feared. The tavern keeper pushed his change towards him but Aldred shook his head and, instead, pushed another penny towards the portly man in the stained apron.

'Keep it and here's another if you point out a man named Tedman for me.'

'I don't want any trouble; Tedman would have my guts for identifying him to a stranger.'

So saying, he pushed the coins away from him again. Aldred was at a loss what to do next, short of calling out the name and seeing who responded, when the man standing next to him scooped up the coins and pointed to a thin youth in dirty yellow trousers and a brown tunic sitting at a table with three others at the far side of the room.

'Thanks, friend,' Aldred muttered and made his way to the table.

'I'm looking for a man named Tedman. I have an opportunity for him to make some money,' he told the shifty looking quartet as he sat down on the bench opposite Tedman.

All four men eased their daggers in their scabbards, a trick Aldred knew only too well. It meant they were preparing to draw them quickly. Aldred smiled and placed a pouch containing a few small coins on the table.

'This is just to prove that I am serious and not trying to trick you.'

The young man who the man at the bar had said was Tedman grabbed the pouch and shoved it out of sight. The others protested but he told them in graphic terms to be quiet.

'What do you want with Tedman?' the man asked.

'I believe you know a street girl named Synne?' Aldred asked.

'Maybe,' he said cautiously, then added, his curiosity piqued, 'she disappeared; do you know where she is?'

'Outside,' Aldred replied, 'with a score of my men.'

Aldred exaggerated the number who had accompanied him just to make sure that no one did anything stupid. The four, who had started to rise to go and see for themselves, sunk back onto their benches.

'Very well,' Tedman said eventually as the silence lengthened, 'what do you want and how much are you prepared to pay for it?'

'Synne says that someone is offering a fair sum in gold for news of a man called Edgar. I want to know his name and whereabouts.'

Tedman relaxed and smiled smugly.

'You know where Edgar, son of the whore who keeps the brothel on Woolgate, is?'

Tedman's smile widened exposing his blackened, missing and rotting teeth. Aldred wondered idly how they had got into that state in such a young man. He must be in a lot of pain; such a man could be illogical and dangerous.

'I may do, but that's my business. I will pay you to tell me who is offering the reward for him.'

'How much?'

'Ten silver pennies.'

Tedman laughed, but there was no mirth in it.

'You must take me for a fool. I don't care how many men you say you have outside, you will tell me now where Edgar is or my friends and I will remove your testicles from your body.'

'I wouldn't do that if I were you,' a voice said softly in Tedman's ear as he felt the point of a knife prick his side just about where one of his kidneys lay.

At the same moment his three companions felt someone put their hands on their shoulders and, at the same time, a small stabbing pain in their sides. Cedda, Wictred and two other warriors had quietly entered the tavern and bought a beer whilst Tedman and his cronies were engrossed in conversation with Aldred, so they hadn't noticed the four make their way across the crowded room to where they were sitting.

'Kill me and you'll never know who's offering the reward,' Tadman said, thinking that would keep him from harm.

'Oh, I don't suppose it's much of a secret. If I was offering a reward I would want it announced far and wide. The trouble is that it's been six years and many will have forgotten or not have been in York at the time. Only you seemed to have had the perseverance to remain on the lookout for Edgar; you and your gang of street urchins.'

Aldred took out his own dagger and started to clean his nails with its sharp point.

'Now I'm in a hurry so I'd prefer it if you told me in exchange for ten silver pennies. If not, I'll stay another day and find out another way. It won't concern you though because you'll all be floating down the Ouse with your throats cut.'

'You wouldn't dare kill us here,' Tadman blustered, 'you'd never get out alive'

'No, but you have to leave sometime and I don't suppose that however many bully boys you get to escort you can tackle my armoured warriors, all of whom are battle-hardened and have been trained by the Normans.'

Tedman nervously looked at the hauberks that Aldred and his men wore under their cloaks and, although they had left their helmets and swords outside, he didn't doubt what the young Northumbrian had said. The Norman knights had gained quite a reputation on the continent and even Tedman had heard about them.

He nodded. 'Very well, but the price is fifty silver pennies.'

'Twenty and that's my final offer.'

'No, not enough, forty then.'

'Perhaps you don't understand what the word final means. Accept twenty or we walk out of here and wait for you outside, and I'm well aware that there is a back entrance.'

Tedman's shoulders slumped and he nodded. Aldred took a second pouch from Ceadda and passed it to Tedman under the table. None of them wanted others knowing what was happening. Twenty silver pennies was a rich enough sum to start a fight with every man in the place trying to grab it.

'The man you want is Kætilbiǫrn the goldsmith. Ask anyone for his workshops in Gulsmedgate.'

'Thank you. Now that wasn't too difficult was it?'

Aldred got up to leave and his companions sheathed their daggers out of sight under their cloaks.

'Oh, by the way, if I find you have played me false my ship's crew and I will come looking for you and there won't be anywhere to hide.'

Tedman didn't respond. He waited until the warriors were leaving and then spat on the floor. It broke the tension and the four started squabbling over the twenty silver pennies.

ϮϮϮ

It wasn't difficult to find Kætilbiǫrn's workshop the next morning, but before Aldred set out with Edgar bound and gagged in a handcart to keep him quiet, he had questioned him. He was curious why the man would risk capture by coming back to a place where he had a hefty price on his head.

At first the man wouldn't talk; not even when Aldred threatened to kill his mother. There might be a bond of filial loyalty there, but it was a weak one, at least on the son's side. It wasn't a threat that Aldred would ever carry out; he didn't attack women, or children if he could help it, but Edgar wasn't to know that.

However, he decided to talk after Ceadda had taken him to a horse trough and, whilst the crew of the birlinn kept away the curious, he repeatedly held Edgar's head under water until he was close to drowning. After the third such immersion Findlay's agent decided that he nothing to lose by talking.

After he'd finished his tale Aldred told Ceadda that he needed to warn Erik Håkonsson about the threat to the north of his domain. Aldred's uncle might be the Earl of Bernicia but Erik was lord of all Northumbria and he could call on over twice the number of men that Eadwulf could raise on his own.

Edgar laughed when he said this.

'King Malcolm has already bought Erik's neutrality. You won't get any help from the quarter,' he said with a satisfied smirk.

'Then we need to warn Cnut,' Aldred decided. 'I don't suppose that he wants to bring the border with the Scots any closer.'

The problem was that Cnut was preparing to march against Eadric Streona who he'd retained as Earl of Mercia. The ever treacherous Eadric had betrayed Cnut's trust and had risen in revolt against the new king's rule. No doubt he expected his loyalty to be bought back by additional grants of lands but Aldred had a feeling that this time he'd run out of lives.

Mercia was far more important to Cnut that Lothian, or even Bernicia as a whole. Moreover one of Aldred's men had overheard gossip that Erik Håkonsson was about to depart to join Cnut with his housecarls to help put down the revolt.

Kætilbiǫrn turned out to be a plump merchant who liked to adorn himself with jewellery. He might call himself a goldsmith but he was in reality a merchant who employed others to do all the work. At first he was suspicious and took some convincing that Edgar was indeed the boy who'd killed his own son six years ago. Once he was satisfied he tried to haggle the reward down.

Aldred, who was pre-occupied with the threat to Lothian, had no patience for Kætilbiǫrn's games and he told him in no uncertain terms that he would take Edgar back to his ship and sail away with him if he didn't pay him the full twenty pounds of gold there and then.

Even then the merchant tried to prevaricate, saying that it would take him time to amass such a large sum. Aldred was no fool and was aware that the fat man was hoping to gather enough ruffians to overcome Aldred and the few warriors he'd brought with him without paying him a copper coin.

'Ceadda hold this fat oaf's hand palm down on the bench, would you.'

Kætilbiǫrn squealed in alarm as Ceadda did as he was bid and Aldred drew his dagger. One of the apprentices tried to sidle away to raise the alarm but Wictred stepped in front of him and pointed his sword at his throat. No one else moved after that. Aldred held his dagger over the plump hand and asked Kætilbiǫrn quietly which finger he would like him to sever first.

That was enough for the man to honour the pledge he'd made and weigh out twenty pounds of gold. It took all the ingots in the workshop and most of the gold ornaments that his apprentices were working on to make up that sum. Kætilbiǫrn was in tears by the time that Aldred had finished.

Aldred put the coffer containing the gold in the handcart and covered it with the sackcloth that had previously concealed Edgar. He shoved Edgar towards Kætilbiǫrn and wished him a pleasant day as he and his men filed out.

'Oh, and if you even stir from here in the next hour or try and send men after us, the next time I draw this dagger will be to cut your throat.'

☩☩☩

Kætilbiǫrn was evidently not a brave man; or perhaps he was loathe to earn the reputation as a man who renegaded on a deal, but they left the dock and sailed back down the Ouse without any problems. Now Aldred's money worries were over for some time to come but the next problem was how to return to Duns without opposition from his uncle.

With the information he'd learnt about Malcolm's planned invasion and Erik Håkonsson's abandonment of Bernicia to its fate he felt that Eadwulf should be grateful for his support, but he knew that was too much to hope for. He was more likely to kill him out of hand. He needed someone to advise him on how to make Eadwulf listen.

He mulled over what to do for some time then the solution came to him.

Chapter Six – Bebbanburg

Autumn 1017

He should have thought of his grandfather before, but the truth was he barely knew Bishop Aldhun, the father of Uhtred's first wife, Ecgfrida. Aldhun and Uhtred had fallen out when he had put aside Aldred's mother in order to marry Sige, the daughter of an influential Dane in Deira when Uhtred had become Earl of Northumbria. It was a necessary political move as part of Uhtred's strategy to unite Bernicia and Deira under his rule, but Aldhun had never forgiven him. That didn't mean he wouldn't help his grandson though, or so he hoped.

Aldhun had been the last bishop of Bernicia to be ordained as Bishop of Lindisfarne, the original base of Christianity in Northumbria. After numerous Viking raids the bishop and the monks had fled the Holy Island of Lindisfarne carrying the coffin of the blessed Saint Cuthbert with them. After years of wandering they had settled at Chester-le-Street but then, with Uhtred's help, Aldhun had moved his seat to Durham and had become its first bishop.

As far as Aldred knew, he was still bishop, though he had to be quite old now. As the most influential person in Bernicia after Earl Eadwulf, his support would mean a great deal.

Durham was on the River Wear but was some distance inland from the coast. Aldred's steersman thought that it was probably navigable as far as Chester-le-Street but that was some six miles north of Durham. Furthermore he would hardly have a use for a birlinn at Duns, so he decided to sell it and use the proceeds to buy horses.

It wasn't as easy as he'd expected. The birlinn was an excellent example of its kind but it was a warship which required a large crew to man it. Merchantmen, like the knarrs, only required half or dozen or so to sail them. However, the threat of pirates and Vikings in the North Sea was ever present and so eventually a wool merchant bought it to protect his convoys between Northumbria and Flanders. He wouldn't pay anything like its true worth, however, and Aldred also had to dig into his chest of silver to purchase the horses he needed.

With these he was luckier. There was a horse fair taking place in Sunderland at the mouth of the Wear and he managed to purchase enough stallions of the right size for his warriors and mares for Uuen and the ship's boys as well as a dozen pack horses and a pony for Synne. He knew he would need spare horses in due course, but what he had bought would have to do for now.

The men gossiped about his extravagance in buying a pony for a servant girl. He couldn't say why he had developed a soft spot for Synne, except that he was determined to try and make up for the rough life she'd led so far.

The steersman had declined to join them. He said that he hated horses and was never happier than when he was at sea, so he stayed with the birlinn. It was an impressive cavalcade that rode out of Sunderland the following morning. Aldred and Ceadda led the forty men accoutred as Norman knights, except for the round shields which they'd retained in preference to the kite shaped ones that the Normans had taken to using. By now they were used to the heavier chainmail hauberk, which protected the legs down to the knees as well the upper arms.

Aldred's banner of a black wolf's head on a red field was carried proudly by Wictred; in contrast to the yellow background which had been used by the lords of Bebbanburg for centuries and which was still used by Earl Eadwulf. Half of the mounted warriors rode behind Aldred, then came the servants, Synne and the pack horses and finally the other score of warriors. Aldred wasn't expecting trouble but nevertheless he sent out a pair of scouts ahead of the column and another pair at the rear to make sure they weren't being followed.

The ride south took less than two hours and Durham came into sight just after the early morning sun disappeared behind grey clouds. The light wind had also become brisker and Aldred guessed that rain was on the way. At this point the Wear looped around the hill on which Durham stood in an almost complete circle. The tongue of land that led into the town was no more than three hundred yards wide and it was spanned by a palisade with towers at each end and two in the middle either side of the gates.

As Aldred's men rode towards the gates they were closed in their faces and archers appeared the towers on either side.

'What is your business here and why do you come dressed for war?' a voice called down from the right hand tower.

'I am Bishop Aldhun's grandson, Aldred of Bebbanburg. Is my grandfather well?'

'Aye, he is, but why are you dressed like that if you are Northumbrians?'

'The armour and helmets were a gift from the brother of King Cnut's queen, Emma of Normandy.'

Whoever was in charge seemed suitably impressed by that and shortly afterwards the gates swung open and an old man wearing a simple black habit with a gold pectoral cross on his chest walked out carrying a crosier and attended by several monks and half a dozen members of the town watch.

Aldred dismounted and walked towards the old man, who had to be Aldhun. It had been some time since he'd seen his grandfather. The bishop's grey hair was now wispy and his equally grey beard was longer than he remembered. He knelt before him and took the bishop's frail right hand in his. The skin resembled spotted parchment but the grip was firm. He kissed Aldhun's ring and got to his feet, only to be embraced by the elderly cleric. The hug was as strong as the grip had been. Aldhun might look as if he was at death's door but appearances lied. He seemed fit and robust for a man his age.

'I never thought to see the only surviving male member of my family again. It is good to see you boy.'

The words *only surviving male* suddenly struck Aldred. Were there other female relatives then?

'How is my mother? Does she live still?'

'No, I fear not. I received word last month that Ecgfrida died during an outbreak of the plague. Her daughter, Sigfreda, is your half-sister, or course, but I've never even seen the child. '

'I'm so sorry, grandfather,' sounded inadequate but it was all he could think of to say.

Aldred felt guilty because he hardly remembered his mother and had rarely even thought about her in recent years. He'd been barely nine when his father had divorced Ecgfrida and he'd been brought up by his father's second wife, Sige, until he left home to start his education and, after that, his training as a warrior.

He had vaguely heard of Sigfreda. She was the daughter of Kilvert, the thane Ecgfrida had married after Uhtred had divorced her. Like his grandfather, he'd never met her.

'I'm sure you won't have heard yet; Sigfreda has recently become betrothed.' He paused for effect. 'To Eadwulf.'

Aldred's first reaction was to protest that she was the man's niece, but then he realised that there was no blood tie between them.

At least I've still got you,' Aldhun said, but he made it sound as if he was a poor second best to his mother. 'Come up to the monastery with whoever you need to keep with you, but your men had better camp here.'

'On the field of the dead?' Aldred said dubiously.

'No, they are all buried over there. You won't find their ghosts over on the east bank.'

He said it derisively, as if only children should be afraid of the spirit world. Practically all Aldred's men were Christians, but most were very superstitious and their belief in the pagan pantheon wasn't entirely dead.

That evening Aldred told his tale to his grandfather whilst they ate in the bishop's hall, together with the abbot and the prior and a twelve year old novice called Beda, the elder son of Leofwine, Ealdorman of Durham. Beda was over the age when the sons of nobles usually began training as a warrior and Aldred had asked about this when they had been introduced.

'I am not my father's favourite son,' Beda had replied with some heat. 'My mother was divorced by my father so that he could marry a younger, and richer, woman. Her son, my half-brother, has been already been named as heir to the vills my father owns and he intends to ask the king to confirm him as the next ealdorman when the time comes, so there is little other option open to me but to become a monk.'

'Is that what you want to do,' Aldred had asked.

'No, I want to be a warrior, but my father has neglected to find me a place with a noble prepared to sponsor my training.'

'It's true,' Aldhun had explained. 'Beda doesn't have the vocation to become either a monk or a priest. He's always up to mischief and I know that's because he's bored.'

'And that's why he's dining with us? In the hope that I might train him?'

Aldhun had nodded but, despite the hopeful look on Beda's face, Aldred hadn't responded and had instead told the company what he'd learned in York.

'I take it that you want me to take these dire tidings to Eadwulf at Bebbanburg?' the bishop asked when Aldred had finished his tale.

'I think he's more likely to listen to you and, in any case, my beloved uncle would probably part my head from my body if I went to Bebbanburg.'

'Very well, but on one condition,' Aldhun said, 'you take the boy off the church's hands.'

Aldred looked at Beda again. He'd been impressed when the boy hadn't thrown a fit of the sulks when he hadn't taken the bait and offered him a place the first time the bishop had suggested it.

Instead he'd eaten his meal quietly, glancing hopefully at Aldred from time to time.

'Very well, you can join my former ship's boys who are now being taught to become warriors.'

ᛏᛏᛏ

Aldhun was feeling very stiff and weary by the time that the fortress on its impressive outcrop of basalt rock hove into view. He was now in his late fifties and riding made every bone in his body ache. Nevertheless, he had eschewed travelling in a carriage. He owned one but he found the jolting around in a conveyance that was little more than an unsprung cart with a roof to be even more uncomfortable than sitting astride a horse all day.

He was escorted by his chaplain, the Prior of Durham and six of Aldred's warriors pretending to be in the bishop's service. Aldhun didn't keep warriors himself and he would rather use the silver they cost for what he regarded as more useful purposes, like the relief of poverty. To disguise their true identity, the six chosen wore traditional Anglo-Saxon byrnies and helmets and had painted their shields blue with a yellow cross: the emblem of the See of Durham. Wictred led the six. He unfurled the bishop's banner and held it high as they approached the gates.

Aldhun's mood was sombre and apprehensive as he rode into the fortress and along the roofless tunnel to the second gate. This space had been designed by a previous lord of Bebbanburg so that, if the outer gate fell, the attackers would be caught in a confined space where they could be slaughtered from above.

As the bishop rode up the slope to the second gate a few raindrops fell on him and he was reminded of the passageway's lethal purpose. By the time that he had dismounted, with help, outside Eadwulf's hall the few spots had turned into a downpour.

Aldred's uncle appeared at the entrance to the hall and feigned astonishment at the identity of his visitor.

'What bishop, have you come to excommunicate me for my wanton and lustful ways?' he asked sarcastically.

'Can we get in out of this damned rain before we exchange pleasantries, my lord earl?'

'Of course, my dear Aldhun. We don't want you to catch a chill and die, now do we? Please come in.'

He gave the bishop a sardonic grin and stood aside so that Aldhun could enter and go to the central hearth to dry himself. His chaplain and Wictred followed him inside whilst the rest took the horses off to the stables.

The bishop looked about as he warmed his hands and his damp garments started to steam as they dried out. The last time he'd been in the hall, when Uhtred had been earl, was many years ago but little had changed except that the hall seemed shorter and he could have sworn that there had been two hearths in those days. Then he realised that Eadwulf had sealed off the far end with a full hight partition. Presumably he kept the newly created area as private quarters for himself and his women.

This outer hall was obviously just used by the steward and his clerks to administer his lands and to receive guests. Aldhun knew that Eadwulf's housecarls and the other men of the garrison lived in the warriors' hall or in the village with their wives and families.

'Well, bishop, what brings you to Bebbanburg?'

'Two things, Eadwulf, but before I explain what they are might I sit and rest my old bones and have some refreshment after the long journey from Durham?'

'Do you intend to stay the night?'

'You think I came all this way to see you and then propose to start back again as soon as we have spoken?' Aldhun asked incredulously.

'No, I suppose not, damn you. You're not sleeping here though, you can stay with the priest in the village.'

'And the rest of my party? I doubt that the good father will have room for all of us.'

'Ask the thane to find them lodging,' he said rudely. 'Now what do you want?'

'A chair, stool or bench, and something to eat and drink?' the bishop prompted quietly.

'What? Oh, very well. Hluda!'

A girl who couldn't have been more than twelve appeared from the far room dressed only in a man's tunic which was far too big for her. Aldhun was shocked at the sight and looked away, trembling with rage. He might have had a daughter in the days when such things were not looked on with disapproval by the Church, as they were today, but such flaunting of flesh, and in such a young child, make him feel sick.

Eadwulf smiled at him in an unpleasant way.

'Yes, I know what you're thinking. Hluda should have more modesty, but as she is here to keep me company in bed, there seems little point in dressing her.

'You must have other servants!' Aldhun thundered. 'Ones who could serve a bishop without causing so much offence.'

'Of course, but I wanted to see the expression on your face.'

He laughed and waved the child away; a minute later an old man brought Aldhun a stool and a boy handed him a glass of mead and a plate of bread and cheese.

'Now, to business; I haven't got all day.'

'What have you heard about King Malcolm recently?'

'Nothing much, why? As long as the barbarians stay in the north I'm not much interested.'

He spat into the fire to emphasise the point.

'Perhaps you should be. Malcolm is preparing a great army to invade Lothian and make it part of his kingdom once and for all. He already has Edinburgh and its shire. Now he wants the rest. He may not even stop at the Tweed.'

'How do you know this? It can't be true. He learnt his lesson a dozen years ago at Durham.'

'Yes, by an army from all Northumbria led by a great warrior.'

Eadwulf flushed at the oblique reference to his brother. He'd been part of the conspiracy to kill Uhtred and he didn't like to be reminded of that inconvenient fact.

'Earl Erik will bring the army of Deira to my aid,' he said, quite flustered by now.

But Aldhun shook his head.

'Malcolm has already bought Erik's neutrality. There will be no help coming from York.'

'How do you know all this? How do I know that you're not trying to deceive me?'

'I hear things,' the bishop said airily.

'From whom? Come on, you could be making this up for all I know.'

'Why would I do that?'

'I don't know; because you detest me and want to make me run around like a headless chicken?'

'I have several sources, but the main one is my grandson.'

'Your grandson?'

It took a minute for the penny to drop.

'You mean Aldred, that little runt! Why on earth should I believe him?'

'Because he's just come from York. He captured an agent of Findlay of Moray at sea and took him back to York where he had a price on his head.'

'And this agent just spun him this yarn out of the goodness of his heart, did he?'

'No, Aldred was going to kill the agent's mother if he didn't.'

Eadwulf sat staring into the dying flames of the fire before he was disturbed by a slave throwing more wood onto it.

'Where's Aldred now?'

'At Durham with his warband.'

'Warband? What warband?'

'Forty Northumbrians armed and trained as Norman knights by Duke Richard.'

'I see. I need to speak to him and find out exactly how much he knows.'

'That would be sensible, but arranging such a meeting might be a little difficult,' Aldhun said tentatively.

'Why? I'll give you a safe conduct for him.'

'I seem to remember that his father was under the impression that King Cnut had given him a safe conduct when he went to his death at the hands of Thurbrand Styrsson.' He paused before adding, 'and others.'

Eadwulf flashed him an angry look but said nothing.

'What do you suggest then?'

'I said I had two matters to discuss with you. The other is Aldred's inheritance.'

'I'm appointed as Earl of Bernicia and that includes being lord of Bebbanburg. Does he intend to challenge the king over that?' Eadwulf scoffed.

'No, not Bebbanburg; Duns, Norham and Carham, which were my gift to his father. It is customary for the eldest son to inherit the property of a dead thane.'

'After paying the inheritance tax due,' Eadwulf added with a cold smile.

'How much is that?'

Before Eadwulf could prevaricate and say he'd have to find out, the voice of the steward in the corner interrupted them.

'Four ounces of gold or the equivalent value in silver, my lord.'

Whilst Eadwulf gave his steward an annoyed look, which the other man ignored, Aldhun pulled out a small ingot of gold from the pouch at his waist.

'That's a pound of gold, take a quarter of it and give me back the rest,' he told the steward.

'Yes, lord bishop,' the man said as he came across to collect the bullion ingot.

'From Kætilbiǫrn the goldsmith,' he said, seemingly impressed, after looking at the mark on the underside of the ingot. 'At least I won't have to check that it hasn't been adulterated. The man is hard and avaricious, but he's honest.'

'This is the deed confirming the transfer of the three vills, Lord Eadwulf. Just affix your seal here if you would,' Aldhun said with a smile, beckoning the steward to bring wax, a candle and the earl's seal to him.

'Good, now that's over and done with, can I suggest that you meet your nephew at Duns in a week's time?'

'How do I know that I can trust him?' the earl asked, feeling that he'd been manipulated in a way he didn't quite understand.

'You can trust him in just the same way that I know he can trust his uncle,' Aldhun said with a smile. 'Besides, I'll be there to see fair play.'

Chapter Seven – The War Council at Duns

December 1017

Various senior churchmen, ealdormen and thanes had arrived at Duns over the past two days and Aldred had made a note of each as they arrived. Some thanes came with just a servant whereas each of the ealdormen brought most of their housecarls as an escort. The areas of dry ground between the myriad of small streams that lay to the south of Duns were full of leather tents. Thankfully the weather was cold but dry and so the area hadn't yet been turned into a morass of mud by the feet of men and horses.

He'd been pleased to see that the abbots of Tynemouth and Jarrow had come to support the Bishop of Durham. There had been a bishop and a monastery at Hexham for centuries but it still hadn't been rebuilt after the last time that the Vikings burnt it to the ground and the former diocese was now part of Durham. All nine ealdormen were present, together with some fifty thanes. Only Aldred's uncle had yet to arrive.

As the morning wore on the sky darkened, matching Aldred's mood. Several of the gathered nobles demanded that they start the council without Eadwulf but Aldhun advised patience. Bread cheese, ale and mead were served to the throng gathered in the small hall at Duns to keep the impatient men quiet.

Aldred scarcely recognised the girl who brought refreshments to the high table where he sat as host, together with Aldhun and the three most senior of the ealdormen. It had been three months since he had last consciously looked at Synne, the street urchin from York. Over that time her scrawny body had filled out, she had grown a little in height and her blond hair had grown back and, although it was still the length of a boy's, she looked much more like a thirteen year old girl, and a pretty one at that. Even her small breasts were now quite noticeable, unlike the flat chest he remembered. He was uncomfortably aware that he felt attracted to her; something he chastised himself about. It was his uncle who liked young girls, not him.

He surreptitiously watched her whilst listening to what Aldhun was saying and, when she went into a corner and started to talk to young Beda, their intimacy made Aldred feel jealous.

Thankfully at this point the noise outside indicated the arrival of Eadwulf and those sitting at the high table rose to their feet as the Earl of Bernicia strode into the room. Two of his housecarls preceded him, shoving men out of the way to make an unnecessarily large passage through the throng for their master and the dozen housecarls who followed him.

'Uncle, welcome,' Aldred said with an insincere smile. 'We're all glad that you could join us.'

Aldred indicated the empty chair next to him and invited him to take a seat with a wave of his hand, which Eadwulf ignored. Instead he stood at the front of the low dais on which the table sat and let his eyes travel over the men who stood in front of him.

Apparently satisfied, he turned back to those behind him.

'It isn't seemly for the Earl of Bernicia to sit amongst thanes and ealdormen,' he stated haughtily. 'Of course, you may remain bishop but I'd be obliged if the rest of you would join your fellows in the main body of this poor excuse for a hall.'

Aldred and the three senior ealdormen were furious but, as Eadwulf's warriors moved towards them, evidently intending to remove them by force if necessary, they had little choice but to obey. They descended to stand in front of the rest with as much dignity as they could muster. There were angry murmurs in the hall at Eadwulf's high handed action, but there were also quite a few sniggers. The voices died away and Leofwine of Durham spoke into silence of the hall.

'That was thoughtless and stupid of you, Eadwulf. We need to unite if Bernicia is to survive, but that was the action of a man who seems bent on causing dissention and disharmony. It certainly wasn't the act of a man who is fit to lead us.'

'You will be quiet,' Eadwulf thundered. 'I was appointed by the king to rule Bernicia as I see fit. Ealdormen come under me and, if I so wish, I can ask the king to appoint others in your place. Be very careful what you say in future or you will suffer my wrath.'

'Can you imagine your brother, Uhtred, behaving like a spoilt brat?'

This came from Iuwine, Ealdorman of Berwickshire, one of the two remaining shires in Lothian.

'Silence, silence I say, or I will have my housecarls remove you by force.'

Eadwulf had gone red in the face with rage and four of the warriors who had accompanied him moved towards Leofwine and Iuwine, presumably intent on carrying out their master's orders.

Bishop Aldhun had watched the sudden disintegration of the war council into farce with increasing dismay. Now he got to his feet and pointed at the housecarls.

'Stop where you are. This is the height of folly, my lords. We're here to decide how best to deal with a full scale invasion by the Scots. I can remember what it was like eleven years ago when they ravaged Lothian and the rest of Bernicia and they would have taken Durham had it not been for Earl Uhtred. Let's concentrate on the reason we are all here, instead of allowing our emotions to get the better of us.'

He sat down but the housecarls didn't go back to the periphery of the hall until Eadwulf nodded his head. Aldred breathed a sigh of relief. His own men were waiting outside the hall just in case Eadwulf tried to do anything idiotic but, had he been forced to call them, then people would have been killed and wounded and that was the last thing he wanted.

Not trusting himself to speak, the earl waved his hand at the bishop, indicating that he should tell the council the situation as he saw it.

'My lords, all that I know was told to me by my grandson, though parts of his tale have since been confirmed by others. I suggest that, rather than relate it second hand, he should tell you what he has discovered.'

Aldhun ignored the savage glare that Eadwulf gave him and sat down again. Eadwulf was about to say something but evidently thought better of it as his nephew came and stood on the dais and, turning his back on the two sitting there, addressed the throng in front of him.

'My main source is a man named Edgar, the agent of Findlay, Mormaer of Moray. Findlay had sent him to York to find out whether the invasion that King Malcolm intends to launch against us next spring was likely to succeed. Apparently Findlay is in two minds about supporting Malcolm in this venture, even though the King of Scots holds Findlay's eldest son, Macbeth, as hostage.

'What he learned in York was that Earl Erik had already been bribed by Malcolm not to come to our aid. We are therefore on our own.'

Uproar greeted this statement with many calling Erik Håkonsson a traitor and others yelling that you could never trust a Dane.

Aldred held up his hands for quiet and, after the bishop had banged his crozier on the floor several times, relative silence returned.

'I also learned that Owain the Bald, King of Strathclyde, will be joining Malcolm's attempt at conquest, just as he did in 1006. It therefore seems that we will be facing a sizable army, many more than the numbers we can raise at any rate.'

'Is there any indication when we can expect this attack?' one of the other ealdormen asked.

'No, but you can't muster thousands of men without there being some signs. My guess would be in the spring.'

'Your guess,' the sneering voice of his uncle came from behind Aldred. 'How do we know that this isn't a whole farrago of lies and speculation? What is it based on? Where is this agent from Moray?'

Aldred slowly turned and stared his uncle in the eye. The man refused to meet his stare and, instead, looked past him at the nobles.

'For all we know this is all a ploy to ingratiate yourself with us after fleeing Northumbria following your father's unfortunate death. That in itself looks suspicious.'

'My family and I fled because we know you had a hand in his murder, uncle, and I was warned that you wanted me and my brother Eadulf dead. However,' he said turning back to face the nobles, 'none of that matters at the moment. Much as I detest you, we need to band together and cannot afford to fall out amongst ourselves.'

He paused and then called out 'Ceadda, Synne, come here please.'

Ceadda emerged from the door and made his way through the crowd whilst Synne made her way from the servant's quarters, demurely looking at the floor. Ceadda was attired in his Norman armour, complete with hauberk and a helmet which appeared different to the Anglo-Saxon type. It was beaten from one piece of iron instead of being segmented which made it much stronger. The ridged nasal was riveted onto it. Unlike Eadwulf's housecarls, who wore leather arming caps under their helmets, Ceadda wore a leather lined chainmail coif under his helmet which protected the sides of his face, his neck and part of his torso as it came down over the top part of his hauberk.

Compared to other housecarls he look much more intimidating. Synne, in contrast, looked every inch an innocent young girl.

'Synne, what do you know of Edgar?'

'I was paid to keep a lookout for him at his mother's brothel as Kætilbiǫrn the goldsmith had offered a sizeable reward for him. Edgar had killed Kætilbiǫrn's only son years before. I didn't know who he was then, but when a stranger came to the brothel I was sent to follow him. Unfortunately he captured me and sold me as a ship's boy to the skipper of a merchantman. Later he came aboard himself and bought his passage back up to Scotland.

'We had just cleared the Ouse estuary when Lord Aldred's birlinn came alongside. I told him that Edgar had a price on his head and the man tried to kill me. Lord Aldred took Edgar and me aboard his ship and I returned to York with him. We took Edgar to see Kætilbiǫrn and he handed him over for trial in exchange for the reward. That's all I know, lord.'

'I questioned Edgar and eventually he confessed that he was an agent of Mormaer Findlay of Moray,' Ceadda now took up the tale. 'He'd been sent to find out if Erik of Northumbria would stand against Malcolm if he invaded. Apparently Findlay was chary of supporting his king if it was likely to end up in a disaster like the Scot's last invasion in 1006. In York Edgar had learned that Erik had been bribed by Malcolm to keep Deira from supporting us; in exchange Malcolm has sworn not to venture south of the River Tees.'

When the uproar that followed this had died down, Aldred cleared his throat and let his gaze travel over the faces in the hall. Perhaps there were one or two who looked sceptical but most now seemed convinced that what he'd told them was true.

'What happened to Edgar?' one of the thanes asked. 'Why not bring him here to face us so that he could confirm what we've heard is true?'

'Because he was worth a lot of money in York and needed to face justice there.'

'How do we know that what he told Ceadda was the truth?' another asked.

'Because Ceadda is very good at getting the truth out of people, and because I threatened to kill his mother if he didn't tell us all he knew.'

'Would you have done?'

'That's irrelevant; it wasn't necessary in the end.'

'It seems that you have convinced everyone that the threat is real, nephew,' Eadwulf said from behind him, his scepticism evident in every word. 'It'll soon be dark and it's started to rain. I suggest we let everyone go back to their tents and reconvene back here after breakfast tomorrow.'

After people had begun to leave Eadwulf got up and came around the table to speak to Aldred.

'I don't like you, boy, and I know you don't like me; but I suggest we call a truce and work together until we've defeated Malcolm.'

'It's not that I dislike you, uncle, though I do; it's that fact that you were involved in the plot against my father that I can never forgive.'

'You can't know that,' Eadwulf said dismissively.

'Oh, but I do. There were two witnesses who escaped from the ambush and they both saw you there, although you were too cowardly to actually fight against him yourself.'

Eadwulf's hand went to the hilt of his dagger but he suddenly found Ceadda's mailed fist clamped around it.

'Not a good idea, if you want to live,' the housecarl whispered in his ear.

'For now I will serve under you but, once Malcolm is defeated, you are a dead man walking, as is that sheep's dropping Thurbrand Styrsson,' Aldred told him, his face only inches form Eadwulf's.

He stepped back and smiled sardonically.

'In the meantime you are welcome to stay in my hall, uncle, but you may prefer the security of your own camp.'

ṪṪṪ

All sign of the previous night's rain had cleared by dawn and Duns awoke to a clear, if cold, morning. As men emptied their bladders and bowels and got campfires started Aldred led his forty housecarls out of his fortress. They were all dressed as Norman knights with the single exception of their round shields. The long spears they held on high were decorated with a small pennon coloured red and black and Wictred carried Aldred's banner of a black wolf's face on a red field.

Everyone gathered at the edge of the camp to watch as the horsemen formed up in two ranks and started to trot towards the camp. The trot changed to a canter and then, as they lowered their spears, to the gallop. Some men started to retreat in panic whilst others uncertainly gripped their weapons and held their shields in front of them.

At the last moment the line split into two and turned to gallop past the startled nobles and their servants. They returned to their starting position and repeated the exercise, except that this time they charged as a wedge formation. This time they all wheeled to the right and came to a halt.

Aldred rode out of the formation and halted his sweating horse in front of the gawping crowd and pulled his helmet from his head.

'I'm sorry if I interrupted your breakfast, my lords, but I wanted to demonstrate what a relatively small group of mounted warriors can do in battle. The wedge can break a shield wall or break through a mass of ill-organised Scotsmen, whereas a charge in line, men riding knee to knee, is virtually irresistible, especially when deployed against the flank of the enemy.

'The demonstration is over. I look forward to seeing you in the hall shortly where Bishop Aldred will celebrate mass before we continue our deliberations.'

Eadwulf had watched the mock attack with some alarm. He'd heard of the success that Duke Richard had had with his heavy cavalry but he hadn't realised what a formidable weapon they could be until today. He'd dismissed his young nephew as not much of a threat to him before the meeting at Duns; now he would take him a little more seriously.

ттт

Findlay of Moray was uneasy. Edgar had never reappeared and he thought that he might have betrayed him until word reached him that the man had been hung in York for a murder committed some years previously. It seemed completely unconnected to his mission for Findlay, but you could never be too cautious. Edgar had been the perfect agent because he was a Saxon and a native of York; he had the contacts and didn't stand out like a Scot would. The muster for the invasion of Northumbria could only be a few months away now and Findlay didn't know whether to answer it or stay well clear.

He was used to discussing such problems with his wife, who had proved a useful sounding board over the years, but her judgement was flawed because their son was a hostage. His solution to that was to produce another child and hope that this one wouldn't be another daughter, but his wife flew into a tantrum at the suggestion.

'What Findlay? You want me to give you another son because you may have to condemn Macbeth to death to give you freedom of action? You are a callous, cold-hearted man and, if I ever loved you, I certainly don't now. If you think that I'm going to allow you near my bed until our son is safely back where he belongs you're a bigger fool than I thought you were.'

'Don't you dare threaten to deny me the marriage bed, wife. I'm your husband and if I want to bend you over the high table in the hall and plough you until you give me another son, God help me, I'll do so,' the mormaer snarled in response.

'Go ahead, you only demean yourself by such threats. If by some mischance you do get me pregnant, then I'll get rid of the child just to spite you, you foul old goat.'

Findlay was angry but his common sense had not completely deserted him. He realised that threats weren't going to work so he tried another tack.

'Then I'll get rid of you and marry someone who will give me another son,' he said with a self-satisfied smile.

His wife realised that it would be all too easy for him to put her aside and force her to enter a monastery as a nun. She might be King Malcolm's eldest daughter but she was far from certain that she could rely on his protection if it didn't suit his interests. Findlay might get rid of her anyway once he found out that she was going through the change of life, admittedly rather earlier than was usual. She wouldn't be giving birth to any more sons - or daughters. That's why it was so important to her that Macbeth was restored to them alive and well. He was probably the only person who would insist that Findlay looked after her into old age.

'Instead of lusting after some young wench, you should be ready to fight alongside Malcolm and demand our son's return before the fight. Then you can hold your men back until it's clear which way the victory will go.'

'Pah, you don't know Malcolm. He won't release Macbeth just because I turn up. He's not a fool; he knows I could do exactly what you suggest. No, he'll hang onto the boy until I play my part and victory is certain. That's why I need to leave behind me a pregnant wife; so Malcolm has less of a hold over me.'

'Very well, I'll lie with you again.'

His wife didn't really have an option. She knew that copulation wouldn't have the result he desired but, like most men, conception was a mystery to him and she could pretend until he went away. That would stop him discarding her for now. If he returned he would, God willing, bring her son back with him. If he didn't return, then she would be a rich heiress. The best outcome would be for Findlay to be killed and for Macbeth to be restored to her as the new Mormaer. Yes, she decided, she would pray for that.

†††

'My lords, let us analyse our enemy's strength,' Bishop Aldhun said the next day when the council resumed.

Eadwulf, who had been about to ask the same thing, scowled at him. He thought of reminding the bishop who was in charge but realised just in time that would seem like whining.

'Iuwine, I think you have the best grasp of the situation over the border?' Aldhun asked.

'Thank you, lord bishop. Hacca of Edinburgh will be forced to take the field against us as he is now Malcolm's sworn man, but I have been in communication with him recently and he has given me some idea about Malcolm's position,' the Ealdorman of Selkirkshire replied. 'As many of you will know, the Scots' kingdom is divided up into seven mormaerships: of these one, Caithness and Sutherland, has been conquered by the Norse and another, Ross, is under threat from them so Malcolm can't call on any men from there. The Mormaers of Buchan and Angus are in a land dispute so I doubt if either will want to send many men south. That leaves Atholl, Fife, Moray and, of course, Edinburgh.

Hacca estimates that, together with Moray, Malcolm could probably muster between three and four thousand men. It's true though, that many of these will be young and untried in battle. In addition Owain the Bald will undoubtedly march to join his cousin, Malcolm. Again, he cannot afford to leave the north of his kingdom or the Isles weak because of the ever present threat posed by the Norse. He faces open revolt against his rule in Galloway and he will have to leave behind a sizeable force in case the Gallovidians take advantage of his absence. He daren't trust the Norse in Cumbria either but there are rumours that he is trying to bribe the Norsemen to join him. With them he could probably afford to bring some fifteen hundred men to the fray.'

A stunned silence lay heavily over the assembly when Iuwine finished speaking. An army of around five thousand men was a huge; twice what Bernicia had raised.

'My lords,' Aldred spoke into the silence. 'Earl Uhtred once delayed Owain's force and severely mauled it whilst it was on its way to join Malcolm when he defeated King Kenneth and seized the throne. I suggest that we could do something similar this time.'

At the mention of his hated brother's name Eadwulf started from the stupor into which he seemed to have sunk and scowled at Aldred.

'I will decide what is and is not to be done to defeat the menace we all face, nephew.'

'What's your plan then, lord earl?' a voice called out from somewhere in the middle of the room.

'Who said that?' Eadwulf yelled.

'I did,' the young man who now pushed his way to the front of the crowd was powerfully built and richly dressed. 'Ceolfrith, son of Ulfric and Thane of Norham.'

Aldred looked at the man with interest. His father had fought and died with Uhtred two years previously and so, officially, Coelfrith wasn't a thane but his deputy at Norham; not that he had ever appointed him formally. However, he wasn't about to challenge Ceolfrith's right to call himself a thane in public. It didn't matter in any event because all three of Aldred's vills in Bernicia had been transferred back to the Diocese of Durham – not that Coelfrith would know that yet.

The young man had to be about seventeen years of age, three years younger than Aldred, but Ceolfrith looked older than that. The last time Aldred had seen him had been four years ago when he toured Bernicia with his father, Earl Uhtred. Then the boy had been a stripling of thirteen and Aldred marvelled at the change that a few years had wrought.

'I will not have people calling out willy nilly. If you have a serious contribution to make to this council you will put your hand up and wait to be invited to speak by me, is that clear?'

Ceolfrith stared at Eadwulf until the earl was forced to break eye contact. Then he slowly put his arm in the air and asked again what Eadwulf's plan was.

'That's what we are here to discuss,' the earl replied curtly, feeling his anger threatening to overcome him.

'Then what, pray, is wrong with Lord Aldred's proposal that we attack Owain's army on the march? My father told me about

Uhtred's tactics and they seemed to work well. They attacked their camp at night and darted in to attack the baggage train during the day. My recollection is that they killed at least two hundred for negligible losses themselves and Owain arrived too late to take part in the battle. Of course, Malcolm won the battle without him and killed both Kenneth and his son, but that's not the point. Not only did it weaken Owain but the morale of his men must have been at rock bottom.'

'I too think the plan has merit,' Gosric, Ealdorman of Selkirkshire, called out.

Eadwulf, whose temper had been slowly rising during the exchange now lost it completely.

'Silence, silence I say. You will all keep quiet and only speak if I say so!'

He was on his feet, leaning on the table with one hand and banging on it with the other. He leaned forward to glare at the nobles in front of him, his face a mask of fury.

'Enough of this nonsense. When we know where Malcolm is, we will muster and face him in open battle, not attack from the shadows like cowards. I will let you know where and when to assemble and you will all bring every man and boy over the age of twelve capable of bearing a weapon.'

'You intend to face Malcolm with an army composed of inexperienced boys and old men?' Aldred asked incredulously. 'They will be slaughtered. The boys haven't yet been trained to fight and will run and old men are too slow and feeble to stand against a warrior in his prime.'

'You will keep your opinions to yourself,' his uncle snapped at him. 'One more word and I will arrest you.'

'On what charge? I'm trying to save you from losing the war before it's even started.'

'Treason,' Eadwulf yelled, now completely losing control of himself.

'Perhaps we should all calm down,' Bishop Aldhun said into the tense silence. 'It might be useful to be aware, Lord Eadwulf, that a messenger has been sent by Lord Aldred to his step mother, the queen's daughter, asking her to use her influence with King Cnut in an effort to get Erik Håkonsson to act in defence of his earldom.'

The reminder of his nephew's royal connections was enough to cool Eadwulf's temper somewhat but he continued to mutter imprecations against Aldred as he slowly resumed his seat.

'The problem is that Cnut is committed to putting down the revolt by the Mercians led by their earl, Eadric Streona,' Gosric said. 'Compared to that, Northumbria is unimportant.'

☨☨☨

No one in Duns was aware of it at the time, but Cnut had managed to capture the faithless earl and he was now languishing in a dungeon in London awaiting trial and execution. However, Cnut had had another problem to deal with. He had decided, now that Mercia had been pacified, that the time had come to disband most of the army he'd raised for the conquest of England. His quandary was that he'd promised the Danes payment for their service to him and his treasury was depleted. As his former enemies were now his subjects, he couldn't allow the army to plunder his kingdom at will to take what was owed to them; which they were likely to do if they weren't paid.

He would have to levy a new tax to find the money, but it would be very unpopular. Raising even more to send warriors north to deal with the Scots was out of the question.

'What will you do?' Emma asked him when they were alone.

Ælfgifu had taken Aldred's letter asking for help to her mother and she, in turn, had taken it to her husband.

'There's not much I can do. I don't want Malcolm tearing chunks out of my kingdom as soon as I'm secure on the throne, but I can't afford to alienate Erik Håkonsson by ordering him to assist that fool Eadwulf; he's too powerful for me to make an enemy of at the moment.

'Furthermore, my brother Harald is ill and likely to die, if my agents' reports are accurate, and so it looks as if I'll have to sail back to Denmark soon to prevent anyone else from seizing the crown when he dies. With Håkonsson now living here, I must also make sure that Norway remains subservient. So you see that the north of Northumbria is the least of my concerns right now, Emma.'

'Yes, I understand. My daughter's stepson is resourceful from all that I hear, but I'm not sure that even he will be able to halt Malcolm's march south without help, and I doubt that the indolent fool of an uncle of his will be of much help; he's more likely to be a hindrance.'

Cnut frowned. He had liked Eadwulf when they'd been young men but that was because he'd been a good drinking and whoring companion. He suspected that his wife was correct; he wouldn't be much use on the battlefield, but it was too late to do much about that now.

ϮϮϮ

The rest of the day at Duns was as unproductive as the morning had been. All that they'd established was that the maximum numbers of nobles, housecarls and other trained warriors they could muster was some four hundred and fifty, excluding Aldred's forty horsemen. Everyone agreed that recruiting boys of twelve and thirteen would be counterproductive, but even if every boy and freeman over the age of fourteen came with their weapons to join the fyrd they could only add perhaps another two thousand to that number, and a third of those would be next to useless as they'd never been trained in the basics of fighting in a shield wall.

The only promising statistic was that nearly four hundred of the fyrd possessed and could use a bow. They were a mixture of hunting bows and the more powerful war bows, but even the former could bring down a stag at fifty paces. If they could do that to a deer, they could do it to a man. Few of the Scots, and even fewer of the Strathclyde Britons, possessed armour, making the archers' job much easier. Even helmets were the exception rather than the rule.

The other advantage that the fyrd had was that, in addition to helmets, most owned a large Saxon round shield whereas the Scots used the much small targe or else an oblong Celtic shield. Neither gave the protection that the Saxon shield did, which was three feet in diameter.

Eadwulf had said little during the latter half of the proceedings, leaving it to the bishop to lead the discussion. However, at the end he got the last word by ordering everyone present to be ready to come to the muster point within one week of the summons. The muster point was to be the site of the ancient Royal Summer Palace at Yeavering in the Cheviot Hills.

'At least he shows some sense,' Iuwine muttered to Aldred. 'If we can draw the Scots deep into the hills we might be able to defeat them.'

'I agree,' he replied, 'but I fear he's chosen it because it isn't too far from Bebbanburg and from there he can advance towards whichever invasion route Malcolm choses. If he does that, he'll lose the advantage that the hills give us.'

'I hope you're wrong, but I fear you're not. The man is an idiot, so is Cnut for appointing him instead of you to be our earl.'

'Be careful, lord. That's treason,' Aldred whispered. 'Though I suspect that at this precise moment Cnut may be regretting his decision.'

'I thought your plan to harass and delay Owain's Britons was a good one, by the way. I'm sorry that you'll not be able to carry it out.'

'Who said I can't,' Aldred said before turning away to thank the bishop for his efforts to keep the council focused.

Chapter Eight – Scouts and Skirmishes

April/May 1018

Winds whipped around the stronghold of Cadzow standing high above a gorge overlooking the Avon Water. Dumbarton had been the base for the kings of Strathclyde for centuries but Owain the Bald had moved to his other fortress as it was better placed for the muster. He sat morosely drinking horn after horn of ale and brooding about his situation as the shutters rattled and smoke was blown back down into the hall from the hole in the roof. He had an ominous feeling that he would be the last King of Strathclyde.

In the time of his ancestors Strathclyde had been one kingdom amongst many. The Scots of Dalriada to the west, the various Pictish kingdoms to the north and east and Northumbria to the south had hemmed it in, but gradually Strathclyde had expanded.

A man whose ancestors had been from Dalriada now sat on the throne of the united Pictish kingdoms. Dalriada itself had disappeared a century and a half earlier, partly being absorbed into Strathclyde. The rest had been settled by Norsemen from the Orkneys and Ireland who had pushed the inhabitants – the Scots – further east into Pictland. Ironically the kingdom of the Picts was now called Scotland, although the Scots themselves no longer had a homeland of their own.

Cumbria, once part of Northumbria, was also part of Strathclyde now. However, Norsemen from Ireland formed an ever increasing portion of the population along its coast and were beginning to move inland, driving out the native Britons.

Two of Owain's sons had died during Malcolm's ill-fated invasion of Northumbria twelve years previously and the third had been killed when he fell from his horse. One of his daughters had married and produced a son but he was only two years old and not a contender to succeed him. The boy would be lucky to reach adulthood if Malcolm, King of Scots, saw him as any sort of rival.

Owain slumped in the great chair that served as his throne glumly considering the future. The letter he held in his hand ordered him to bring all the warriors he could muster to join him in the conquest of Lothian. He was old and Malcolm was his nearest adult male relative. The man had made no secret of the fact that, when he succeeded Owain, he intended to merge Strathclyde into his own kingdom. If he fell in the coming war Malcolm would hardly mourn his loss.

His cousin had obviously learned the lessons of the past. Although Malcolm's oft repeated desire was to push his southern border down to the Tees, he was enough of a pragmatist to know that he had no realistic chance of conquering such a large chunk of Northumbria; at least not if he tried to swallow it in one go. For now his aim was to move the border from the Forth down to the Tweed.

'And what does the high and mighty Malcolm offer me for my help?' Owain asked no one in particular in his drunkenness. 'A worthless strip of land between Galloway and Selkirkshire.'

He had already tried to settle this area with Britons displaced by the encroaching Norse but Eadwulf, at the time an outlaw but now the Earl of Bernicia, had slaughtered his settlers and driven them out. Perhaps if he gave the area to his Cumbrian Norsemen they might have more luck in hanging onto it. However, that wasn't really of much use to him. He had little luck in collection taxes from the Norse in his kingdom as it was; any attempt to impose a levy on new settlers in that remote wilderness would be the height of stupidity.

He re-read Malcolm's missive again but he had trouble focusing on it in his inebriated state and soon gave up. He knew what it said in any case. Malcolm expected him to arrive at the muster by mid-May with fifteen hundred warriors. He had no idea how his cousin thought he could persuade men to serve him when he could offer no plunder, slaves or livestock as an incentive. Malcolm had made it clear that, as Lothian was to be a part of his kingdom, its population and the value of their lands was to be preserved as much as possible. An uninhabited wasteland was of no use to him. Perhaps, if his Norsemen were to be offered land they could provide a substantial part of his army?

The place where they were to meet was deep inside Lothian. That puzzled Owain. Perhaps Malcolm didn't want to have to supply Owain's army until he had to, especially as foraging was prohibited? Provisions for so many men was something else that would cost Owain more than he could afford. The real solution – that Malcolm planned to trap the enemy between the two armies – never occurred to Owain's befuddled mind.

ϮϮϮ

'We've received reports that a good proportion of the Norsemen who have settled in Cumbria sailed up to Carlisle a few weeks ago,' Wictred told Ceadda one cold and miserable morning in late April.

Spring was late in arriving and the weather was more like the middle of winter.

'It looks as if Malcolm is beginning his muster then. Lord Aldred should be here, not visiting his grandfather in Durham,' Ceadda fretted.

Aldred had gone south to visit Bishop Aldhum because the old man was ill and he had asked to see his grandson before it was too late. The Thane of Duns had been gone for two weeks and Ceadda prayed that it wouldn't be too long before he returned. Uncertain what to do in the meantime, Ceadda paced up and down, examining the options.

'We need to call the muster ourselves,' he said finally.

'Shall I send a message to Bebbanburg?' Wictred asked uncertainly.

'What? No! Aldred doesn't want his uncle to know what he's planning. Eadwulf will have his own men watching Malcolm if he has any sense. Let's just hope that what Lord Aldred intends works.'

Two days later Aldred returned to Duns, much to Ceadda's relief. He called a meeting of his senior commanders as soon as he'd washed the dust from his face and hair and changed his clothes.

'First you need to know that the bishop, although not well, is not yet near death. He has little faith in Eadwulf's ability to defend Lothian against Malcolm but will continue to pray for our victory. Whether Malcolm is successful in taking Lothian or not, he hoped that Malcolm will respect Church property and allow the Diocese of Durham to retain its lands in Lothian.

'With that in mind, he has decided that it would be best if Duns, Norham and Carham now reverted to the ownership of the Church. That way he hopes that the three vills won't be seized by the Scots. In their place he had granted me title to a number of vills belonging to the Diocese in lower Teesdale, the most valuable of which is Aycliffe. For the moment, though, he has given me permission to lead the fyrd from my old vills in Lothian.

'However, none of that is important for now. We need to mobilise as many horsemen as we can in order to attack Owain on his way east.'

Three days later Aldred had assembled a total of fifty five horsemen, forty of whom were dressed and equipped like Norman knights. Most were his own housecarls but they were supplemented by Kenric, Ceolfrith and their mounted warriors from Carham and Norham. They wore the shorter byrnies instead of hauberks and carried lighter spears. Twenty of the horsemen carried bows in addition to their other weapons. Aldred left his wolf's head banner behind. It wouldn't be long before Owain discovered who his nemesis was but there was no point in advertising his identity.

The next day one of his scouts rode in to report that the Strathclyde host was on the move from Cadzow.

'How many and what types of warriors?' Aldred asked him brusquely.

The scout, who was a thirteen year old boy still training to be a warrior, was flustered by his lord's tone but he did his best to answer.

'Probably around fifteen hundred, lord. The bulk of them, perhaps as many as a thousand, wore no armour, though a few had helmets, and their weapons were like those of our fyrd: a few swords, lots of spears, axes and the odd scythe and pitchfork.'

The boy swallowed nervously before continuing.

'Perhaps a hundred had hunting bows but there were some four hundred well-armed warriors who looked like Danes.'

'Not Danes,' Aldred muttered. 'Norsemen. Did you see King Owain?'

'Yes, I think so, lord,' the lad stammered. 'There was a covered cart immediately behind the vanguard, quite separate from the rest of the baggage train; and there was a man carrying a banner beside the cart. It was red with what looked like three silver flowers embroidered on it.'

'Yes, that's the banner of Strathclyde. So it looks like Owain is too old or too ill to ride. Thank you, boy. You've done well. What's your name?'

The young scout flushed with pleasure at the compliment and stood slightly taller, thrusting his chest out in pride.

'Colby, lord.'

'Go and get something to eat and drink, Colby. I'll remember you.'

'Thank you, lord.'

'Oh, one last thing. I presume that this army was marching north towards Stirling?'

'Oh no, lord. They were heading south-east.'

'South-east? Are you certain?'

'Positive, lord. I waited until they were crossing the Avon Water to make sure.'

'That means they may be heading for Selkirk. But why do that if Malcolm is still fifty miles to the north near Stirling?'

'Perhaps he isn't and Eadwulf either doesn't know he's on the move or has just forgotten to tell us?'

'Wictred, you and Colby ride to Stirling and find out where Malcolm is. I don't need to tell you to take care and avoid all habitation; but I need to know as soon as possible. Now get moving.'

ϮϮϮ

Wictred was five years older than Colby but the boy had the knack of assessing the landscape and choosing the best routes to avoid the skyline so Wictred let him lead. The warrior had left behind his stallion, his hauberk, lance and shield. Like the boy he was dressed in a leather gambeson and rode a rouncey: a normal riding horse.

Colby led them along the southern edge of the Lammemuirs and into the Moorfoot Hills where they camped by a small loch. That night they ate stale bread and cheese washed down with water. A fire would be seen some distance away so they wouldn't be able to eat anything hot until they returned to Duns. Wictred debated whether one of them should stand watch, but the chances of being attacked were remote and they both needed their sleep if they were to remain alert the next day.

The following morning they moved ever westwards, climbing into the Pentland Hills in the early afternoon. So far all they had seen was the odd shepherd boy keeping watch over flocks of sheep. That night they made another cold camp by a small river that Colby said was called the Auchter Water,

Dawn brought with it a thick mist which would make navigation difficult. They pressed on in what they hoped was a north-westerly direction but it was too dangerous to ride without being able to see the way ahead and so they had to lead their horses. Both felt frustrated at the slow progress they were able to make when time was of the essence.

They heard the noise of an army on the move before they saw anything. The sun was beginning to burn off the mist, but it would be some time before they would be able to see any distance. The distant sound of men talking, the occasional clash of metal on metal and the tramp of numerous feet came at them out of the whiteness but they were incapable of deciding which direction it came from.

They stood still for an agonisingly long time as the sounds seemed to swirl all around them. Suddenly a gust of wind blew away the mist for long enough for them to see a column of men snaking along the bank of a small river off to their left. They were on the side of a hill and so the marching men wouldn't see them unless they looked up. Then the mist closed in again.

'Owain's army,' Colby whispered to Wictred. 'Did you see the banner?'

The older scout nodded. The scrap of material had hardly moved in the wind, sodden by the mist and hanging limply on its pole, but it was a dark red colour; Malcolm's standard was blue with a white saltire.

The King of Scot's standard dated back a hundred and fifty years to the battle of Athelstaneford. A force of Scots and Picts led by King Angus MacFergus had raided deep into Lothian but were trapped on their way home, encumbered with slaves and plunder, by a strong Northumbrian army. However, Angus had a vision the night before the battle in which St. Andrew, who had been crucified on a saltire - a diagonal cross - came to him and promised him victory. On the morning of the battle a cloud appeared in the otherwise blue sky which resembled a saltire. Thus inspired, the Picts had routed the Northumbrians and won the battle, escaping with their booty. Afterwards the white saltire on a blue field had been adopted by Angus as his banner and subsequent kings of Scots had continued to use it.

Having found the Strathclyde army Wictred was in two minds about what to do. Aldred would find knowing Owain the Bald's current whereabouts useful but his mission had been to find Malcolm. In the end he sent Colby back to Duns and pressed on alone towards Stirling.

†††

Colby and the other scouts came back to where Aldred waited to confirm that the army of Britons and Norsemen had camped for the night on a tributary of the River Clyde called the Mouse Water. Their camp stretched from the outskirts of a village called Lanark to a farmstead named Cleghorn and had no defences, nor did they appear to have set any sentries. As they were inside the boundaries of the shire of Edinburgh they presumably felt safe. Aldred and his men would soon disabuse them of that idea.

The night was cloudy and the only light came from the various campfires along the banks of the Mouse Water. The fires silhouetted those who still sat talking by the warmth of the flames as the evening turned chilly but the various groups lay down to sleep and the once bright fires became no more than dying embers.

Aldred and his men divested themselves of their armour and, armed only with the short sword known as a seax, they emerged from the dark of the forest and crept towards the sleeping camp. Only the nobles, chieftains and the Norsemen had tents and Aldred's men avoided these, concentrating on the men sleeping in the open. They all used the same technique: a hand over the mouth to stifle any sound and a quick slash across the throat to sever one or both of the carotid arteries. The fifty men worked quickly and they had killed four men each on average before one of the sleeping Britons woke. At first his sleep befuddled mind couldn't comprehend what he was witnessing, but then he realised with horror what was going on and yelled a warning at the top of his voice.

As soon as the alarm was given Aldred and his warriors abandoned their grisly task and fled back towards the trees. One or two ran into Britons struggling to their feet and grabbing their weapons but a quick thrust into the belly or a slash at a leg enabled the Northumbrians to get clear. To Aldred's dismay two of his men got trapped by a group of Britons and died fighting but, even so, they managed to take down four of the enemy before they were overwhelmed.

His men were jubilant. They had killed over two hundred of Owain's men for the death of two of their own. Nevertheless Aldred felt the loss of his two housecarls keenly. They had been with him for several years and he regarded them as almost brothers. He prayed that his next attack would be less costly.

Owain didn't move for the rest of that day whilst they held a service and buried the dead in ground newly consecrated by the priests travelling with his army. That night they set sentries all around the periphery of the camp. Aldred wasn't so stupid as to try another infiltration though. This time his target was the oiled leather tents of the leaders and the Norse warriors.

His twenty archers took up position at the edge of the forest some seventy yards from the nearest tents. There were three sentries near them but they were inexperienced farmers and never saw the men crawling towards them until it was too late. With the nearest sentries out of the way Ceadda lit a fire in the bottom of a barrel so that it would remain concealed. The archers quickly filed past, lighting the rags soaked in pig fat tied to their arrow heads, as they went. The fire arrows flew into the oiled leather tents and soon twenty or so were well alight. Each bowman sent a second arrow into another tent before Aldred gave the order to withdraw.

No one gave chase, they were too busy trying to douse the fires and rescue the men who'd been sleeping inside. Aldred had no way of knowing how much damage the fires had done but Owain knew. Twelve warriors had been burnt alive, all of them Norsemen, another score had been badly scorched and would be no use in battle for some time, if ever again. Worse of all for Owain, two of his nobles had also been roasted alive. However, the losses weren't as serious as the effect on his men's morale.

The next morning the dead were hastily buried and the army moved on, heading for the Pentland Hills. Owain sent out scouts ahead of the column and to each flank. However, they disappeared and never returned. Once off the road the king had to abandon his carriage and ride, something he found very uncomfortable at his age. He became even more uncomfortable when it started to rain in the late morning. The water that fell was ice cold and it was interspersed with showers of hail; unusual for that time of year. His men regarded it as a bad omen and their morale sank even lower.

Having abandoned the wagons of the baggage train, everything had to be carried by slaves, servants and his warriors. This further slowed the column and by midday they had scarcely made four miles from the ford over the Mouse Water. The column had bunched up to cross over the next river, the North Medwin, when suddenly the hundred or so who had already crossed were attacked by horsemen.

Aldred's housecarls, dressed as Norman knights, were something the Norsemen who constituted the vanguard hadn't encountered before. They hastened to form a shield wall as the horsemen charged along the river bank in wedge formation but they hadn't closed up tightly enough when the wall of armoured horsemen hit them, their long spears finding their way past shields to strike chests, faces and limbs. The Norsemen in the front row were flung back into those behind and the whole centre crumpled.

Aldred had picked his target carefully. He was a giant wielding a two-handed battle axe. Had he been able to bring the axe head down onto the stallion's head, as he intended, Aldred would have been flung over its head into the mass of Norse warriors and his death would have been certain. Luckily the giant couldn't reach his target before Aldred's spear point struck the middle of the man's chest.

The impact nearly tore the spear from Aldred's grasp, but he held on grimly as the point cut through the links of chain mail, the padded leather gambeson underneath and then smashed into the giant's ribcage. It was a jaggedly broken rib that penetrated his heart, rather than the spear point, but the effect was the same. The dead axeman was thrown back into the rows behind, knocking five men to the ground. Aldred let go of his spear and drew his sword as his stallion trampled over the men who'd been floored, crushing bones and skulls.

By the time Aldred had his sword in his hand he was through the shield wall and he struggled to turn his horse. Once he'd done so, he cantered along the rear rank cutting and hacking at the demoralised Norsemen.

Within minutes the shield wall had broken apart and his mounted housecarls were slaughtering the remaining Norse. He saw one of his men dragged from his horse and killed but he was the only one before the Norsemen broke and splashed back across the ford towards the rest of the stunned Strathclyde army.

The archers dismounted and sent three volleys of arrows into the backs of the routed Norse. Only a few made it to safety. Aldred's archers sent a final volley into the mass of men crowded along the far bank and then, just as Owain yelled at his army to cross the ford and attack Aldred's men, the archers mounted and the Northumbrians rode away.

By now nearly half of the Norsemen were dead or seriously injured and the remainder thirsted for revenge. Despite Owain's insistence that they stay with the main body, they left that afternoon in pursuit of the horsemen who had wreaked so much damage.

†††

Wictred missed the boy's company as soon as Colby had left him to return to Duns. Somehow it had seemed safer when there were two of them, even if the other scout was a half grown boy. He knew it was ridiculous; Colby wouldn't have been of much use if they had run into trouble, but the feeling of increased vulnerability remained. Consequently he was more cautious and made slower progress that he would have done had the boy still been with him.

He followed a small river for a while until a tall hill hove into view. He decided it was worth exposing himself at the top, although it was a risk, because of the view he'd obtain. It took him an hour to get there but the flat lands beyond lay open to his gaze. There were a few farmsteads and on the horizon he could just make out the pale sun glinting on water which he correctly assumed was the western end of the Firth of Forth.

He racked his brains for what he'd been told of the area into which he was heading. Stirling itself lay some thirty five miles away as the crow flies. Unfortunately the area between his present position and Stirling was fairly heavily populated and so the best way to approach Stirling would be from the south-west. That meant taking the longer route across the wetlands between Galsgow and Falkirk until he reached the Carron Valley. From there he should be able to get close enough to Stirling to see whether a great host was encamped there.

However, he mused, what if there was no-one there? It could mean that the army hadn't yet started to congregate, or perhaps it could be because Malcom had already left. If so, he was fairly certain that they would head along the south bank of the firth towards Edinburgh.

At some stage Malcolm would want to link up with Owain the Bald and Wictred had seen for himself that the Strathclyde force was heading for Selkirkshire, far to the south of Edinburgh. He sat down and allowed his horse to crop the sparse grass on top of the hill whilst he tried to make sense of it all.

Eventually he came to the conclusion that Malcolm was planning a two pronged attack on Lothian with the Strathclyde army coming in from the west and Malcolm striking south from Edinburgh. Eadwulf would doubtless hear about the army in the west first and move to intercept it, marching along the Tweed valley. When Owain blocked Eadwulf's advance along the Tweed, Malcolm could then attack the Northumbrians in the flank and overwhelm them.

The more he thought about it, the more certain he was that it was the only strategy that would explain Owain's current direction of movement. Of course he couldn't be certain until he'd located Malcolm.

He looked to the north once more. He was far too far away to be able to see movement along the southern shore of the Firth of Forth but if he rode slightly east of north he should eventually come to the hill fort at Cockleroy above the town of Linlithgow. From that vantage point he should be able to see the coast road fairly well. He set off in the right direction guided by the sun's position and the time of day. However as the afternoon wore on it became more difficult to navigate as he had to rely on the sun's fitful appearance in the increasingly cloudy sky.

When the sun disappeared for good he decided that it was best to camp and hope for a brighter morning. He found a small river and settled down for the night. He didn't know exactly where he was, but in fact he was only a few miles miles south of the old hill fort which he sought.

Some sixth sense woke him; perhaps his horse had whinnied softly or some small sound had alerted him, but he knew that someone was moving stealthily close by. Wictred's hand closed on the hilt of his dagger and he slowly drew it from its sheath. Another small sound, perhaps the gentle rustling of fallen leaves disturbed by a carefully placed foot, drew his eyes to a small figure dark against the slightly lighter outline of a bush.

The figure remained stationary for a couple of minutes, then, presumably reassured by the quiet, it moved again towards Wictred's horse. The warrior lay stock stil, trying to decide if the person was alone or whether there were more of them in the darkness. He couldn't detect any other movement or sounds, other than the scurrying of small animals and the hoot of an owl, and he decided that whoever was out there was alone.

The figure reached the tree to which Wictred had tied his horse and started to untie the knot. Silently the young warrior pulled aside his blanket and arose from his makeshift bed. As the intruder worked hurriedly to untie the knot, Wictred's arm encircled his slight body and the edge of his dagger drew blood from a nick to his neck.

The horse thief was even smaller than Wictred had supposed, probably just a young boy. He was so thin that he nearly managed to wriggle free of Wictred's arm until the man pushed the dagger harder into the lad's throat and drew more blood.

'Hold still or I'll kill you, so help me God.'

The boy started weeping and stuttered 'don't kill me as well.'

'As well as who?'

'The rest of my family.'

'I'll not harm you, but only if you give me your oath not to run away if I let you go. Do you trust me?'

'I suppose you would've have killed me straight away if you were going to, wouldn't you?'

'I just want to know why you were trying to steal my horse.'

'To get away from here, of course. Before those bloody Scottish bastards kill me like they did the rest of my family.'

Ah, Wictred thought, it sounds as if my theory about Malcolm heading for Edinburgh might be correct.

'But this is the shire of Edinburgh isn't it? Part of the King of Scots realm?'

'Perhaps, I don't know. All I do know is that a group of men came to our farmstead and started to steal our livestock.'

Wictred took his knife from the boy's throat but kept a firm hold on his arm.

'Tell me,' Wictred said, sitting down and pulling the boy down beside him.

'When my father and brother protested they killed them. For a moment I was rooted to the spot in horror but then I realised that there was nothing I could do, so I ran away and hid in the trees. I heard my ma and my two sisters screaming,' he sobbed. 'Then it went very quiet and the bastards set fire to our home. I crept back when I was sure they had gone but my mother and sisters were just blackened corpses.'

Wictred held the weeping boy in his arms, at something of a loss as to how he could comfort him.

'I didn't know what to do,' he said eventually, 'so I just hid in the forest and went to sleep. When I woke up it was dark and I was thirsty. I headed towards the river and then I saw the horse. I thought you might be a bloody Scot but it was worth the risk. If I could steal your horse I could ride away to safety.'

'Can you ride?' Wictred asked surprised.

'Yes, of course. My father taught me as soon as I was eight.'

'How old are you now?'

'Ten. You haven't told me who you are if you're not one of the bastards who killed my family.'

'I'm a housecarl who serves the Thane of Duns. My name is Wictred.'

'An Angle, like me?'

'If you are an Angle. What's your name boy?'

'Oeric.'

Wictred had to smile. The name meant ash tree. The boy looked more like a willowy sapling than a sturdy ash.

'Tell me, Oeric, do you know if a large army of these Scots have passed this way heading east?'

'Father said he'd heard that thousands of Scots were heading along the coast road so I suppose so.'

'Yes, it all ties together. The men who attacked your farmstead must have been foraging. I've got to get back and let Lord Aldred know.'

'What about me?' Oeric almost wailed.

Wictred hesitated. He needed to ride as fast as he could but his conscience wouldn't allow him to just abandon the boy.

'You can sit behind me but you'll have to hold on tight.'

As they rode Wictred wondered what would happen to Oeric now. He had no family and he was too young to be of use to anyone as a worker. Still it wasn't his problem.

Chapter Nine – A Game of Cat and Mouse

June 1018

Malcolm was infuriated and he wasn't a man who hid his displeasure. He had brought enough supplies with him so foraging wasn't necessary. He was determined that the people of Lothian would welcome him as their king and he had warned his nobles and chieftains that looting or persecution of the inhabitants wouldn't be tolerated.

Therefore when he saw small parties of his men slipping away and then returning to the column hours later with livestock and carts loaded with plunder he was furious. When they camped that night he had his bodyguard seek out the leaders of the foragers and the next morning he hanged half a dozen of them from trees beside the road. The mood was sombre as his men marched past the bodies as they slowly twisted in the breeze off the sea, their faces blue with protruding tongues and their trousers stained with faeces. It would have been of little comfort to Oeric, but one of those strung up had been the leader of the raid on his family's farmstead.

ϯϯϯ

Hacca, Ealdorman of Edinburgh, looked balefully at the messenger sent by Malcolm.

'You know what this says?' he asked.

'Yes, lord. You are to muster the warriors and fyrd of Edinburgh and join the king's army when they arrive here in a few days' time.'

'Am I then required to wage war on my fellow men of Lothian?' he asked in disgust.

'Only if Selkirkshire and Berwickshire don't submit, lord,' the messenger replied impassively.

'As I'm told they have already answered the muster called by the Earl of Bernicia, I suspect that's highly unlikely, don't you?'

'I'm only the messenger, lord.'

Hacca looked at the fifteen year old youth standing in front of him.

'You said your name is Duncan Mac Crínán, did you not? The only Crínán I've heard of is the hereditary lay abbot of Dunkeld who is married to Bethóc, daughter of King Malcolm. Is he your father?'

'Yes, lord,' the youth said, shifting uncomfortably from one foot to the other.

'So you are one of Malcolm's grandsons?'

Duncan nodded and Hacca sucked his teeth. Malcolm had no surviving sons and, apart from his cousin, Owain of Strathclyde, the king's closest relatives were his three maternal grandsons: Duncan, his younger brother Maldred, and the thirteen year old Macbeth. As Malcolm didn't like or trust Macbeth's father, Findlay, it was no secret that Duncan was likely to be his successor.

'Then I would be very surprised if you weren't privy to your grandfather's plans. If I am to help you, I need to know what those plans are. I have taken an oath to serve King Malcolm but my people see the Scots as invaders and won't fight alongside them, whatever I say. Rumours are already spreading that Malcolm's men are pillaging and raping their way along the south bank of the Forth.'

'It's true that some men have disobeyed the king and have raided nearby farmsteads; however, the king has hanged the ringleaders to emphasise his determination to stop that sort of behaviour.'

'I see. That's encouraging, but I'm not a fool. If Malcolm hasn't dangled the carrot of loot and slaves before his army, what has he promised them for their support? They're not here just because he asked them nicely.'

'Those thanes who support Malcolm will be allowed to keep their land; those who oppose him will see everything they own confiscated and distributed amongst Malcolm's army.'

'Thank you; that has the ring of truth about it. And what about the Strathclyde army? What has Malcolm promised Owain the Bald?'

'How do you know that Owain is involved?'

'I told you earlier not to take me for a fool, Duncan. I already know that Owain is heading for Selkirk.'

'If you want to know what the king's strategy is, then I suggest that you ride back with me and ask him.' He paused before adding, 'lord.'

Hacca thought for a moment. His instinct was to join his fellow Anglians and hope that together they could defeat Malcolm, but the truth was he had no faith in Eadwulf's leadership. If Aldred had been the earl he would have been more confident of victory.

'Very well, I will come with you and renew my oath of fealty to King Malcolm and discuss what role my men and I are to play.'

†††

'Where are they now?' Aldred asked Colby.

The boy had eventually stumbled across Aldred at an old Roman fort in the valley of the Upper Tweed. He had very nearly been caught by a group of Norse warriors mounted on a variety of horses that they had obviously stolen from local farmsteads. However, because he was lighter, better mounted and not weighed down by armour, his horse had managed to outrun his pursuers.

'They were about four miles away when I first saw them,' the boy replied, 'in the hills to the south-east of the junction of the Tweed and Harris Water. I was intending to hide in the Roman fort when I found that you were here.'

'What of Malcolm?'

'That's why Wictred sent me to find you. His army is moving along the south bank of the Firth of Forth, presumably heading for Edinburgh.'

'That makes sense. He'll want to make sure that Hacca supports him. He won't want a stronghold like Edinburgh in hostile hands if he really intends to make Lothian part of his kingdom.'

'Then why is Owain heading so far south?' Ceadda asked. 'Surely they'll want to combine their forces before they face the Bernician army?'

'Because he intends to trap my beloved uncle in a pincer movement,' Aldred replied with a grim smile.

'Pincer movement?'

It wasn't something that Ceadda had heard of before.

'Yes, I think that the plan might be for Owain to block Eadwulf's advance and then for Malcolm to attack him from the flank or the rear.'

Ceadda nodded.

'Yes, I can see that could be disastrous, even if numbers weren't in Malcolm's favour. But what can we do to stop it?'

'We have to defeat Owain and stop him being the anvil to Malcolm's hammer, and the first step towards that goal is to eliminate the Norsemen.'

ϮϮϮ

The fyrd were slow to respond to Eadwulf's summons. April was traditionally the month when ploughing and fertilising were completed and sowing the new crops took place. The next few months were devoted to weeding and scaring the birds away; tasks that could safely be left to the women and children. Therefore it wasn't until the end of the month that the thanes and their men started to arrive at the muster point at Yeavering Bell. By then he had received reports that Malcolm was at Edinburgh but no one seemed to know if the men of Strathclyde were with him.

The earl was quite pleased with the numbers who had answered his call to arms. He hadn't been certain that everyone would but, apart from some five hundred thanes and their housecarls, well over two thousand men of the fyrd were present. Admittedly a few hundred of them were half-trained boys and elderly men, but they would be making up the numbers at the rear, not fighting in the front ranks.

Hacca might have been obliged to join Malcolm but that hadn't stopped him from sending a message to Eadwulf telling him that Malcolm had less than three thousand men. However, Hacca had pointed out that Findlay of Moray was expected to bring another eight hundred with him. With those reinforcements, Malcolm's army would outnumber Eadwulf's force by five to four.

That was bad enough, but Owain the Bald was thought to have another fifteen hundred, including hundreds of Norse warriors. His scouts had been unable to discover where Owain was, but they were certain that he hadn't joined Malcolm as yet. As if that wasn't bad enough, Aldred had failed to answer the summons with his horsemen and his fyrd. That had infuriated him beyond measure and he vowed to charge his nephew with treason as soon as he could get his hands on him. For all he knew Aldred might well have joined Malcolm as an act of petty revenge against his uncle.

ተተተ

Colby and two other scouts lay flat in the grass at the top of Pykestone Hill watching the score of mounted Norsemen in the valley below them.

'I think Lord Aldred had hoped for more,' Colby muttered to no one in particular.

'Well, these twenty will have to do. Ready?' the oldest of the three asked. 'Then let's go.'

The three slid back down the reverse slope until they were out of sight and then mounted their horses. They nonchalantly walked their horses along the ridge that ran north-east from the summit.

After a hundred yards or so they came in full view of the Norsemen but evidently they hadn't spotted them.

'Bloody useless lot,' one of the Northumbrian scouts remarked. 'They should have seen us immediately if they were any good at their job. We need to attract their attention before it's too late.'

The three started to talk loudly amongst themselves and, with the wind in an easterly direction, it carried the sound faintly to the men in the valley below. Suddenly the Norsemen urged their horses into a canter up the slope towards the scouts. The three pretended that they were unaware of any danger and carried on chatting and ambling along the ridge. Colby pretended he'd suddenly seen the enemy horsemen and pointed them out to his companions. With cries of alarm they turned their horses and rode over the ridge into a small valley to their right.

The Norsemen gave a try of triumph and kicked their horses into a gallop to chase their quarry. They hared after the three scouts paying no attention to their flanks. By the time they had realised that Aldred and fifty mounted and armoured men had appeared over the crest to their right and were now only a hundred yards from them, it was too late, or so Aldred thought.

The Norsemen turned away from Aldred's charge and urged their horses up the opposite slope. The Northumbrians slowly gained on the fleeing Norsemen and a few stragglers were caught and cut down, but the majority reached the crest safely.

The one advantage that Aldred's warriors had was the stamina of their stallions and as the tired Norsemen's horses went over the crest the Northumbrians were close behind the main body.

Aldred realised at once that the Norse scouts weren't as useless as they had made out. As his housecarls poured over the crest they hauled their horses to a halt in confusion. On the reverse slope not a hundred yards away were a hundred and forty Norsemen drawn up as a shield wall. The twenty mounted Norsemen, having led their quarry into the trap, parted to ride to the flanks of the shield wall, dismounted and formed up at right angles to the centre. What

Aldred had fondly imagined was a trap into which he'd lured the enemy horsemen turned out to be quite the opposite.

ተተተ

Aldred had a split second in which to decide what to do. The shield wall was moving to envelop him. If he acted at once he could retreat and, with luck, most of his men would be able to get away safely. However, presenting their backs to the advancing enemy would expose them to thrown spears and, for all he knew, a hail of arrows.

Besides he had never been one to shy away from a fight and he was damned if he was going to start now.

'Form wedge,' he yelled kicking his own horse forward.

Ceadda moved to his right side and Wictred his left whilst the others closed in to form the rest of the formation. There was little space available in which to build up momentum but they managed to reach a canter before they crashed into the middle of the oncoming shield wall.

The Northumbrians had the advantage of charging downhill whilst the Norse were below them walking up the slope weighed down by armour. Aldred picked his target: a man armed with spear and shield and, with the twin advantages of a longer spear and thrusting from well above the man, he managed to strike the space between his helmet brim and the top of his shield. The point smashed his cheekbone and ricocheted off it, entered his eye socket and killed him instantly.

Instead of letting go of his spear, Aldred hauled back on his stallions' reins and the beast reared up smashing its iron clad hooves into two men in the second row, breaking bones and crushing a skull. The stallion came back down onto all four legs and barged the bodies out of the way. They were thrown into the last rank of the shield wall and several more men were knocked to the ground. The horse snorted its anger and tried to bite the face of another of the enemy, who swiftly retreated out of harm's way.

Suddenly Aldred was in the clear and, much to his astonishment, he was unharmed and had even managed to retain his grip on the spear

Ceadda and Wictred followed Aldred, their fine chainmail hauberks splattered with gore from the men they'd killed, widening the gap as they did so. By the time the rear rank of the wedge formation had fought its way through the enemy, the centre of the shield wall was a mass of mangled corpses and screaming wounded.

The men at the rear of any shield wall were the youngest and least experienced. Their task was to push against the front ranks to prevent them from being forced back. They were not usually called upon to fight themselves. Realising that the Northumbrian mounted warriors were now behind them, they turned to face them. As they were doing this, the more experienced warriors tried to force their way through the rear ranks to resume their position facing the enemy. Chaos ensued.

They were now charging uphill so the momentum of the horsemen didn't have the same shock effect. All the same, they rode into a disorganised rabble instead of a proper defensive line. Once more the men on foot were unable to counter the horsemen and, although Aldred's men didn't have the cohesive impact they had enjoyed during the first charge, the Norse were demoralised and bewildered.

This time Aldred did let go of his spear when he'd skewered the warrior in front of him. He had his long handled axe dangling by its leather thong ready and a second after he'd let go of the spear he had grasped the haft of the axe and chopped it down, splitting the helmet of a man who was trying to kill him with a sword.

As he did so he felt a blow on his shield and he turned to look down at an axeman who was trying to pull his weapon free. Aldred smiled mirthlessly. Had they been more experienced, the Norsemen would have tried to kill the horses rather than the men riding them. He swung his own axe overarm and felt the jar as it embedded itself in his attacker's shoulder. As the man fell away

Aldred had difficulty in keeping hold of his axe. He couldn't let go because of the thong securing it to his wrist and he started to panic. It came clear just in time but he felt a sharp pain in his wrist as he rode clear of the fight.

He gritted his teeth, ignoring the injury, as he turned to charge back into the melee once more, but he saw that it wasn't going to be necessary. The Norse line had broken and many were fleeing downhill. Those who remained put up a good fight but the result was a forgone conclusion.

Leaving Ceadda to finish the last groups of fighters off, he sent half his men after the routed Norsemen. Aldred took no pleasure in watching them chopping down panicked men as they tried fruitlessly to outrun the mounted housecarls. By the time that they had reached the stream in the valley below only a dozen Norseman were still alive.

Aldred impatiently allowed Uuen to examine his wrist. Thankfully it was no more than a bad sprain and his servant applied a cold compress. He tried to convince his master to wear a sling but he knew Aldred would refuse, so he didn't try very hard.

Aldred should have felt elation at his stunning and totally unexpected victory, but instead he felt remorse at killing so many brave warriors, coupled with grief as eight of his own men had been killed.

Two hours later they had tied their own dead to spare horses and collected the Norsemen's armour and weapons. At least now his fyrd would be well protected and armed. They had been told to muster at Duns and then make their way to the monastery at Melrose. Aldred might have effectively eliminated Owain's Norse contingent – his best fighting force – but that still left a thousand Britons marching to support Malcolm.

He slept fitfully that night, partially due to his sore wrist, but more because he was probing his scheme to defeat the rest of the Strathclyde army for flaws. He knew how lucky he had been that day. He had ridden into a trap and had won, despite the odds. He didn't think for one moment that he could be so fortunate again, but he had to try. Without Owain, even his fool of an uncle might be able to defeat the rest of the Scots. Always provided that Findlay could be persuaded to return to Moray, of course.

As he tossed and turned he fretted over the task facing him. On top of everything, he wouldn't be able to use his right hand for a time. He prayed that the sprain would have healed sufficiently before it was time to put the next stage of his plan into operation.

At dawn the next day Uuen had to help him to mount, which irritated him beyond measure; then he led his men towards Owain's last reported campsite.

Not all his men went with him. Wictred and Colby headed in the opposite direction to keep an eye on Malcolm's army.

Chapter Ten – The Peace Envoys

July 1018

'You've no doubt heard that Malcolm and his barbarians have invaded Lothian?' Kætilbiǫrn asked Thurbrand, the son of the late Jarl Styr.

As a goldsmith Kætilbiǫrn needed protection for his goods and Thurbrand was happy to provide it, for a price. Thurbrand could have expected to have inherited his father's lands but the two had never got on. Many years before, shortly after Uhtred married Thurbrand's sister Sige, Uhtred, as Earl of Northumbria, had to give judgement over a land dispute between Styr and his son. Thurbrand had also accused his father of adultery. Uhtred had found against Thurbrand and in favour of Styr and had also fined the son.

Thurbrand never paid the fine and fled to Denmark where he had become one of Cnut's companions. He had subsequently returned with him when Cnut launched his conquest of England. Later he had conspired with Eadwulf to murder Uhtred while he was on his way to submit to Cnut.

The assassination of such a prominent English noble had embarrassed Cnut and both Thurbrand and Eadwulf had been banished from court for a while. However, when the uproar over Uhtred's murder had died down, Cnut made Eadwulf Earl of Bernicia in his brother's place and Thurbrand had been given the large triangle of land lying between the Humber Estuary and the North Sea. Although part of it was marshland, other areas were fertile farmland with no less than twenty five separate vills and farmsteads.

Thurbrand was called the Hold, a nickname of Danish origin for a noble ranking between a thane and an ealdorman. As a result the area where his estates lay became known as Holderness; ness - meaning nose - the shape of the peninsula. In addition to farming, Thurbrand's other activities included hiring out his housecarls to provide protection to those rich enough to pay for them, and seafaring. Thurbrand owned several knarrs for legitimate commerce and he used two small longships to escort them. However, he wasn't averse to employing them for the odd spot of piracy when the opportunity arose.

He was well aware that Aldred had sworn to kill him for his part in Uhtred's death but, as Duns was at one extremity of Northumbria and Holderness the other, he didn't feel particularly threatened. The fact that Eadwulf was Aldred's lord increased his feeling of security. He was certain that Eadwulf would find some way of eliminating Aldred.

When Kætilbiǫrn told him of the Scots' invasion he felt even more secure. If Eadwulf didn't kill Aldred first, there was every possibility that the wretched man might die in battle against the Scots.

However, Thurbrand had completely forgotten that Uhtred had another son, Eadulf. As his mother was Sige, Thurbrand's sister, the boy was also his nephew.

†††

At first Eadulf had found life in London boring. He was surrounded by women for a start: his step mother, Ælfgifu, his half-sisters, Ealdgyth and the baby Ælfflæd and, of course, Queen Emma and her ladies. He felt ignored and out of place. Since Emma was now heavily pregnant, he supposed that there would soon be another baby on which his step mother would lavish her attentions.

His only male companion was Fiske, his body servant. Fiske was now fourteen and, although he looked after his master diligently, they had little in common and Eadulf sensed that the Norse boy was as bored as he was.

Eadulf had escaped from his mother and the maids, a not infrequent occurrence, and had made his way down to the stables, his usual place of escape whenever he got the chance. The stable boys knew him well and liked him. He didn't treat them like dirt, as most sons of the nobles at court did. Fiske had followed him and kept a discreet eye out to make sure he didn't come to any harm.

On this particular day there was another boy there about Eadulf's age. Like him, he was richly dressed and obviously wasn't a stable hand. He seemed to be waiting for something and then one of the grooms brought two saddled horses around the corner.

'Where do you want go riding today, Gunwald?' the groom asked as he helped the boy into the saddle of a small grey mare.

Eadulf suddenly felt very envious. He hadn't been outside the royal complex since his arrival.

'Let's head west today,' the boy replied with a smile.

'Can I come too?' Eadulf suddenly found himself asking.

'Who are you?' Gunwald asked with a frown. 'I haven't seen you before.'

'My name is Eadulf and my step mother is the queen's daughter, Ælfgifu.'

'Oh, I see. I'm Gunwald, the natural son of King Cnut.'

Eadwulf looked at the other boy with interest. He knew that Cnut had two sons by his first wife – three year old Svein and two year old Harold - but this was the first he'd heard about the king having a bastard.

'Why haven't I seen you at court before?'

'Because my father doesn't like to parade me in front of his new wife. I am being fostered by one of his companions, a man called Bjorn Svensson whose estates are up in Deira. However, my foster father has been called to London as one of the advisers of Queen Emma whilst the king is away in Denmark.'

The two boys looked at each other and Gunwald was tempted to invite the other boy to join them but he knew that would get him in trouble unless Eadulf had permission.

'Look, I go riding most days if I can. Why don't you ask the Lady Ælfgifu if you can come with me? I'd enjoy the company of a boy my age. Ealdorman Bjorn has a son, Sigurd, but he's only eight and hasn't learned to ride properly yet. He does give a good impression of a sack of flour on a horse, though. '

Eadulf had laughed at Gunwald's wry description of his foster brother and decided he liked him. He watched them ride across the cobbled courtyard and out of the gate in the palisade that surrounded the royal enclosure before he made his way back to the queen's chambers. He knew that he would be scolded for disappearing yet again so now was not the time to ask if he could go riding. Besides he needed a little practice before he displayed his skills to Gunwald. He had looked like a natural rider and it had been several months since Eadwulf was last on his pony. Perhaps he could persuade someone to give him a few lessons first. At that moment he spotted Fiske watching him and beckoned him over. Fiske was a good rider and he was more than happy to do what Eadulf asked of him.

†††

Gunwald's foster father, Bjorn, had left Deira unwillingly. He was the Ealdorman of Beverley and he was in dispute with Thurbrand the Hold over two vills in the Wolds, the area to the north of Holderness and to the east of York. Both Hornsea and Brandesburton had been included in the lands granted him by King Cnut but Thurband had produced charters, undoubtedly forged, showing that the two vills had been granted to Thurbrand by Sweyn Forkbeard, Cnut's father. With Cnut out of England and Bjorn himself in London it would be all too easy for Thurbrand to seize his lands by force and argue in the courts later.

When word reached London in late March that the Scots were preparing to invade Lothian Queen Emma felt compelled to do something but she felt impotent. She had no army she could send north without her husband's permission and, given the current impoverished state of the royal treasury, that wasn't very likely. She therefore called a meeting of the council.

The room used for meetings of the inner council was located in a separate building called the Exchequer which also housed the offices of the chamberlain, the steward of the household and the various clerks responsible for all aspects of managing the kingdom and the lands personally owned by Cnut. It was a timber structure built on stone foundations and lay fifty yards from the queen's chambers.

The area between the two was often a sea of mud but duckboards had been placed between them so that Emma didn't risk getting covered in dirt, or even perhaps losing a shoe, between the two.

She was perfectly familiar with the meeting room. Like the rest of the administration building, it was lit by windows, over whose frames thin skins had been stretched. This allowed in a modicum of light whilst shielding the occupants from prying eyes.

The walls were decorated with the shields and banners of four previous kings; from Emma's first husband, Æthelred, to her present one, Cnut. The other two were Cnut's father, Sweyn Forkbeard and Emma's stepson, Edmund Ironside.

As she took her seat at the head of the table, with difficulty because of her swollen belly, she cast her eyes around those who had attended. Two were Anglo-Saxon archbishops - Wulfstan of York and Lyfing of Canterbury – and four were Danish nobles: Thorkell the Tall, Earl of East Anglia, Bjorn and two other ealdormen.

'Thank you for attending this meeting of the king's council, my lords,' she began.

One might have expected her to be nervous as this was the first time that she'd chaired this council but, as the sister of the Duke of Normandy and wife to two kings, she was well used to her status and exuded confidence.

'As I'm sure you're aware, Malcolm of Scotland is in northern Lothian with a large army. It's probable that he intends to move south into English Lothian; why else would he be there in such force? I have now learnt that Owain the Bald and the army of Strathclyde have already invaded the western part of Selkirkshire in English Lothian.'

There was a buzz around the table. The information about Owain was new to everyone present.

'May I ask how you know about the invasion of Selkirkshire, lady?'

'A birlinn arrived last night from Berwick upon Tweed with a message from Aldred, the son of the late Earl Uhtred. He is attacking Owain on the march and seems to have had some success. He says that he only has a small force, but his aim is to delay Owain further and, if possible, prevent his army from linking up with Malcolm. It remains to be seen what he can achieve in reality. Meanwhile I understand that Earl Eadwulf is raising an army to oppose Malcolm.'

'What is the Earl of Northumbria doing about the invasion of his territory, lady?' Bjorn asked.

He had hoped for the earldom himself and had bitterly resented it when it went to Erik Håkonsson instead. Consequently there was little love lost between the two Danes.

'Apparently nothing,' Emma replied brusquely. 'But you already know that, Bjorn.'

'One hears rumours, lady, that Erik may have been bribed by Malcolm,' Lyfing of Canterbury began.

'We are not here to listen to gossip and title tattle my lord archbishop,' Emma cut him off before he could say more. 'The question is, what can we do to halt Malcolm's invasion?'

'If Earl Erik isn't prepared to act, lady, then I'm not sure what we can do.' One of the ealdormen said with a sneer.

'As I understand it, this Lothian has been disputed for some time. Didn't King Edgar, father of Æthelred, give Lothian to Kenneth the Second, King of Scots, a little while before his death?'

'Yes, but on condition that Kenneth came and swore fealty to Edgar as his superior,' Emma replied. 'He failed to do so and officially the treaty was never formalised, allowing the then Earl of Bernicia to reclaim it after Edgar's death. It has been a bone of contention ever since. More recently it has been split into two with the northern part being part of Scotland and the southern two shires remaining part of England.

'My view, and I suspect that of the king,' she continued, 'is that the present border between the shire of Edinburgh and the rest of Lothian is ill defined. It would be better to re-establish it on the Firth of Forth in due course but, in the meantime, we might have to accept the River Tweed as the boundary.'

'Lothian encompasses more than the land north of the Tweed, lady,' Archbishop Wulfstan said in alarm. 'The Tweed runs well to the north of the Cheviot Hills but Lothian includes the land bounded by the Tweed in the north, the Cheviots in the south and Cumbria, which is now part of Strathclyde, to the west. The Tweed only forms the boundary between Berwick and a vill called Carham.'

One of the reasons for the archbishop's concern was that one of his largest monasteries – Melrose – lay just south of the Tweed but well inside the boundary of Lothian. The abbey, the diocese of Durham and indeed his own archdiocese also owned numerous estates in the part of Lothian south of the Tweed.

Queen Emma thought about what Wulfstan had said. If all of Lothian was ceded to the Scots, not only would the area south of the Tweed be lost, but there would still be no clear boundary between the two kingdoms west of Carham. This would inevitably lead to numerous disputes in the future.

'Thank you for your advice, archbishop. I hope that between them Earl Eadwulf and Lord Aldred can defeat Malcolm, but if not, he needs to be convinced to stay north of the Tweed. Someone will need to go and negotiate with him.'

She looked around the table before coming to a decision.

'My lord archbishop, would you and Ealdorman Bjorn act as my emissaries for this difficult task?'

Bjorn looked startled whereas Wulfstan merely bowed his head in acknowledgement. He was an obvious choice; Bjorn less so. He was an ealdorman of Northumbria but his lands, and therefore his interests, lay a good two hundred miles south of the River Tweed.

'You do me much honour, lady,' Bjorn said smoothly, 'but perhaps your relative through your daughter's marriage, this Aldred, might be a better choice.'

'Aldred will have just fought against Malcolm; not the most sensible choice I'd have thought,' Emma said tartly. 'No, Bjorn, you are my choice to assist the archbishop to salvage what we can from this situation.'

☨☨☨

'I won't be able to go riding with you after today,' Gunwald told Eadulf as they rested their horses after racing along the north bank of the River Thames. Both the groom and Fiske had accompanied them but remained at a discreet distance.

Gunwald had won but then he was the more experienced rider by far, though the other boy was improving quickly.

'Oh,' Eadulf said, unable to hide his dismay. 'Why, are you tired of winning all the time?'

'No,' Bjorn's son laughed. 'You have improved a lot over the past month and I enjoy riding with you and, if I'm honest, your company generally, especially since we started to learn the basics of swordsmanship together. No, my foster father is being sent on a mission to Northumbria and he thinks it will be good experience for me if I go with him.'

'Really?'

Eadulf's mind was racing. The only thing he liked about living in the king's palace was the time he spent with the king's bastard. His earnest desire was to rejoin his half-brother Aldred and now he saw a way of achieving this.

'You know my brother has estates in Bernicia; I would dearly love to see him again. Do you think your foster father would take me with you?'

'I'm sure he would be agreeable if I ask him, but I'm not so sure your mother and the queen would be so happy to lose you.'

Eadulf's heart sank. At nearly nine he was beginning to think of himself as a man. He was taller than Gunwald and looked more like ten or eleven, but that made little difference to how Ælfgifu saw him. However, the queen had just given birth to a son who she had named Harthacnut, meaning Cnut the Tough, and her mind and that of Eadulf's stepmother were on the political implications of his birth.

Ælfhelm, a former Earl of Deira, had a daughter, Elgiva. As earl Ælfhelm had been indolent and ineffective and therefore King Æthelred had him disposed of so that he could make Uhtred Earl of all Northumbria. The king also had Ælfhelm's sons blinded, which had enraged the people of Deira and made Æthelred even more unpopular.

When Sweyn Forkbeard seized the crown he married his son, Cnut, to Elgiva to increase his acceptance in the North. Once Cnut was secure on the English throne she became less significant politically and he divorced her in order to marry Emma of Normandy. Nevertheless, Elgiva remained important as the mother of Cnut's two eldest sons – Svein and Harold.

'The king will be pleased that you have presented him with a son, lady,' Ælfgifu said as she took the baby away to give to the wet nurse.

'Yes, I'm sure. I suspect that Elgiva will be less pleased. Harthacnut represents a threat to her sons.'

'You think that she intends harm to him?' her daughter asked in alarm.

'Not physically, no. But she will plead with Cnut for him to name one of her brats as his heir.'

At that moment one of Emma's maids entered the room and stood nervously at the door.

'Yes, what is it?' Emma asked peevishly.

Normally she treated her servants politely but she was still suffering discomfort from a difficult birth and was not in the best of moods.

'Ealdorman Bjorn is asking for a word with Lady Ælfgifu.'

The maid's reply was brusque to point of rudeness and the queen glared at her until the girl dropped her eyes and added 'lady,'

'I thought that he'd have left for Northumbria by now,' Emma complained to her daughter.

'Mother, you know perfectly well that he and Archbishop Wufstan are sailing for York tomorrow.'

'Yes, of course. Oh, I do wish that the king was here. I hope that I'm doing the right thing by negotiating with that barbarian Malcolm.'

'It may not come to that; Eadwulf might defeat him and send him packing.'

'Huh,' Emma snorted. 'The man is an indolent coward; worse than Elgiva's father, Ælfhelm, was.'

'I agree, he has worse traits too. Cnut should have made Aldred earl instead of him.'

'Yes,' Emma said sarcastically. 'Hindsight is a wonderful thing. You had better see what Bjorn wants.'

When Ælfgifu returned ten minutes later she was biting her lip and looking worried.

'What did he want, and why are you looking so concerned?'

'He has asked if he can take Eadulf with him as a companion for his ward, Gunwald.'

'Cnut's bastard? I'd almost forgotten about him. What did you say?'

'I said I'd think about it and give him an answer this evening.'

'You treat that boy like a baby. He's a big strapping lad now, out riding or learning to be a warrior every chance he gets. It's not even as if he's your son. It's time to give him some independence.'

'I suppose you're right but I've brought him up as if he were my own child. It's difficult to let him go, especially to travel to the

North where there are all sorts of dangers, not least his damned uncle.'

'Well, he hasn't managed to kill Aldred yet, despite his threats. He's all mouth and no guts.'

'I do hope you're right, but there are other dangers, like the Scots.'

'Don't worry. He'll be with Wulfstan and Bjorn.'

'You think I should let him go then?'

'It's your decision, not mine.'

'If it was Harthacnut in eight or nine years' time, would you let him go?'

'I don't suppose that the king would allow me a say; but, yes. This is a dangerous world and we don't do those we love any favours by trying to mollycoddle them.'

'I suppose that you're right.' Her daughter said reluctantly. 'I'll let Bjorn know and go and say goodbye to Eadulf.'

ϮϮϮ

'There's a sail away to the west,' Eadulf called down from his perch near the top of the mast.

He and Gunwald were too small and weak to carry out most of the tasks of the ship's boys, one of whom was Fiske, but the two young boys stood their watch as lookout. Now Eadulf's sharp eyes had discerned a sail as a smudge on the horizon.

Bjorn was travelling in his own snekkje – a small longship with a dozen oars each side -whilst the archbishop and his entourage were being conveyed north in a knarr with a dozen horses. A second warship was escorting them in case they ran into pirates. This craft wasn't a snekkje, but one of the largest longships in Cnut's fleet – a skeid - with thirty eight oars a side. It carried a crew of eighty five; over twice as many men as Bjorn's snekkje. The greatest threat of pirates was from the Continent and so the skeid was sailing to the east of the other two ships.

'There's a second one now,' Eadulf called down.

'Can you tell where they're headed?' Bjorn shouted back.

'Ahead of us, I think, but it's difficult to be sure yet.'

'Well done, Eadulf. Stay up there and keep an eye on them. Let me know when you can tell what type of ship they are.'

Bjorn smiled grimly to himself. They were passing the mouth of the River Humber some seven or eight miles to the west of them and the likelihood was that these were Thurbrand's two snekkje. If so, they were in for a nasty surprise. The big skeid was still hidden from the oncoming ships by the horizon. The problem was letting the skeid know that pirates were in sight to the west.

'Change our heading a little to the north east so that we close on the knarr,' he told the steersman.

Once they were in hailing distance Bjorn explained the situation to the captain of the knarr. He in turn turned his ship and headed closer to the skeid and shouted across what Bjorn had told him. There was a flurry of activity on the longship and the sail came down and was stowed on the deck ready to be raised again quickly. Now the big ship wouldn't be visible to the oncoming snekkje until its hull appeared over the horizon, and even then only if the enemy lookouts had sharp eyes.

Both Bjorn's ship and the knarr spilled wind from their sails so that the rowers in the longship could keep up with them without tiring themselves out. It also meant that the two pirate ships would close with them more quickly.

When the snekkje were two miles away Bjorn calculated that they would soon be able to see the skeid and ordered the steersman to turn towards the pirate ships. The knarr would be of little use in a fight and so it continued to sail north. The skeid also turned towards the pirate ships and raised its sail to catch the wind from the south east.

The captain of the nearest enemy ship now realised that he had sailed into a trap. His snekkje turned through one hundred and eighty degrees and headed back the way it had come in a vain attempt to reach the safety of the harbour near the entrance to the

Humber Estuary. The sudden change of course caught the second snekkje by surprise and its captain made a fatal error. Instead of tacking through the wind, the ship's boys were caught unawares and mishandled the sail. It backed against the mast and the ship lost way, coming to a standstill. By the time the crew had hauled it around to catch the wind again Bjorn's ship was less than a mile away and the big longship was coming up fast.

The skeid ignored Thurbrand's rearmost snekkje, other than sending several arrows into its rowers, and sailed on after the other pirate ship. The outcome of that particular fight was never in any doubt.

Bjorn's snekkje had a crew of thirty warriors whereas the enemy ship was a little smaller with only a dozen oars a side. As his ship came alongside Bjorn gave the signal and four grappling irons snaked across to secure the other ship. Axemen on the other ship managed to sever two of the ropes but Bjorn's men pulled the two ship's together before their quarry could sever the remaining two.

Bjorn jumped onto the other ship's deck closely followed by his men. All of them were housecarls and experienced fighters; the crew of the other ship also contained warriors but many of the crew were hired thugs and petty thieves who proved no match for Bjorn's men. Within fifteen minutes all the pirates bar one were dead or had surrendered.

The captain had retreated to the stern and seemed determined to die fighting. Bjorn pushed his way to the front of his housecarls as they surrounded the lone pirate. He grunted in satisfaction when he recognised the young man shouting insults at him.

'Well, well, if it isn't Edgar Thurbransson. The days when you father could prey on merchant shipping with impunity has come to an end.'

'Bjorn! I thought you were in London living the soft life at court.'

'You thought wrong. Make your peace with God before you die, Edgar.'

'My father will ransom me.'

'What? So he can build you another ship to carry on with your piracy? No, this is your last day on earth, Edgar. I only wish your father was here so that he could join you on your journey to Hell.'

Bjorn could see the fear in the young man's eyes. He knew that Edgar was only seventeen but he was just as bad as his father and England would be better off without him. He therefore had no compassion for him as he stepped forward and thrust his sword towards Edgar's chest. The youth acted as Bjorn had expected and raised his shield to protect his torso. At the last moment Bjorn dropped the point and thrust it onto the space between the bottom of his opponent's byrnie and his knee.

He felt the point glance off his adversary's thigh bone. As he pulled it out Edgar screamed and his leg collapsed under him. He dropped his sword and the shield hung uselessly from his left arm as the pain overtook him. Bjorn was about to finish him off but out of the corner of his eye he noticed Eadulf with the ever protective Fiske by his side watching from prow of the other ship.

'Boy, this is the son of the man who killed your father. Do you wish to kill him?'

Eadulf licked his lips nervously. One part of him was revolted by the idea of killing someone but he had grown up hating the two men responsible for his father's death and the thought of killing Thurbrand's son excited him. He therefore nodded eagerly.

Fiske helped him down onto the deck of the other snekkje. Bjorn thrust a dagger into the boy's hand and stood aside. Eadulf looked down at Edgar kneeling in a growing puddle of his own blood. He'd lost so much that his face was turning white and it wouldn't be long before he died anyway.

For a moment Eadulf felt compassion for him, but then he remembered how this man's father had slaughtered his own father together with forty of his warriors. Hate replaced pity. At that moment Edgar collapsed, the light going out of his eyes. Eadulf knew that he had to act then or lose the respect of Bjorn and his men. Even Fiske encouraged him by whispering 'now Eadulf' in his ear.

He knelt beside the prone body and thrust the point of the dagger under Edgar's chin and up through his mouth and into the base of his brain. He had expected the sharp point to slide into the dying youth easily, but he had to push with all his might to cut through skin and tissue.

As the light went out of Edgar's eyes, Eadulf slowly got to his feet, his trousers and tunic covered in blood, and spat in the face of the corpse. Bjorn's housecarls cheered and two of them lifted him onto their shoulders. The remorse and shock he'd initially felt at killing his first man, especially a defenceless youth, disappeared as he glowed with pride at the approval of these hardened warriors.

The feeling didn't last, of course, and that night he wept as reaction set in. At dawn he'd been a boy with few cares or worries; now he had killed and had become harder as a result. Gunwald had congratulated him, of course, but it had come between them somehow. Perhaps the other boy was jealous, Eadwulf thought, but the truth was that they were both still very young and what his friend had brought himself to do frightened Gunwald.

Chapter Eleven – Defeat of the Norse

Mid July 1018

Thurbrand didn't know what had happened to his eldest son or his two ships until one of his housecarls, a man called Aart, brought a shepherd from a village called Kinsea near Spurn Head to see him.

'Tell Lord Thurbrand what you told me.'

'I was on the cliff top three days ago, lord, watching my sheep when I saw your two snekkje tack around Spurn Head and head out to sea. I wasn't paying much attention but the next time I looked I saw that they were heading towards two ships near the horizon who were sailing northwards. Some of the lambs were playing a bit too near the cliff edge and so I sent my two dogs to drive them back to safety.'

'I'm not interested in your bloody sheep. What did you see?' Thurbrand yelled at him.

'Yes, lord. Sorry, lord. The next time I looked a third ship, a much bigger one, had appeared and it and one of the original two ships heading north were now heading towards your two snekkje. The third ship – a knarr I think, continued to head north.'

'Did you see any devices on their sails?'

'What, oh. Yes, I think so. I couldn't see the knarr's sail but I saw the other two quite clearly: the smaller ship had a striped sail, green and yellow, and the other sail was plain with a red crown embroidered on it.'

'Bjorn and Cnut,' Thurbrand whispered to himself.

He could understand his son wanting to attack one of Bjorn's ships but not one of the king's; what was the boy thinking of?

'What happened next,' Thurbrand asked, but he knew the answer already and his heart sank.

'Well, the one with the green and yellow sail attacked one of the snekkje. The longship completely ignored it and sailed on to catch the leading snekkje. They must have overcome your men, lord, because half an hour later the two strange ships sailed away leaving your two ships aflame. They burnt for a while then they sank below the waves. I'm sorry, lord.'

'What, yes. Thank you. You may leave. Aart, give him a silver penny for his trouble.'

The housecarl looked at his lord in surprise. It wasn't like him to reward the likes of the shepherd. He was more likely to have been sent on his way with a kick. However, Aart knew only too well what the sea battle meant. Edgar had been Thurbrand's favourite son and he would be feeling his loss keenly. He made a swift exit, knowing full well that Thurbrand's grief would soon result in him striking out at anyone within range.

He had two other sons, Carl and Arne, but as they were only eleven and nine, he hadn't taken much interest in them before this. That now changed and he filled their ears with his hatred of Ealdorman Bjorn.

†††

Aldred surveyed the motley bunch of men who stood in front of him. They ranged in age from twelve to late forties and they were equipped with everything from rusty swords to two-handed scythes. They were the one hundred and twenty eight men who comprised the fyrd of his three vills: Duns, Norham and Carham.

'Behind me,' he said, gesturing to two wagons laden with weapons and armour, are the spoils of war: helmets, leather gambesons, byrnies, swords, daggers, spears, axes and shields. Some of the chain mail will need repairs and much of it will need blood and other substances cleaning off them. There are blacksmiths and even an armourer amongst you who can held with the repairs. Wash the muck off and then use sand to get rid of the rust.

'Make sure that what you take is a good fit. My housecarls will help you, and they will also ensure that there is no squabbling over the better items. The army of Strathclyde, or what's left of it, are about fifteen miles away. At their current speed that means we have a maximum of three days before they reach us. In that time you will be taught how to form up as a shield wall and, more importantly, how to fight in one.

'The one exception is the archers. The few who own a war bow and those who know how to use a hunting bow will join my mounted housecarls. Once the enemy form up, we will charge them in the flank and inflict as many casualties as we can before withdrawing. Inevitably the more hot headed will chase after us. Your job is to wait in ambush and pepper them with arrows.

'If that doesn't dissuade them, my horsemen can charge again to give you time to fade away. Our aim is not to fight them in battle – they have four times our numbers – but to whittle down their strength and their morale with as few casualties on our side as possible. Does everyone understand? Right let's get started.'

When Kjetil and Hakon came back to tell Aldred that the vanguard of Owain's army had sacked Melrose and were now moving into the hills to the east he decided that it was time to put his plans into operation.

'Has there been any change to their numbers?' Aldred asked after he had sent Uuen to summon Ceadda, Ceolfrith and Kenric.

'We've seen a few slipping away, lord, but there haven't been any reinforcements if that's what you mean.'

Aldred grunted in satisfaction. If Owain's men were deserting him that was a sure sign that morale was low.

'The other thing we've noticed is that the order not to pillage seems have fallen by the wayside. Every day forage parties go out and we've seen plumes of smoke in the distance.'

'That either means that they are low on supplies or Owain is losing control.'

Just at that moment Ceadda and the others arrived. There was no tent for them to meet in; Aldred and his men were travelling light and his quarters were at the base of a large oak tree that had only recently come into leaf. Like his men, he slept on the ground wrapped in his cloak.

'Tomorrow we confront Owain and hit him hard, but today we'll take the horsemen and deal with these forage parties. I want each of you to take ten men and track a forage party. Stop them from burning anymore farmsteads if you can, but make sure that no-one returns to their main army. Not only will that reduce their numbers, but it will further demoralise the rest. Go and get the men ready to leave; Kjetil and Hakon will lead us to where their main body is. Hopefully Colby, who's still watching them, can tell us in which direction the foragers have gone.'

Aldred was riding beside Ceadda when Kjetil, who was riding a few hundred yards ahead of the rest with Hakon, came galloping back.

'There's a party of the enemy less than half a mile away, lord.'

Aldred cursed. He should have realised that one of the forage parties might be heading towards them.

'How many?'

'About twenty, all on foot.'

Aldred looked around him. They were crossing a stretch of open meadow dotted with shrubs. There was a wood straight ahead of them about two hundred yards away. Suddenly Hakon appeared waving his arms. That could only mean the Britons were close behind him.

'Ceadda, take your men and ride around in a loop so that you cut off their line of retreat. Ceolfrith, you go with him. Kenric, your men will form the second rank. The rest of you form extended line and prepare to charge.'

Ceadda and his group rode off the track and into dead ground whilst the rest formed up. A minute after the last man had taken his post the forage party appeared at the edge of the wood. Aldred and his horsemen sat, not moving as the last of the enemy cleared the wood. They were so intent on talking and joking amongst themselves that they didn't notice the line of mounted warriors blocking their path at first. When they did they froze in consternation. Then someone had the sense to order them to flee back into the woods.

Just at that moment Cetta's twenty horsemen appeared from the gully where they were in hiding and rode across the track, blocking their retreat. Without a sound Aldred raised his spear on high and pointed it at the would-be foragers. The horses started at a walk, then went directly into a canter before increasing the pace to a gallop. At the same time they levelled their spears.

This had taken less than a minute and in that time the Britons had dithered, not knowing whether to charge the line of horsemen watching them silently from just in front of the trees or to defend themselves against the charging warriors. The sight of the oncoming horsemen was too much and, almost as one, they turned and charged into Ceadda's men.

Horsemen are most effective when they use the shock effect of a charge at full tilt. They are most vulnerable when they are stationary. However, what the score or so of Britons hadn't seen was that the rear rank of Ceadda's men had dismounted. They were all bowmen and now they stepped forward in front of the horsemen and sent a volley at low trajectory straight into the yelling Britons.

Half a dozen of them were hit, some by more than one arrow, and fell to the ground. A second volley of arrows struck them before the rest had covered another ten paces. Now half their number were dead or seriously wounded. The charge petered out just as Aldred's men hit their rear.

The Britons broke; some managed to escape but others were cut down by the horsemen as they fled whilst the archers went amongst the Britons, cutting the throats of the wounded. The victors quickly gathered up what little wealth the corpses had on them for distribution later and then resumed their journey.

ϮϮϮ

Wulfstan and Bjorn made their way through York's narrow streets towards Earl Erik's hall. They were accompanied by Wulfstan's chaplain, who was there to record their conversation with Erik, and six of Bjorn's housecarls.

They got as far as the main gate in the palisade before two sentries crossed their spears and demanded to know who they were.

'It's sad day, my son, when a housecarl of the Earl of Northumbria doesn't recognise the Archbishop of York,' Wulfstan said quietly.

'I'm sorry, lord archbishop, but why do you come here with so many armed men?'

'Ealdorman Bjorn and I are the emissaries of Queen Emma, Regent of England in the absence of King Cnut. Now are you going to let us pass or do you want to be arrested for treason?'

'Will you wait here whilst I let the earl know of your presence?'

'No,' Bjorn replied. 'It is not for the likes of you to obstruct us. Now stand aside or my men will part your head from your body.'

The housecarl glared at Bjorn but nodded to his fellow sentry and reluctantly they allowed the group through the gates. The hall was unmissable. It was the only structure built of stone in the compound. Like Bishop Aldhun's hall at Durham, it was two stories high with the main hall at first floor level up some narrow steps built into the side of the building.

Once more their way was barred by a housecarl at the bottom of the steps.

'Wait here,' Bjorn instructed their escort whilst Wulfstan told the sentry at the bottom of the steps to inform his master that an embassy from Queen Emma were waiting to see him.

Erik Håkonsson was about to eat with his wife when the sentry came into the hall and whispered in his ear.

'What is it Erik?' she asked, annoyed that their meal had been interrupted.

'Archbishop Wulfstan and Bjorn of Beverley are waiting to see me, apparently on a mission from Queen Emma.'

'Emma, what can she want?'

'Cnut foolishly left her as regent when he sailed back to Denmark. I told him that he should have appointed me but he wouldn't listen.'

'Do you think that this is to do with the Scots' invasion?'

'What else? I should never have taken Malcolm's bribe, but I didn't think that Cnut was interested in the far north.'

He chewed his lip and then got up and went to the door.

'My dear Wulfstan, what a pleasure it is to see you again, and you too Bjorn. Please come on up.'

Even he was well aware that the welcoming smile on his face must appear false. Beside him stood his wife, Gytha, who was Cnut's sister. For the king to have given Erik her hand in marriage was a sign of great favour; however, she was hardly someone that Erik would have chosen for himself. Apart from the fact that she was ugly she was domineering and so far had failed to bear any children, something that Erik regarded as her most serious failing.

It wasn't as if she had any influence with her brother either. Sometimes Erik suspected that he had been glad to see the back of Gytha; certainly he'd made no effort to visit her or even contact her over the three years that they had been wed.

Gytha joined them at the table and, once they were all seated, Erik cut through the hypocritical pleasantries and asked what had brought his unwelcome guests to York.

'Apart from the fact that it's time that I visited my archdiocese, you mean?' Wulfstan replied.

'I know that my brother keeps you busy as a law-giver and administrator so it must be difficult to balance that with your duties here and, of course, in the diocese of Worcester,' Gytha remarked sharply before her husband could reply.

Wulfstan had remained as Bishop of Worcester when he was made Archbishop of York and her remark was a not so subtle dig at the income he received from both in return for which he did little.

'But did I hear correctly; you are here as representatives of the queen?' Erik asked, giving his wife a warning look.

'Yes, lord,' Bjorn nodded. 'We are tasked with making peace with King Malcolm and securing the northern border.'

'A laudable aim. Of course, I would have taken the field against him myself but I fear that thenobles of Deira have little love for their counterparts in Bernicia and they would not march to support them.'

'You surprise me, lord,' Bjorn replied with a scowl. 'My fellow ealdormen and I would have followed you to oppose the Scots. We have no desire to see the northern border of England any closer than the Forth. Even the Tweed is too close and the Tees would threaten us even more. We have to bear in mind that Strathclyde has now infiltrated the shire of Lancaster and so threatens us from the west. If we aren't careful one day the Scots and their allies will rule everywhere north of the Humber and the Mersey.'

'You exaggerate, Bjorn. It may be sensible to allow the Scots to take Lothian – after all it has been fought over for the past century – but I'm am assured that Malcolm has no ambitions south of the Tweed.'

'Assured by whom, Earl Erik? By Malcolm? And you trust him, do you? Are you aware that Lothian stretches much further south than the Tweed; from Cornhill Lothian's border marches due south as far as the Cheviot Hills? Once he has those the way is open down Redesdale all the way to the Tyne.'

Erik had never been further north than the Tees but he was well aware that the Tyne wasn't that much further on; Durham was the only stronghold between the two. What Bjorn had said gave him cause for concern, but the man was one of his ealdormen and he wasn't about to have his inferiors berate him.

'Watch your tongue! You have no right to speak to me like that.'

'In his capacity as the Queen Regent's emissary I think he probably has,' Wulfstan said quietly, 'but as the second most senior churchman in England and one of the king's most trusted advisers, I would certainly like to know why you are so certain that you know Malcolm's mind.'

Erik was astute enough to realise that he had revealed more than was wise. By saying that he was certain that Malcolm wouldn't come south of the Tweed he had given away the fact that he must have been in contact with the Scottish king, or at least his representative. Furthermore he had mistakenly thought that the region of Lothian lay wholly north of the River Tweed. He realised that he'd been wrong footed on both counts.

'What exactly is your mission?' he asked rather more brusquely than he had intended.

'That rather depends on the outcome of Malcolm's invasion,' Wulfstan said carefully. 'If he manages to wrest Lothian from our control, then we are to conclude a treaty conceding the land between the Forth and the Tweed, but no more. In return he must swear not to encroach further on Cnut's kingdom.'

'And if he is beaten by Eadwulf?' Gytha asked.

'Do you really think that's likely, lady? From what I hear, the only hope we have lies with Uhtred's son, Aldred; if only he was in command instead of his uncle,' Bjorn replied with a grimace.

ϮϮϮ

The gale driven rain lashed the fortress of Bebbanburg standing on its basalt rock at the edge of the North Sea. Below the eastern cliffs the waves crashed against the rock, sending salt laden spray high in the air where the wind blew it, together with the rain, over the palisade and into the area in front of the earl's hall.

Eadwulf was reluctant to venture outside where his housecarls waited for him to join them. It was time to ride to the muster at Yeavering Bell, the site of the ancient royal palace in the middle of the Cheviot Hills. It wasn't only the foul weather that delayed him. He had recently married his betrothed - Sigfreda - and, experienced fornicator that he was, he had never enjoyed introducing a young girl to his rather novel ways of enjoying sex as much as he had

Sigfreda. Knowing that she was his nephew's half-sister made it even more pleasurable for him.

The girl's mother, Ecgfrida, had never forgiven Uhtred for casting her aside and had dripped poison into Sigfrida's ear about Uhtred and his family ever since she was a baby. Now Sigfreda stoked the fires of hostility against Uhtred's sons, especially Aldred, that already burned in Eadwulf.

Of course, he would love the opportunity to outlaw his nephew. Aldred's popularity was a threat to the earl's position and his recent successes against Owain had further enhanced his reputation. It seemed that Eadwulf was placing his animosity against his nephew above the need to defeat the invaders. The earl's judgement had always been clouded by his jealousy of his late brother, Uhtred, and his yearning to wipe out his brood but, Eadwulf's hatred of Aldred had grown even greater since the council at Duns.

He thrust into his wife one last time and groaned as he climaxed. She feigned an orgasm to coincide with his, though in truth he had never managed to satisfy her. He was too self-centred to think of her needs and she relied on the willing services of someone else for that. At least this time he was making love naturally instead of indulging in one of his perversions.

He rolled off her and yelled for his body-servant to come and help him dress. The boy who entered was a fifteen year old Irish slave called Aodghan - an appropriate name as it meant little fire and he was Sigfreda's secret lover. She made little effort to cover her nakedness and Aodghan's eyes roved over her body, wishing that he wasn't leaving with his master. He was in love with Sigfreda and would do anything for her. He found himself wishing his master was dead so that he could stay in her bed for ever.

Instead he had to help the bad-tempered earl to dress and put on his byrnie. Once he had fastened the thick oiled cloak around Eadwulf's neck with a gold broach, he took one last look at Sigfreda, gave her a half-hearted smile and followed her husband out of the hall and into the rain.

Sigfreda pulled on a shift and wrapped a bearskin cloak about her to go and wave Eadwulf off. However, her eyes kept drifting to Aodghan, who blushed and looked down bashfully under her bold scrutiny. She fondly imagined that her affair with the young slave was a secret, but little escapes the notice of the other slaves and the housecarls. Several chuckled to themselves as they saw the exchange between the two. Then the cuckolded earl kicked his horse into a trot and they rode out through the gates and down onto the road that led into the Cheviots.

ƬƬƬ

'I'm not sure that it's a very good idea,' Ceolfrith said, stubbornness written all over his face.

Aldred looked at him with surprise. It wasn't the reaction he'd expected. When Ceadda also looked unconvinced he began to doubt himself. The plan seemed to him to give them the best chance of further reducing Owain the Bald's numbers. The King of Strathclyde had grown ever more wary of night attacks and pinprick raids on his column on the march as it moved ever closer to linking up with Malcolm Forranach.

Such a strategy had had its day; Aldred risked losing too many men if he persevered. He needed a different approach and he thought he'd found it. When his closest companions disagreed he wondered if he was growing overconfident. His latest plan was certainly bold and carried a high degree of risk, but he'd been confident of its success. He still was but he had to convince his men.

It would be incorrect to say that Ceolfrith, Kenric and Ceadda followed Aldred blindly; they had always been fully involved in deciding tactics but up until now they had accepted his basic ideas and had concentrated on honing the fine detail. Now they seemed totally opposed to the latest plan he'd proposed.

There was some urgency if he wanted to strike another significant blow against the Britons of Starthclyde. His uncle had just sent word to him that Aldred was to join his army immediately or he would declare him a traitor.

'Have I ever failed you?' Aldred said, looking the three of them in the eye in turn. 'This is our only chance of destroying Owain's contingent as a fighting force before we have to go east to join the main Bernician army.'

He couldn't bring himself to say Eadwulf's name; the sound of it tasted too bitter in his mouth. He had vowed to kill Eadwulf after Uhtred's death and the desire to do just that grew stronger with every passing day. However, he wasn't so blinkered that he didn't realise that the overriding priority was to thwart Malcom's territorial ambitions.

Perhaps Eadwulf would fall in battle? That was a vain hope; he couldn't see his craven uncle risking his own life. He wasn't the type to lead from the front. In any case, Aldred would rather he survived so that he could have the pleasure of killing him himself.

'You are relying on Owain walking into your trap. If he has the sense to send part of his army to outflank us or cut off our retreat we'd be slaughtered,' Kenric said.

'Even if he doesn't do that,' Ceadda added, 'he still has a thousand men; we'd be outnumbered by six to one. It's too risky, lord.'

'A thousand demoralised men, reducing all the time as every night deserters make for home.'

'Even so,' Ceolfrith said, 'a victory would restore their self-confidence and rob Bernicia of some of its best warriors. Owain isn't the main enemy; Malcolm is.'

'Without Owain's Britons, Malcolm's forces will be matched by ours,' Aldred pointed out.

'Not if Findlay's men of Moray join him,' Ceolfrith pointed out. 'Then they'll outnumber us quite significantly.'

'Ah, yes. I'm glad you mentioned that. I have a little task for Wictred. He can take Kjetil, Hakon and Colby with him.'

Chapter Twelve – Macbeth the Red

July 1018

Wictred and his three companions halted their horses in the trees well away from the track they'd been following. Having found a suitable clearing, they unloaded the packhorse and set up camp. Confident that they were still over a day's ride away from the area where Malcolm's army was reported to be, they gathered wood and started a small fire to cook the rations they'd brought with them. Not having eaten since they had chewed some stale bread and cheese before leaving the previous night's campsite, they were all looking forward to the stew of dried meat, lentils and root vegetables.

Suddenly Colby, whose hearing was the best of the four, held up a warning hand and Hakon kicked soil over the fire to put it out without having to be told. There was no doubt about it. A minute later the other three could hear the jingle of harness and the sound of human voices coming from the track they'd been following that day.

Silently the four scouts put on their helmets, picked up their weapons and shields and made their way through the trees towards the sound. Whoever was travelling along the track wasn't bothering to move quietly and so the odd crack of a twig and other small sounds made by the scouts passed unnoticed.

When they could see movement along the track they stopped, still within the shadow of the trees. Night wasn't far off and it was almost certain that the armed men marching along the track would camp soon. Wictred estimated that it was a strong foraging party of

Scots who'd had a successful day, judging by the abject collection of slaves and number of livestock that they were driving along.

The four waited as the last of the main body passed. There was a sizeable gap between them and the next group. It consisted of some thirty captives, mostly women and children, guarded by five Scots.

'Kill all but the youngest,' Wictred whispered in the ears of his companions.

Quickly they strung their bows and selected their best arrow. They picked their targets and a second later four arrows hit the Scots leaving the survivor, who didn't look older than fourteen, looking around in abject terror. The scouts stepped out cautiously, checking that the enemy group in front of them had heard nothing.

Just at that moment ten more Scots rounded the corner; evidently a rear guard. It would be difficult to say which group was the more surprised. The captives were only bound at wrist and neck and a quick witted girl yelled at her fellow prisoners. They charged the surviving guard and knocked him to the ground, sitting on him whilst one of them used her bound hands to pull his dagger form its sheath.

She launched into a frenzied attack on the young Scot, reducing his body to a mass of blood and mutilated flesh before cutting the other women and the children free.

Meanwhile the rear guard had gathered their wits and charged towards Wictred and his three friends. They were still forty paces away when four arrows tore into them. There wasn't time to pick individual targets and only two were killed. The oncoming Scots hesitated for a split second, which gave the archers a chance to string another arrow. This time only one was killed but two were wounded: one in the thigh and one in the shoulder.

Wictred and the two Norse boys pulled out their swords and swung their shields around from their backs. Colby was too young to wield a sword but he was the proud possessor of a seax. The four ran silently towards the unwounded Scots. For a moment the enemy stood there and Wictred was afraid that they'd flee, but instead they charged towards them, yelling in rage.

The four scouts stopped once they were certain that the Scots weren't about to flee and formed a small shield wall. The leading Scot, a giant of a man wielding a double handed axe, raised it intent on killing Wictred, but Colby darted in from the side and thrust his seax into the giant's armpit. The man bellowed in fury but he was crippled; his left arm fell uselessly to his side and the axe dropped to the ground.

Colby tugged furiously to free his seax but he lacked the strength; it was stuck fast. Just as another Scot jabbed his spear at him, he dropped to the ground and rolled out of harm's way. The boy still had a dagger and he ripped it free before cutting both the hamstrings of his attacker. The Scot screamed and fell on top of Colby.

By the time that Wictred had dispatched both the axeman and the man on top of Colby the two Norse youths had finished off the last few Scots. A minute later, having cut the throats of the wounded, the four returned to the captives. Unfortunately Wictred's instruction to keep the last Scot alive had patently been ignored. The four scouts looked at the remains of the Scot, who can't have any older than Colby, and felt sickened. It wasn't caused so much by the gory body – a warrior didn't last long if he was squeamish – but it was the fact that the mutilation had been carried out by a young woman.

Wictred had wanted to question the Scots boy and gave vent to his anger so fiercely that the women and children cowered away from him. Fortunately he realised that this wasn't getting him anywhere. The rest of the forage party could return any minute to find out where the back of the column had got to and they had to get away from there. After hurriedly dragging the bodies out of sight and giving the women and children the Scots' weapons, the scouts returned to their campsite whilst the former captives headed in the opposite direction. Wictred would like to have given them some food but they only had enough for the four of them for another three days as it was.

One thing he did learn before the two groups parted company was that the road the forage party were following led to Melrose and its monastery.

ϮϮϮ

Malcolm was getting impatient. He had been camped at Melrose, on the opposite bank from the monastery, for two days and so far there was no sign of either Owain the Bald or Findlay of Moray. He had few horsemen and those he had, apart from his own bodyguard, were mainly nobles and chieftains. However, he did have a score of scouts mounted on shaggy mountain ponies. He had sent them out both days to check the approaches to Melrose but they had failed to find anything.

'You had better hope that your father has the sense to join me, boy,' the king said to Macbeth, who was standing in front of the ornately carved chair that served Malcolm as a throne on campaign. 'Or he'll receive a present of your head in a basket.'

'That's hardly likely to make him a more loyal subject is it,' Findlay's son replied impudently, which earned him a punch in the stomach for his pains.

'One more comment like that and you'll not grow up to be a man whether your father turns up or not,' Malcolm said angrily. 'Get him out of my sight before I do something I might regret.'

Malcolm watched sourly as the two warriors who had been assigned to look after Macbeth pushed him roughly out of the tent. The king would never admit it but he was nervous. He had never forgotten the humiliating defeat that Uhtred of Northumbria had meted out to him at Durham a dozen years ago. He acted as if victory over Uhtred's brother was a forgone conclusion in public but he was far from sure of that in private. He needed Owain and Findlay, not only to bolster his numbers, but to provide their experienced warriors. Many of his own army were youths who had never faced an armed man in anger.

The men of Moray hadn't taken part in the ill-fated attack on Durham and Owain was bringing hundreds of Norsemen, or so Malcolm believed. He was well aware that Eadwulf wasn't anything like his brother, Uhtred; indeed, his nickname of Cudel referred to his spineless nature. Nevertheless Malcolm was well aware that he had plenty of experienced ealdormen and thanes, including Uhtred's son, Aldred.

He paced about the large leather tent that served as his living quarters gnawing his lower lip as he tried to imagine what had happened to the armies of Strathclyde and Moray. His grandson and acknowledged heir, Duncan, son of the king's eldest daughter Bethoc, entered at that moment and wondered whether to leave again before his grandfather became aware of his presence. From the look on Malcolm's face, he wasn't in the best of moods.

'Well, what is it?' Malcolm barked, annoyed at being disturbed.

'I thought that you'd like to know that Findlay of Moray has been spotted in the Pentland Hills, lord king.'

'The Pentlands? They're what? The best part of forty miles away?'

'I'm not sure of the distance but the scouts who found them said that it would take them at least three days to arrive,' Duncan said.

'And that's if Findlay is in a rush to get here, which I doubt he is.'

'At least we know he'll reach us before we have to fight the Northumbrians. The latest reports say that they are still camped in the Cheviot Hills some forty or fifty miles away,' Duncan said, trying to lift his grandfather's spirits.

'Um, but where's Owain? Duncan, take as many scouts as you can find and ride west along the western valley of the Tweed until you find him. When you do, tell him to get a bloody move on. Clear? Off you go; you leave at dawn.'

ϮϮϮ

Wictred and his companions crested the hill above the monastery, which lay south of the Tweed at Melrose. They crawled on their bellies so as not to be seen against the skyline until they were in the shadow of the hilltop. Someone would have to know they were there to spot them now.

The Scots' camp sprawled over the north bank and, judging by the number of tents, they estimated the enemy numbers at a little over two thousand: a little less than earlier reports had suggested. Colby sucked his teeth.

'How in the name of all that's holy are we meant to find one boy amongst that lot, let alone rescue him and escape without being killed?'

'There are Benedictines from the monastery moving about the camp,' Wictred pointed out. 'We could disguise ourselves as monks.'

'Apart from the fact that none of us have a tonsure,' Kjetil pointed out.

'That can easily be remedied,' Wictred said with a grin, pulling out a sharp knife.

The monastery had not been pillaged by the Scots, but nevertheless it kept its main gates firmly closed and barred. The monks tending to the sick and injured left by the monastery's postern gate but that was also kept locked when not in use. The four scouts hid in a nearby house, having tied up the elderly man and woman living there. Wictred hoped that someone would find them, but not until they were well away from Melrose. They waited until they saw a monk leaving through the gate and then pulled him into the house as he walked past. He too was bound and gagged after stripping him of his habit. It was a bit large for Wictred, the tallest of the four, but it would have to do.

They had passed the time shaving the crown of their heads with sharp knives and so Wictred, his disguise complete, undid the postern with the monk's key and slipped into the monastery. He waited until two monks entered the timber building across the courtyard in front of him and then walked boldly towards the church. He intended to hide in there until dark and then try and find the store where spare habits were stored.

However, as he rounded a corner he bumped into a novice coming the other way. The boy was about Colby's age and size.

'Oh, I'm sorry, brother. I should have looked ...' the young novice began to say.

He didn't have a chance to complete the sentence before Wictred clamped a hand over his mouth and dragged him into a narrow alley between two buildings. He held his knife to the novice's throat and slowly removed his hand.

'Cry for help and I'll kill you. Don't worry, I just want information.'

The boy nodded, his eyes wide with fear.

'Where do they keep the spare habits?'

'What? Spare habits? Why?'

'I've no time to explain, just tell me.'

'You're with the Northumbrian army, aren't you?' the boy said excitedly. 'Take me with you. I hate being a novice but my father insisted. I want to be a warrior and fight the bloody Scots.'

Wictred wasn't sure whether to believe him, but the eager look on his face seemed genuine.

'Very well, if you help us I'll take you with us. Now show where the habits are kept.'

The boy said that his name was Osric and he started to chatter excitedly until Wictred told him to shut up in no uncertain terms. Osric led him to a small hut next to what he said was the refectory. Unfortunately the door was locked and it was in full view of anyone crossing the courtyard in front of the church. However, it was a wattle and daub building.

Wictred chipped away and at the mixture of dried mud and straw that made up one of the infill panels at the rear of the hut until he'd made a hole big enough for Osric to slip though. A minute later he re-emerged pushing several black habits through the hole ahead of him. Wictred selected three that he thought would roughly fit his three companions and pushed the rest back into the hut. The next problem was reaching the postern gate carrying the habits without arousing suspicion.

'Why don't we wear them?' Osric suggested.

Two minutes later a slightly more rotund Wictred locked the postern again and returned to the house where the others were hiding. He introduced Osric as the other three clambered into their habits. Then the novice noticed the trussed up monk sitting in a corner. With a cry of glee he went over and kicked the monk hard between the legs. The man emitted a muffled cry of pain through his gag and doubled up on his side.

'I take it you have a grudge against him?' Hakon asked with a grin.

'Let's just say it's wise not to let him get you on your own, the old pervert.'

Wictred smiled in relief. He was devout and hadn't liked trussing up a monk. Now he felt much better about it.

'Have you been into the camp?' he asked Osric as they sat down to a meal of bread and cheese – all they could find in the old couple's house.

'Once, to accompany Brother Irwyn. He's our herbalist and I was tasked to carry his basket of potions, remedies and ointments.'

'Did you see a boy of about thirteen, a noble's son who would probably be escorted?'

Osric shook his head and then stopped.

'Wait, there were lots of boys around, of course, servants and the like; even many of those carrying weapons looked to be quite young, but there was one boy washing down by the river and three bored looking warriors on the bank who appeared to be waiting for him.'

The four scouts looked at each other. That sounded if it might be Macbeth. They had no description of him, other than the fact that he was nicknamed the Red.

'What did he look like?' Wictred asked.

'The most noticeable thing about him was his long red hair,' Osric replied. 'Of course, there were many men and boys in the camp with various shades of hair from ginger to dark bronze, but this boy's hair was what drew my attention to him. It was bright red.'

'That sounds as if it's probably our boy. I don't suppose you saw where he went after he had bathed?'

'No, but I did see him later.'

'Where?'

'In King Malcolm's tent.'

'Really? Is that where he's living?'

'I suppose so. Brother Irwyn was treating the king's grandson, Duncan, for a rash. He did so in an area off the main tent and there were two beds in there. The boy with red hair was sitting on the other bed.'

A smile of triumph crossed Wictred's face. What had seemed an impossible mission now looked as if it had at least some chance of success.

†††

Macbeth was bored and fearful at the same time. He had been treated well as a hostage, but then he had expected to be as the king's grandson. However, he had nothing to do all day in camp. It had been slightly better when the army had been on the move as he was allowed to ride, even if his escort had held a leading rein tied to his horse's bridle. For the last three days they had been camped waiting for the two other contingents to join them and there was nothing to occupy his time.

The fact that there was no sign of his father wasn't good. He might be Malcolm's grandson, but the king had two other grandsons and Macbeth was convinced that he would carry out his threat to behead him if his father failed to join him before the forthcoming battle.

That night he retired to bed as usual after he had eaten. His cousin Duncan and the rest of the nobles would continue drinking and telling bawdy stories for several hours yet and, as the tent's internal walls did nothing to attenuate sound, he wouldn't be able to sleep until Duncan stumbled in drunk.

Usually his cousin would ignore him and collapse on his bed before commencing to snore loudly. On other occasions Duncan would insist on regaling Macbeth with stories that the boy had already heard through the tent's walls.

He lay awake cursing the revellers and wishing them all to Hell when he there was a brief lull and he thought that he'd heard a noise coming from the rear wall of the tent. He strained his ears but the brief lull in the racket from next door came to an end. He thought that the noise he'd heard was probably the scampering of a rodent. He hated rats and the thought of the damned things biting his face whilst he was asleep gave him the horrors.

He got up and picked up one of his shoes with which to hit the animal before moving stealthily towards the other side of Duncan's bed. He dropped his shoe and nearly yelled out loud when a young monk appeared in the space between the bed and the tent's outside wall.

'Quiet!' the novice warned, not that they were likely to be heard above the carousing nobles. 'We are here to rescue you and take you to your father.'

'He sent you?'

'Not exactly. I'll explain when we're away from this place. Get dressed as quickly as you can.'

There were numerous questions Macbeth wanted to ask, but he did what he was told and a minute later he and the monk crawled under the bottom of the tent wall. It was still twilight but it wouldn't be long before darkness descended. When he emerged there was another monk crouched outside the tent.

'Well done, Osric. Macbeth, my name is Wictred. I'm a housecarl serving Lord Aldred, the Thane of Duns. He has tasked us with taking you to your father.'

'Why would you do that?' Macbeth started to ask but Wictred cut him off.

'Talk later; we need to get out of here fast. Put this on and put the hood up to hide your hair.'

He handed him Colby's habit. He and the two Norse youths had already gone back to the horses. A group of monks all together would have looked suspicious; besides, if it all went wrong at least someone could go back and tell Aldred.

Wictred and Macbeth walked back towards the ford across the river that led to the monastery whilst Osric followed at a distance. They were nearly at the perimeter of the camp and Wictred breathed a sigh of relief. It proved to be a trifle premature.

'You there, monk,' a voice called in heavily accented English. 'I've got a boil on my arse. Can you lance it and put something soothing on it?'

Wictred stopped; to have continued walking, ignoring the request for help, would have immediately aroused suspicions. He stood there wondering what the devil he was going to do.

☨☨☨

Findlay, Mormaer of Moray, lay in his tent deliberating over the options facing him. Taking his only son hostage had been a stroke of genius on Malcolm's part. He pretended to be indifferent to his son's fate, but the truth was that he loved Macbeth and would do almost anything to save his life.

He was also conscious that he trod a tightrope as mormaer. He had succeeded his brother, Máel Brigti, to become mormaer but Máel had two sons, Gillecomgan and Máel Coluim who had been too young at the time. Now they were young men who were plotting to depose Findlay so that Gillecomgan could become mormaer. If he defied the king, Malcolm could well decide to help his nephews achieve their desire.

However, he didn't see why his highlanders should be asked to lay down their lives to help Malcolm expand his kingdom to the south. When he had called the muster there had been considerable discontent. It was understandable due to the threat from the Norse who had captured Caithness and Sutherland and who were now in a position to invade Moray.

Some of the pressure from the Norse had been reduced when Sigurd the Stout, Jarl of Orkney, Shetland, the Hebrides and Caithness, had been killed four years previously fighting against Brian Boru at the Battle of Clontarf near Dublin. His sons divided his lands between themselves with Einar taking Caithness and Sutherland. He was a bully and taxed his people heavily so he quickly became unpopular. Findlay doubted that they would follow him in any attempt to invade Moray, but he couldn't be certain.

Had he but known it, he needn't have had worried about a Norse invasion. Einar had other things to worry about. He was in conflict with Thorfinn, the youngest of Sigurd's sons who had just reached fourteen and who was now demanding a share in his father's realm.

Findlay had only brought eight hundred men south with him, the remaining part of his army staying in Moray to defend it if needs be. He was accompanied by his two nephews just in case they were tempted to raise a rebellion in Moray in his absence. However, he was well aware that taking them with him was not without its own problems. Gillecomgan and Malcolm mac Máel Brigti were busy sewing dissention amongst his men and some had already deserted to return home. Findlay worried that the trickle could become a flood the further south he went.

If only Malcolm wasn't holding Macbeth a hostage he would have had no compunction in defying him and returning to Moray.

ϯϯϯ

Wictred stood rooted to the spot. He had no surgical tools, no salves and no medical knowledge, other than how to wash and sew up a wound. However, he didn't even have a needle or catgut to do that.

'Well, what are you waiting for?' the Scot asked belligerently, getting to his feet.

The Northumbrian knew that it was pointless trying to brazen it out. If he did that it was likely that all three of them would be caught. He walked towards the man with the boil, the seax he was wearing under his habit bumping reassuringly against his leg.

'Yes, I can lance it for you,' he said cheerfully.

At the same time he gestured for the two boys to carry on towards the monastery. Osric hesitated, reluctant to leave Wictred, but when the man glared at him the novice nodded, acknowledging that Macbeth's safety was of paramount importance.

'Now where's this boil?' he asked when he reached the five Scots around the campfire.

The man obligingly pulled down his trews and bent over to expose his none too clean posterior with a large angry looking abscess on one cheek.

'Yes, this should stop you feeling any more pain,' Wictred said lifting his habit and drawing his seax.

He brought it down across the back of the Scot's neck, half severing his head from his body, then picked up the skirts of his habit and ran as if the devil was after him.

By this time the two boys had reached the ford over the river. In response to Wictred's warning cry, they pulled off their encumbering habits and splashed into the water. When Wictred reached the ford he turned, seax in hand, to delay his pursuers so that Osric and Macbeth could escape.

His sacrifice proved to be in vain. A spear lanced out of the darkness and struck him in the sternum. It chipped the bone and glanced off it to enter his right lung. Wictred doubled over in shock and fell to his knees. A few seconds later one of his pursuers brought an axe down onto his skull, shattering it and cutting deeply into his brain. He died instantly.

Half a dozen Scots dashed into the ford whilst Macbeth and Osric were still wading knee deep in water towards the far shore. The warriors yelled in triumph, thinking that they would soon catch the two fugitives. Osric glanced behind him and saw with dismay that the nearest pursuers were gaining on them. Whilst the two boys were knee deep and struggling against the current, the taller men were slowed rather less by the water.

Macbeth was the fitter of the two and, despite being a year younger than Osric, he was making slightly better progress. Osric's leg muscles felt as though they were on fire. Suddenly Macbeth took off his habit, the lower part of which was water logged and slowing him down. He threw it into the river and it was carried away. However, unlike Macbeth who was wearing his normal clothes, Osric only wore a pair of braies and a coarse cotton undershirt beneath his habit. Monks felt that the chafing of the rough material on bare skin was somehow good for the soul. He was therefore reluctant to divest himself of his habit. He lifted it up instead and, now looking like a maiden with an ardent swain in hot pursuit of her, he began to make better progress.

Nevertheless the Scots were now close behind him and, just when Osric thought that he was bound to be overtaken by the furious Scots, he heard the sound of horses and three riders appeared on the far bank leading two other horses.

'Come on, shift yourselves,' Colby yelled in his treble voice.

Osric and Macbeth redoubled their efforts, their aching legs being given new vigour by the appearance of the three scouts. They reached the far bank and used the last of their energy to haul themselves into the saddle of the spare mounts. A moment later they were galloping away across the meadow towards the trees where they had left the packhorse.

As the effects of the adrenalin, which had been pumping through their system during their flight, faded away, the two boys were left feeling exhausted and had trouble riding at a gallop without falling off. Once safely away from the river they slowed to a walk and the others were forced to do likewise. Then they heard splashing sounds behind them as a dozen or more Scots mounted on shaggy ponies crossed the river in pursuit.

They kicked their horses into a faster gait. A horse can only sustain a gallop for a relatively short period of time but their horses were larger and more powerful than the ponies and even at a moderate canter they started to draw away from their pursuers. Shortly afterwards they entered the trees and made their way back to the campsite.

Dusk had descended by the time they got there and Kjetil, who had taken charge after the death of Wictred, hoped that it would be difficult, if not impossible, for the Scots to follow their tracks. Nevertheless they couldn't stay there. Hakon grasped the lead rein of the packhorse and they rode out of the clearing, heading north-west.

As they rode Macbeth started to ask questions but all Kjetil would say was that their mission was to find Findlay and negotiate his son's return. He wouldn't say what the terms were and when he persisted in demanding to know more Kjetil told him to shut up, pointing out that sound can travel a long way at night. Macbeth was glad to be out of the clutches of King Malcolm but he wasn't sure that he could trust his rescuers. They seemed to have an ulterior motive.

Chapter Thirteen – Aldred's Stand

Late July 1018

Despite their misgivings, the others had eventually accepted Aldred's plan. First he had to lure the Britons onto his chosen battleground. This would be a test of his fyrd's brief training and was perhaps the most risky aspect of the plan. Aldred drew his fyrd up across the road that Owain's army were following and waited for the vanguard to appear.

It was nearly an hour before two of his scouts came cantering back to tell him that the Britons were close behind them.

'There's no vanguard as such, lord,' the senior scout said. 'They are just a rabble though there are a few outriders to warn of an ambush.'

Aldred nodded his thanks and shortly afterwards he could see a cloud of dust approaching; then the first of the Britons, preceded by a few men riding shaggy mountain ponies, appeared.

As soon as the enemy saw Aldred's shield wall blocking their path, they began to chatter excitedly amongst themselves. Suddenly a hundred or so young hotheads ran towards the fyrd. A volley of arrows, shot at high trajectory from behind the ranks of the fyrd, darkened the sky and rained down on the leading Britons, killing and wounding a score or more. It did nothing to deter them, however, and it wasn't until two more volleys had done more serious damage to their numbers that the young Britons came to their senses and decided to withdraw.

Seeing many of their young men and several boys killed by the enemy archers had inflamed the main body and, without any orders, several hundred Britons now charged towards the pathetically small shield wall. Aldred knew that he had to time his next move to perfection. He raised his right arm and then brought it down suddenly. A horn sounded three times and then the signal was repeated. At the same time Uuen waved a blue banner. The shield wall broke apart and the fyrd fled, leaving the archers facing the enemy on their own.

The archers sent one last volley into the oncoming horde and then they ran for their lives. Unencumbered by armour or shields they began to outstrip the spearmen of the fyrd and turned into a narrow valley. The fyrd followed. Now they were only sixty yards ahead of the closest Britons.

Aldred's men and the Britons both laboured uphill towards a narrow saddle between two hills. It was an ideal defensive position with a low ridge of rock at the top which ran halfway across the saddle. Where this ended Aldred's men had dug pits and placed sharpened stakes at an angle the previous day. This made an assault from below difficult. A few of the slower men were caught by the leading Britons, who wasted time hacking their hated enemies into a bloody pulp. It was unfortunate, but it gave the rest of the Northumbrians time to take up their position behind the defences.

The fyrd stood there, sucking in great lungfuls of air and taking the opportunity to drink from their water bottles, whilst the Britons paused uncertainly a few hundred yards below them. They feared that they had been drawn into a trap, and so they had, but not in the way they thought. Owain's army feared that hundreds of Northumbrians would now appear to cut them off, but that didn't happen. They slowly regained their courage and started to shout insults at the shield wall and to bare their backsides at them.

Meanwhile King Owain studied the terrain. On the right of Aldred's defensive line the rock strewn hillside rose almost vertically in a cliff, making a flank attack impossible. A narrow side valley cut through the steep hillside some two hundred yards in front of his position but that didn't appear to lead anywhere and, in any case, it could be a trap. He decided to ignore it. The slope on the other side of the saddle was less steep but it was quite thickly wooded. Owain was faced with a choice. He could either attack the laughably small shield wall in front of him or he could decline to fight and go back to the road. After all, his priority was to join up with Malcolm's army.

However, if he did that his men's morale would suffer even further and there was always the danger that, now their blood was up, his men would ignore his orders and attack anyway. He had nearly a thousand men against one hundred and thirty, so the outcome seemed certain. Furthermore, he wanted revenge for the damage that Aldred had inflicted on his army and his reputation. In the end it was an easy decision and he ordered a general attack.

Aldred sat on his horse at the top of a nearby hill with Uuen, who had a number of other coloured flags at his feet and a hunting horn slung over his shoulder. He watched the men of Strathclyde advance up the narrow valley, just as he'd hoped. Then Owain sent his archers forward to soften up the men facing him. When the gap between the archers, who were running forwards eager to begin slaughtering the Northumbrians, and the main body of Britons grew to around a hundred yards Aldred nodded at Uuen who blew his horn and raised a red flag.

Forty horsemen galloped out of the side valley and charged into the left flank of the startled archers. The mounted warriors cast their spears into them as the archers turned towards the threat and changed their target, but they were too slow. Before the first arrow flew, the horsemen were amongst them, chopping down with sword, axe and mace. None of the archers wore any form of armour, other than a few who had quilted tunics called gambesons, and their only other weapons, apart from their bows, were daggers and knives.

The horsemen had adopted a wedge formation and they drove deep into the bowmen before another blast on Uuen's horn warned them that Owain's spearmen were nearly upon them. They lay about them and used the bulky bodies of their horses to force their way clear of the archers before riding back up the side valley.

They left behind almost half of the two hundred archers dead or too wounded to be able to draw their bows. Perhaps more importantly, the whole of Owain's army were further demoralised by the sudden attack.

Eventually Owain persuaded his remaining archers to advance again, this time with a screen of three hundred spearmen on their left flank. Uuen raised a yellow flag and the advancing bowmen came under fire from Aldred's own archers hidden in the trees on the attackers' right flank. They sent arrow after arrow back at their attackers but Aldred's men were half hidden by the foliage and protected by the tree trunks, so few found a mark.

Several hundred men armed with spears, swords and axes left Owain's main body and ran towards the trees, eager to kill the archers but they just retreated deeper into the wood, leaving behind several of their number high up in the trees who began to pick off individual Britons as they appeared below them. The retreating archers kept stopping to bring down one or two of their pursuers as they retreated deeper into the wood, adding to the enemy's losses.

Eventually the Britons got weary of being picked off one by one and withdrew. The archers high in the trees inflicted more casualties as they desperately fled out of the wood.

Meanwhile Owain had ordered the rest of his army forward to assault Aldred's shield wall. Although they were outnumbered by at least three to one, the fyrd were behind their defences. The covered pits with their sharpened stakes at the bottom, claimed over fifty victims before the Britons learned to avoid them; however, the pits still served a purpose as the attackers were forced to bunch together through the gaps. In spite of the ferocious assault by the Britons the shield wall initially held firm.

However, the line was only two ranks deep and as men in the front rank fell those in the second line stepped forward until their losses meant that gaps in the line began to appear and the Britons began to break through.

Ceolfrith, who was in command of the fyrd, ordered his men to leave gaps directly in front of the pits so that they could reinforce those facing the main points of attack. He sent half a dozen experienced warriors to kill the Britons who managed to get through the line, but nevertheless things were getting desperate.

Another blast on Uuen's horn was scarcely audible above the din of battle. This time he raised a green flag and Aldred's mounted warriors galloped out of the side valley once more. This time they split into two groups. One headed across the valley towards the Britons retreating from the woods to prevent them from reinforcing Owain's main body; the other horsemen charged at the group of horsemen surrounding the King of Strathclyde some two hundred yards behind the main conflict.

The score of mounted warriors bearing down on those fleeing from the woods would have been enough to frighten men who were prepared to receive their charge. As it was the Britons were anything but prepared and didn't even try and defend themselves; they broke and ran. The mounted warriors chased them down the hill far enough to ensure that they would play no further part in the battle and then turned their horses to head back uphill.

Aldred was impressed by their discipline. He was well aware that most horsemen chasing a routed foe would be so fired up that they would keep up the pursuit, hacking down the routed enemy for miles.

Kenric, who was leading the second group of warriors, gave the signal to move into extended line as they neared the mounted group around Owain. The various chieftains and the bodyguards tried to form a line to defend their king but Kenric's horsemen knocked them aside like a gust of wind carrying away chaff. Some fell to the Northumbrian's spears, others were simply barged out of the way by the heavier horses. Several ended up on the ground as their mounts were killed under them. However, there were fifty of them against the twenty Northumbrians.

Kenric fought his way past the first line of the enemy and found himself facing two of Owain's bodyguards. He lifted one out of his saddle on the point of his spear whilst he used his shield to ward off the other man's axe. As he hauled on the reins to bring his horse around to face the second bodyguard Owain raised his sword and brought it down on Kenric's shoulder just as he let go of his spear in order to draw his sword.

He felt nothing for a moment. The chain mail had stopped the sword from cutting into his body, though a few metal links had broken, but the blow had been hard enough to break his collarbone. Then the pain hit him and he had to bite his tongue to stop himself from screaming in agony.

He was completely vulnerable and it would have been the work of a second for either the king or the bodyguard to have killed him at that moment, but Ceolfrith had seen Kenric's predicament and drove his spear through the back of the bodyguard.

Owain dug his heels into his horse and was making good his escape when another of the Northumbrians rode into him, sending his horse to its knees. Owain was thrown out of his saddle and landed hard. He lay there badly winded and unable to move.

Ceolfrith saw him on the ground but didn't know who he was; to him he was just another Scottish chieftain. He thrust down with his spear, breaking Owain's spine. The deflected spear point tore into his right kidney. Ceolfrith pulled his spear free and looked around for another opponent.

Owain wasn't dead but he was crippled and bleeding badly internally. He lay there in agony until his suffering was abruptly ended by the unshod hoof of a horse ridden by one of his own chieftains as he fought a losing battle against two mounted housecarls. The hoof crushed his skull and turned his brain to mush. So died the last King of Strathclyde.

☨☨☨

Aldred was beginning to despair, despite his clever tactics and his men's courage, the Britons' numbers were beginning to tell. He had lost over half his men and, although the opposing strength had been cut to no more than four hundred effective combatants, the Northumbrians were being overwhelmed.

Then a wail of despair reached him as news of Owain's death spread throughout the Britons. They lost heart and, by the time that Aldred had managed to reach the injured Kenric, the enemy were in full flight. Kenric had sent those of his horsemen who had survived to make sure that the Britons kept running, but it wasn't really necessary. Malcolm wouldn't be reinforced by the army from Strathclyde.

Aldred knew that he should be celebrating a great victory, but the loss of nearly fifty dead and over thirty seriously wounded made him question whether it had all been worth it. He had lost six of his mounted housecarls and, even worse, Ceolfrith had been killed in the last moment of the battle. Kenric would recover from his broken shoulder, God willing, but the death of Ulfric's son was a blow.

He shrugged off his weariness; there were the dead to bury and the wounded to treat and then he would have to march to join his wretched uncle. That could wait. His men were exhausted and they deserved a day to recover. He would send a messenger to Eadwulf to let him know what had happened, then he would set off for Yeavering when he was ready. However successful he'd just been, he was well aware that this had been a minor affair compared to battle that was to come.

ተተተ

Kjetil held up his hand and the others halted beside him. Below them in the valley of Gala Water, a northern tributary that eventually ran into the River Tweed near Melrose, hundreds of men were camped on both banks. Judging by the evidence, such as old campfires, tents and the men he could see he estimated that there was something under a thousand warriors in Findlay's host. It wasn't as many as Aldred had expected, but they would still increase the size of Malcolm's current army by a third if they joined him. It was enough for the Scots to seriously outnumber the Bernicians, even without the Strathclyde Britons.

Of course Kjetil didn't know about Owain's death and the elimination of the threat from Strathclyde at that stage. He tried to stop worrying about his lord and how he might be faring and focused on the matter in hand. His job was to stop Findlay joining up with Malcolm; that was all that mattered. He swallowed and tried to quell his nervousness. An awful lot was riding on his young shoulders.

Although he and Hakon were Norse by birth, they had developed a fierce loyalty to Aldred and they were determined to repay the trust he had placed in them by serving him as best they could. He chewed his lip, wondering how best to approach the mormaer. Macbeth edged his horse forward until he was next to Kjetil.

'Perhaps I could make a suggestion?'

Kjetil looked at him with suspicion. Over the past couple of days he had got to know Macbeth and he liked him; however, he didn't trust him. If he was in the boy's shoes he would have been looking for any chance to escape.

Macbeth was well aware that his companions wanted something from his father and that he was no more than a bargaining counter. Of course, he would prefer to return to Findlay's side without any terms and conditions, but Hakon still had a firm grip on the leading rein attached to the bridle of his mare. He had little option but wait until he knew more. It was frustrating, especially as his escort, having found the Moray campsite, seemed at something of a loss about how to proceed.

'My father is religious,' Macbeth continued, 'send Osric down to negotiate with him.'

Osric had lost his habit during their flight from Melrose but Colby was near enough the same size and he still had his; it made a warm robe in which to sleep. The former novice had been glad enough to escape from the rigours and discipline of monastic life and he never wanted to wear a habit again, but Osric could see the sense in acting as their emissary. Monks were sometimes used as negotiators and technically he was still a member of the

Benedictine order. None of the others could pass muster as a monk if they were questioned.

Whilst they set up camp in a wood on the far side of the hills above the Gala Water Osric rode down towards the sprawling campsite. Macbeth had pointed out his father's tent in the middle of the camp, though it would have been difficult to miss it. Quite apart from its size, there was a banner flying outside the tent displaying three silver stars on a blue cloth, the device of the mormaers of Moray.

Before he'd left Macbeth had given him the ring he wore on his left hand to prove that they were accompanied by Findlay's son. When he was challenged at the perimeter of the camp he held up the ring and loudly proclaimed in Pictish that he had a message from Macbeth the Red for his father.

Pictish was a Brittonic language spoken in much of Scotland and was very similar to the language of the Strathclyde Britons. As some of the monks at Melrose were Picts, Britons or Irish, Osric had learned to speak enough of the Brittonic tongue to get by.

At the sight of the gold ring encrusted with three diamonds in imitation of the badge of Moray the leader of the sentries licked his lips and demanded that the boy hand him the ring so that he could examine it more closely. This man's dialect was different to that which Osric was used to, but he understood what he was saying. He might be young but he wasn't naïve. He knew that there was every chance that the man would take the ring for himself and either kill Osric or send him packing.

'No, Lord Findlay will have your head, and those of your friends, once he finds out that you have stolen his son's ring and denied him the chance to free Macbeth.'

Osric's words, stated in a high voice that carried some distance, made the others in the group nervous. However, their leader wasn't so easily intimidated. He drew his sword and pointed it at the novice.

'Let me see that ring now or I'll cut you hand off at the wrist and take it anyway.'

Instinctively Osric pulled his hand back and held it close to his chest.

'Or, I'll kill you and take it from your dead fingers,' the man threatened.

'What's going on?' a voice asked.

The newcomer appeared to be a noble of some sort. Unlike the sentries, who were barefoot and dressed in a saffron coloured length of cloth belted around the waist and draped over one shoulder, this man wore a red tunic of fine wool that reached his knees. Over that he wore a byrnie and had calfskin boots on his feet.

'Lord, this spy is trying to bluff his way into camp by asking for you. No doubt he is an assassin. Shall I take him away and question him?'

The noble looked at Osric, who had now dismounted, and demanded to know if this was true.

'No, lord. I have a message for Mormaer Findlay from his son, Macbeth.'

'You have?' the man asked, surprised. 'Have you come from King Malcolm?'

'Not exactly. Perhaps it would be better if I explained everything to the mormaer in private.'

'Come with me.'

The man in the red tunic started to walk towards the tent with the blue flag outside it; Osric went to follow him but he was still holding his horse's bridle. He could hardly take it into the tent with him, but he didn't trust the men of Moray not to steal it if he let go of it.

Seconds later a man strode up to him and said that Findlay had asked him to take care of his mount. Osric was still uncertain but he handed the reins over to him.

'Now what's all this about a message from my son?' the man in the red tunic asked as soon as Osric had enetred the tent.

'You're Findlay MacRuaidrí?' Osric asked and then felt foolish.

There was a distinct resemblance between father and son if you imagined the face beneath the beard. Futhermore, both it and his hair were red; not perhaps as striking a colour as his son's, but distinctly a brighter shade than most redheads.

'Apologies, lord. I'm Osric, a novice monk from Melrose where King Malcolm is camped,' he explained.

He handed the ring over to Findlay.

'You'll recognise your son's ring, of course.'

'I should do. It was a present from me on his twelfth birthday. Where is he?'

'On the instructions of Lord Aldred, eldest son of the late Earl Uhtred of Northumbria, my companions and I rescued Macbeth from the Scots king's camp and made our way here with him.'

'Why?'

The question surprised Osric and he hesitated, not sure what to say at this juncture. He was about to explain how they rescued Macbeth, not why. He took a deep breath and thought quickly.

'Because Aldred hoped that, with your son no longer a hostage, you would not feel it necessary to assist Malcolm in his bid to conquer Lothian.'

'I see. If that's all there was to it you would have brought my son with you when you entered my camp, wouldn't you? You could even have let him ride in alone having seen him safely here, unless you expected some form of reward. Is that it? Or are you here to negotiate a ransom for him?'

'Not a ransom no. But we risked a great deal to restore your son to you. Our leader was killed, sacrificing himself to ensure that Macbeth could make good his escape.'

'Yes, very noble of you I'm sure. But what is it you want if it isn't money?'

'Your sworn oath to return to Moray immediately without aiding Malcolm's campaign.'

'Ah! I see. Of course. And if I don't agree?'

'Then my companions will take Macbeth back with them for Lord Aldred to make a decision as to his future.'

Just at that moment two men, also dressed as nobles entered the tent. They looked so alike they had to be brothers.

'I don't recall inviting you to join me,' Findlay said icily.

'What's going on, uncle? Who's the monk? He's young to be an emissary,' Gillecomgan said, ignoring his uncle's rebuke.

'We hear that he has news of Macbeth; is that true?' His brother asked.

'Please excuse the rudeness of my nephews, Brother Osric, but they are naturally concerned about the welfare of their cousin. If you would excuse us, I would rather discuss matters with Osric in private.'

He waited patiently. The two brothers looked at each other. They were desperate to know what had happened to Macbeth but Findlay obviously wasn't going to say anything further whilst they were present, and so they left the tent, making their displeasure evident.

'I rather think that my nephews had hoped that my son was dead, then they could squabble over which of them was to succeed me,' Findlay muttered, his distaste for the pair obvious.

Osric was feeling rather out of his depth. A couple of days ago he'd been a novice in the Melrose Monastery, his days devoted to learning, prayer and the more menial tasks involved in running such an establishment. Now he had been given the responsibility to negotiate with Findlay and offer to exchange his son in return for the mormaer's sworn promise to return to Moray. It had seemed straightforward but he now realised that the situation was far from simple. However, he was a bright boy and he was beginning to appreciate the difficulties faced by the man he was talking to.

Findlay had started to pace up and down, lost in thought. He would dearly love to be reunited with his son but the fact that he was no longer in danger, at least in the short term, was the most important thing. His escape from the king's custody meant that in effect he was now an outlaw. Whether or not Findlay joined Malcolm he knew enough of the man's character to realise that he would assume that Findlay was responsible for Macbeth's rescue and he would want revenge.

With the king's hand against him and his two nephews waiting for him to make a mistake the future didn't look too promising. In a lot of ways it would have been better if Osric and his companions had left well alone.

Of course, there was always the possibility that Malcolm would lose the coming battle or that he might even be killed. Even if he won, his army might be so weakened that he would be unable to strike north into Moray, at least for some time to come. He stopped pacing, his mind made up.

'I will ride with you and see my son so that I may say goodbye to him,' he told a relieved Osric.

The request to make sure that his son was alive and well came as no surprise, but saying farewell to him was not what Osric had expected. He naturally thought that Macbeth would be returned to his father's care.

'I want you to take Macbeth back with you,' Findlay explained, 'and send him to a place of safety in England. I will contact this Lord Aldred once it is safe for him to return home, but that may not be until he has reached manhood.'

'But why?' Osric asked, but Findlay wouldn't explain his reasons.

A little later Findlay and two of his warriors accompanied Osric out of camp. Just in case it was a trick Osric led the group to where the others waited via a circuitous route, but they weren't followed. When he realised what the former novice was doing Findlay smiled. The boy was wise beyond his years.

The three scouts got to their feet and quickly mounted ready to fight the three strange warriors accompanying Osric if needs be, but Macbeth gave a cry of joy and ran towards his father.

It was late in the day when Findlay and his men left in one direction and Macbeth and his escort in another. It had taken the mormaer some time to convince his son that what he'd decided was both sensible and necessary.

As he rode back to his camp the thought crossed Findlay's mind that his men were going to be very unhappy if they returned home without reward. Well, now that he'd undoubtedly made an enemy of King Malcolm, there was no reason not to plunder and pillage their way back through Lowland Scotland.

Chapter Fourteen – Prelude to Battle

Early August 1018

Aldred led the remains of his small force down the valley of the River Glen towards Yeavering with a heavy heart. He had arrived at Melrose to find that he had narrowly missed an encounter with the Scots army by less than twenty four hours. The abbot told him that Malcolm had learned of Owain's death and had headed east along the Tweed Valley to seek out and destroy the Bernician army.

The badly wounded remained at the monastery at Melrose whilst he pressed on with his remaining twenty eight mounted warriors and seventy five members of the fyrd. When he arrived at Yeavering he found two surprises waiting for him. He had expected to see Colby and the two Norse scouts but Osric and Macbeth came as something of a surprise.

Kjetil quickly told him what had happed and explained why Macbeth was still with them. He mourned Wictred's death when he heard of it but he was proud of the way that the youth had died. Wictred had been the only one to escape the massacre of Uhtred, other than Uuen, and he felt the loss of another link with his father quite keenly.

When Kjetil had finished his story he was relieved to find out that he'd succeeded in his ploy to deprive Malcolm of reinforcements. However, he needed to make sure Macbeth was safe. He couldn't stay with Aldred and his men. If Malcolm won and got his hands on him there was no doubt that he would be killed in revenge for his father's desertion.

He didn't know whether to be delighted or angry at the other surprise: Synne suddenly appeared. Dressed in a byrnie and a helmet covering her short blond hair he hadn't recognised her at first, but her pretty face was unmistakeable.

'What in the name of all that's Holy are you doing here' he asked her in amazement. 'And why are you dressed like that?'

'I came because I couldn't bear to be apart from you,' Synne replied. 'And this seemed the best way to travel.'

From being an undernourished urchin, good food had transformed her into a pretty young girl over the past few months and her figure had taken on a decidedly female form that even the shapeless byrnie couldn't hide. With a start Aldred realised that he was in love with her. He'd been a fool not to realise it before. He hated being apart from her and when she was present he couldn't take his eyes off her. He had tried to convince himself that he was being foolish; that it was a short lived infatuation with an attractive young girl, but as soon as he saw her again he realised how much he'd missed her and how much he cared for her. What's more she showed every indication that the feeling was mutual.

At first he thought that she'd have difficulty in making the transition from guttersnipe to servant girl, but she was evidently made of sterner stuff. Within a few weeks she had put her past life behind her and as time went on her poise and self-confidence developed. Others grew to respect her and she became popular, especially amongst his housecarls – and not just because she was pretty. They liked her character and personality.

The seven years between their ages didn't seem to matter anymore, nor did their very different backgrounds. He decided in that instant that he would marry her as soon as possible. He considered sending her back to Duns but that was in Lothian and, if Malcolm won, she would be lost to him and goodness knows what her fate would be.

Then he had a flash of inspiration. He'd send Macbeth and Synne to Aycliffe in Teesdale. As his wife, she could take his property over; not only Aycliffe but also the other vills given to him by Bishop Aldhun. However, before he could find a priest to marry them, a summons arrived for Aldred to attend his uncle immediately.

'Why are you so late attending the muster,' Eadwulf barked at him as soon as Aldred entered the earl's tent.

Aldred looked around at the interior. Tent was too insignificant a word for the hall made out of oiled leather. The main space was large enough to house a table and benches to seat ten, a desk and four oak chairs. The floor was covered in wooden boards on top of which lay straw. Off to one side there was a separate chamber with a platform covered in bear and wolf pelts which obviously served as the earl's bed. Another side chamber housed his servants, all of which appeared to be female.

Eadwulf was sitting in one of the chairs and two others were occupied by Iuwine and Gosric, the earldormen of Berwick and Selkirk respectively. The fourth was vacant but Eadwulf made no attempt to invite Aldred to sit in it.

'Did you not get my message, uncle?

The last word was uttered in a manner that made clear Aldred's distaste for the relationship.

Eadwulf flushed with annoyance at his nephew's tone.

'You will call me lord.'

'Yes, lord. Of course, lord. My apologies, lord.'

'Don't be impudent. Well, I'm waiting for an answer.'

'If you received my message you will know that I have spent the past couple of weeks fighting against the army of Owain the Bald,' Aldred pointed out, trying to keep his anger in check. 'Not only did we defeat a force fifteen hundred strong and which contained hundreds of experienced Norse warriors, but Owain is dead. Malcolm won't be reinforced by anyone from the west; nor will Findlay and the men of Moray be joining him. That's what I have been doing whilst you sat here doing nothing.'

Eadwulf got to his feet, his face purple with rage. He went to strike Aldred, who took a pace backwards and put his hand on the hilt of his dagger. He was just as enraged as his uncle was, but he was managing to keep his anger in check – just.

Gosric and Iuwine got to their feet and stepped between the two men.

'We have enough enemies to fight without squabbling amongst ourselves,' Gosric said coldly.

'Besides Aldred would kill you if you laid a finger on him,' Iuwine added. 'You should be congratulating him on his almost unbelievable achievement instead of chastising him,' he went on. 'Would you rather he had been here on time if it meant facing an army of perhaps five thousand; double our number?

Eadwulf glared at the three men for a long minute before he regained control of himself.

'Go on, get out, all of you. Get out!' he shouted before slumping back down onto one of the chairs.

'That man will manage to snatch defeat from the jaws of victory,' Gosric commented as they left the tent.

†††

Early the next morning Aldred went to the cleared area that served the camp as an open air church. Ceadda accompanied him as his groomsman and Synne, lacking any female companion or male relative to give her away, had asked Beda to escort her.

Neither groom nor bride had anything appropriate to wear for the occasion so they dressed in the tunic and trousers, laced to the knee, that they normally wore under their chain mail. If the priest found marrying a man to a girl dressed like a boy unusual he was wise enough not to say so.

It was a fine, warm day and the unusual ceremony had attracted a large crowd of spectators. Everyone knew of Aldred's success against Owain and many had heard that he had also turned back the army of Moray. It was no surprise then that a great cheer went up when he appeared. Men started to chant his name and only stopped when he raised his arms in acknowledgement and signalled his appreciation.

Eadwulf was bedding one of his servants at the time but the repeated cry of 'Aldred' somewhat spoiled the moment. He slapped the girl hard as he found his lust diminishing and kicked her out of bed. He lay there on his front beating his fists against the bed in frustration and anger like a spoilt child.

Just as the ceremony was about to start there was a commotion on the east side of the camp. Aldred tried to ignore it but then an excited murmuring began in the crowd and the priest went and asked someone what was going on. He came back and had a quiet word with Aldred.

'The Bishop of Durham has just arrived with the contingent from Durham,' he told him.

Aldred regarded him with disbelief. The last time he had seen his grandfather he was in good health but he was old and frail. He couldn't believe that he'd travelled all the way to Yeavering from Durham, a distance of some one hundred and fifty miles. Even in a carriage it was a long way for someone as old as Aldhun.

The old man walked into the open-air church leaning heavily on his cozier and embraced his grandson.

'I was coming to bless the army before the battle but I gather that I have arrived just in time to marry you, he said before turning to the priest. 'That is if you don't mind, father.'

'Of course not, lord bishop. It's an honour to meet you.'

Someone brought a chair for Aldhun to sit on whilst he conducted the service. If he was surprised when he was presented to Aldred's betrothed he hid it well. He did, however, keep the homily mercifully short. Aldred suspected that he didn't know quite what to say, other than a few platitudes.

'Where is Earl Eadwulf, isn't he in camp?' he asked after blessing the union between Aldred and Synne.

'He's sulking in his tent,' Ceadda said with a disdainful sniff.

'Well, I had better go and pay my respects,' Aldhun said shuffling off in that direction, followed by his chaplain.

The two housecarls standing guard in front of the earl's tent crossed their spears as Aldhun approached.

'The Earl isn't to be disturbed,' one of them said curtly.

'Do you know who I am?' Aldhun asked him mildly.

'Some priest?'

'Yes, but I'm also the Bishop of Durham. Now, please announce me to Lord Eadwulf. I'm not good at standing at my age so don't take too long or you might risk me cursing your immortal soul.'

The man looked startled and hurriedly lifted the flap and disappeared inside the tent and announced the bishop.

'Who did you say is here?'

Eadwulf's incredulous voice came through the leather wall of the tent quite clearly.

'I thought that the old goat was dead.'

'I'm still very much alive, Eadwulf, and getting rather fed up standing out here,' the bishop called back.

Eadwulf's scowling face belied the welcome he gave Aldhun as he ushered him into the tent and invited him to take a seat. The old man gratefully lowered himself onto it with a sigh.

'I wasn't expecting you, bishop. What brings you here?' the earl asked without preamble.

'I came to bring spiritual support to our efforts to defeat the Scots, of course. Why else would I be here? I'm sure that your men will be encouraged by my presence, even if you're not.' Aldhun replied with a smile that didn't reach his eyes.

He had never liked Eadwulf as a boy and he would never forgive him for his part in Uhtred's death. Had the man confessed and sought absolution Aldhun would have been forced to grant it but, of course, he hadn't. Aldhun didn't suppose that he had ever confessed his sins to a priest. Furthermore, the man's lifestyle flew in the face of everything a devout churchman held dear.

'The word is that Malcolm has left Melrose and is advancing along the north bank of the Tweed. You are hardly likely to stop him sitting here. When will you be moving north?'

Eadwulf did his best to hide his surprise. No one had told him that the Scots were on the move.

'I suggest you leave military matters to me, bishop. It's not your area of expertise.'

'And is it yours?' Aldhun asked, knowing that Eadwulf had never fought a battle in his life.

'Bernicia may be your diocese, bishop, but I am its earl. I will make a decision about our strategy in consultation with my ealdormen. You've no need to concern yourself.'

'I do hope you will include my grandson in your war council. I hear that he has had notable successes against Strathclyde; defeating an army ten times the size of his and killing its king. Having somehow persuaded Findlay of Moray to withdraw, he has effectively halved the size of the enemy's forces. He seems a quite remarkable young man, wouldn't you agree?'

'He is merely a thane. He has no seat amongst his betters,' Eadwulf replied, looking as if he had a wasp in his mouth.

'I doubt that Cnut will forgive you if you lose Lothian because you were too stiff-necked to take advantage of the greatest asset you have. Remember that pride comes before a fall, Eadwulf.'

The bishop rose to his feet with a groan and left Eadwulf to ponder what he'd said.

ϮϮϮ

'Why isn't Aldred here?'

The question was asked by Gosric of Selkirkshire but it was obvious that it was also at the forefront of everyone's mind. Apart from the nine ealdormen the only other person present at the meeting was the captain of Eadwulf's housecarls.

'He's not an ealdorman,' Eadwulf said dismissively.

'No, but he commands a conroi of mounted warriors trained by the Normans, something that the Scots don't have. In addition he has a dozen mounted scouts,' Leofwine of Durham pointed out.

'And he has won a remarkable victory over the Strathclyde Britons,' Iuwine of Berwickshire added to general mutters of agreement from the others.

'I'm your earl and I say he has no place here,' Eadwulf said furiously.

He gazed around the tent, noting the sullen looks on some faces and the contempt on others. He realised that he risked losing the respect of his ealdormen and so, unwillingly, he sent for his nephew to join them.

When Aldred arrived he was accompanied by his grandfather; the elderly bishop leaning on his arm.

'Lord, I thought it might be appropriate for Bishop Aldhun to bless our deliberations,' he said with a disarming smile.

Eadwulf gritted his teeth but tried to smile.

'What a good idea,' he said, failing to hide the sarcasm in his voice.

After the blessing Aldred got up and asked if it would be helpful if he briefed everyone about what his scouts had found earlier that morning. Without waiting for the earl's permission he continued.

'Malcolm left Melrose three days ago and my scouts have just reported that his vanguard is now only seven miles from the vill of Roxburgh. At some point they must have crossed the Tweed. It would seem that they are heading for Berwick. In two days' time I would expect them to have reached my former vill of Carham, now in the possession of the Diocese of Durham.'

Eadwulf chewed his lip, deep in thought.

'What's the ground like south of the Tweed at Carham?'

Aldred wished that Kenric was there but he was at Melrose recovering from his broken collarbone. He had been to Carham - once - but he hadn't paid much attention to the surrounding area. Then he remembered that one of his mounted warriors, an Angle named Oxa, came from Carham.

'I'll send for one of my housecarls who was brought up there. He can describe the area better than I can.'

Eadwulf sat drumming his fingers on the table in front of him and the rest started to talk amongst themselves whilst they waited. When Oxa arrived it was plain that he lived up to his name, which meant Ox. He stood head and shoulders above most men and was built to match. His chain mail hauberk had been specially made for him.

'Oxa, can you describe the land around Carham. Where is the best place for a battle?' Aldred asked.

'Yes, lord. To the west there are low hills and the area between there and the river is quite narrow. Beyond the vill the land opens out into low lying strip fields and pasture for a mile or more before the trees come down almost to the Tweed just before the next vill – Wark.'

'Would you say that there is somewhere for you and the other horsemen to hide so that you could strike the Scots in the flank,' Leofwine asked.

Aldred disliked Leofwine because of the way that he had treated his eldest son, Beda, disinheriting him in favour of the son born to his second marriage, but he was grateful to him for the question.

'Yes, lord. There is a wood some four hundred yards from the river bank. The trees are not too close together so as to prevent horsemen moving through them but they would screen us from sight if we were a few yards back from the front edge.'

'You are thinking of using your horsemen to attack the Scottish left flank?' Eadwulf asked incredulously. 'What difference would two score of you make, against two and half thousand men on foot?'

'You would be surprised how effective they are, lord.' Oxa replied. 'We charged the Britons and the Norse time and time again, throwing spears into them before withdrawing. Unless you've faced a charge by heavily armoured warriors mounted on large stallions you don't know how intimidating and demoralising they can be.'

'I don't want to frighten them; I want to kill them and that's a job for our warriors on foot,' Eadwulf said dismissively.

'With respect, lord. I think you are wrong,' Iuwine said. 'You will recall the demonstration that Aldred laid on at Duns? Aldred's horsemen aren't going to defeat the Scots on their own; of course not. But their intervention will unnerve the Scots and the left flank will crowd to the right, disrupting their attack and thus making the job of our shield wall easier.'

'Especially if we use the massed archers to further unsettle them but concentrating them on our left flank – their right. Thus they will be shooting at the side unprotected by their shields,' Aldred suggested.

'Enough! You are all talking nonsense!' Eadwulf bellowed. 'The archers must be used to blunt their attack head on. Your housecarls are needed to reinforce the front rank and will fight on foot, Aldred.'

'The archers will achieve nothing that way, except pepper the Scots shields with arrows. My men are trained to fight on horseback and they are good at it. You are wasting a unique asset if you ask them to fight on foot,' Aldred replied, doing his best to remain calm.

'Don't argue with me or you'll find yourself in chains for treason,' Eadwulf warned him.

'This is how you intend to fight is it, lord?' Readwald of Jarrow asked. 'What Aldred and Oxa have said convinces me that their plan gives us the greatest chance of victory. I've seen how the Scots fight. They may lack discipline but that doesn't mean that they can't overcome a shield wall. The very fact that they wear no armour means that their youths are light and nimble enough to jump over a shield wall and kill those in the ranks behind. Fighting in the traditional way isn't going to work.'

Other ealdormen shouted their agreement; only those who owed their appointment to Eadwulf supported him.

'Silence, silence I say!' Eadwald was on his feet banging his dagger on the table, his face a mask of fury.

Gradually the hubbub died away. Readwald got to his feet, as did several other ealdormen.

'If your plan is to stand in the middle of a meadow and hope that the Scots can be defeated by a defensive line of the fyrd, then I for one will play no part in it. You are leading us to disaster, Eadwulf. I suspected before I came here that you know nothing about warfare and today has confirmed that opinion only too well. You need to come to your senses and listen to Aldred who, out of all of us, has the most experience, despite his youth. If not, then I and my men will leave tomorrow. At least that way we will be alive to face the Scots when they cross the Tees.'

Readwald walked out of the tent in silence. Three more ealdormen followed him and then four more got up and left. Eadwulf just sat there impotently, wondering what had just happened.

'I suggest that you use tonight to think long and hard about your strategy for defeating the Scots, Eadwulf,' Aldhun said quietly. 'I'll do my best to persuade them not to leave. If I succeed then we'll meet again after mass tomorrow morning. If not..'

He shrugged and left, accompanied by Aldred and Oxa. The remaining ealdormen followed them out.

'I wouldn't want to be whoever Eadwulf choses to sleep with tonight,' Oxa muttered as they walked back to their camp.

Aldhun looked at him quizzically.

'He'll take his anger and frustration out on the poor girl,' Oxa explained.

ϮϮϮ

The next morning Synne, Osric and Macbeth set off for Aycliffe escorted by Kjetil, Colby, Beda and Hakon. Beda had been careful to keep out of the way of his father since the ealdorman's arrival at Yeavering but Aldred thought it sensible to send the boy away nevertheless. Leofwine had supported him against Eadwulf, but he wasn't aware that his son was training to be a warrior with Aldred's men instead of becoming a monk.

It said much about his regard for his eldest son that he had never asked anyone about Beda since he'd left his hall for Durham. The last thing Aldred wanted was to fall out with Leofwine, which would inevitably happen if he found out that his wishes had been flouted.

Aldhun led mass and then he, the ealdormen and Aldred headed off to the earl's tent. Eadwulf hadn't attended mass, but then he never did.

'Have you had time to think about your plans to defeat Malcolm and his Scots?' Aldhun asked.

Everyone had agreed at a brief meeting held after mass ended that it be would less confrontational if the bishop opened the council of war.

'I've decided that I need more time to consider what has been said,' Eadwulf temporised.

'I don't think we have that luxury, lord. We really need to be moving north now if we are to intercept Malcolm at Carham,' Iuwine pointed out. 'It's the best place to fight him this side of Berwick and he will probably reach there some time tomorrow.'

Eadwulf glared at him but he knew that he was right.

'Very well, we will do as Aldred suggests but I will hang him from the highest tree if his plan doesn't work.'

'If his plan doesn't work we'll all be dead,' Gosric said grimly.

Chapter Fifteen – The Comet

7th/8th August 1018

On the night of the seventh of August Eadwulf's army camped on a stream called the Willow Burn where it opened out to form a small lake. They were a mile and a half south east of Carham and the scouts reported that Malcolm's army had halted for the night on the Tweed some two miles south west of the vill.

Aldred found that he couldn't sleep. His mind was on the coming battle but he also thought of the one night he'd spent with his new wife. She was so young that Aldred had begun cautiously, stroking and kissing her gently but Synne had responded with a passion that surprised him. He wasn't a virgin but he had never encountered anyone who was so ardent. He smiled at the memory but then he heard a commotion outside his tent and he went to investigate.

Dozens of people were outside looking up at the night sky. The night was cloudless and the crescent moon shone down bathing the ground below with silver light. The sky was filled with countless twinkling stars but it wasn't either the moon or the stars that had awed everyone. It was a bright comet that streaked across the sky with a very long tail.

It might have been there for some time but the preceding nights had been cloudy. Its appearance on the eve of battle was a dreadful omen. Any comet was seen by the superstitious Northumbrians as a harbinger of doom and destruction. Aldred swore under his breath.

Then Bishop Aldhum appeared, limping with the aid of his crosier, through the growing throng of soldiers, servants and camp followers.

'It's a portent of disaster,' he maintained in a firm voice, 'but not for us; it's for the Scots who have dared to invade our land.'

Aldred could feel the relief wash over the crowd like a wave and he sighed in relief. He didn't believe for one moment that the comet was anything other than a heavenly phenomenon that couldn't possibly affect the outcome of the battle, but he was almost alone in that. Even the ealdormen had been troubled by it.

He wondered what his uncle thought. He wasn't a religious man in any shape or form, but he had a nasty feeling that he might use the comet's appearance to try and convince his nobles that it meant that Aldred's plan was doomed to failure, whatever the bishop said. He would have to wait and see what the morning brought.

He went back to his tent and lay down. Having been unable to get to sleep prior to the appearance of the comet, he now found that his mind was at peace and he quickly drifted off.

†††

Four miles away the Scots had also stood watching the comet in the night sky. If anything they were even more superstitious than the Northumbrians, especially the highlanders. Unlike the Bishop of Durham, their senior churchmen – the Bishops of St. Andrews and of Dunkeld – were as awed by the comet as the meanest servant.

Malcolm was furious. The defeat and death of Owain and the non-appearance of the men of Moray had already sapped the morale of his army. The comet had served to reinforce their growing mood of defeatism. He had to do something and so he sent for his horse.

He rode throughout the vast camp, calling out that God and his son Jesus, had sent a message promising them victory on the morrow. Not everyone believed him, but it gave his men heart and several started to cheer him. The growing mood of optimism was infectious and more and more started to cheer and yell his name – Malcolm Forranach – Malcolm the Destroyer.

Satisfied that he had done enough to counter the appearance of the comet as a herald of disaster for his army, King Malcolm rode back to his tent and went to bed. Unlike Aldred though, he didn't sleep soundly. Despite what he'd told his men, he believed that the comet might well foretell his defeat the next day. After all, things had hardly gone his way so far.

ṪṪṪ

'Lord, the earl has called a meeting in his tent,' Uuen said, shaking Aldred awake from a deep and dreamless sleep.

Aldred looked around him, confused at first and unsure where he was. It was still dark and he could scarcely make out Uuen until his servant lit a candle. Ten minutes later he joined the ealdormen and the bishop in Eadwulf's tent just as the first fingers of dawn appeared in the sky above the hills to the east. The day promised to be fine and sunny, which meant that it would be hot. He made a mental note to ensure that his men filled their water skins to the brim.

Aldred relaxed after various ealdormen had allocated him another forty mounted housecarls serving them and a few of the wealthier thanes. Ealdred hadn't liked it and had made his displeasure felt, but there wasn't much he could do about it. They were his nobles' men, not his.

It would have been nice to have been able to train them first, but at least they should be able to throw a spear from horseback and then turn back into the woods.

The earl finally agreed that two thirds of the archers should be placed on the left flank, but he still wanted the rest placed in front of the shield wall. These few would have to defend the four hundred yards between the woods and the river and so would be stretched rather thin. Aldred knew that it was a waste of good archers but there was nothing he could do about it.

At least the front rank of the shield wall would be found from armoured ealdormen, thanes and housecarls, but the three behind them would be members of the fyrd whose quality as fighting men varied considerably.

The nobles had expected Eadwulf and his own housecarls to take their place in the centre of the front rank but it seemed that the earl had other ideas.

'I need to be behind the shield wall,' he explained. 'From horseback I can see how the battle is progressing and I can send my housecarls to reinforce any point of weakness.'

'Alternatively so that he can flee if the battle is going badly,' Iuwine muttered to Gosric.

Ealdred's decision was not popular and one or two nobles almost accused him of cowardice, but he would not be moved.

'Good,' Eadwulf said, bringing the meeting to a close. 'Get ready to march. I plan to be in position in two hours' time.'

'Don't forget to tell your men to carry full waterskins,' Aldred called out as the nobles dispersed. 'It is going to be a hot day and thirsty men don't fight well.'

ƫƫƫ

Just before midday the vanguard of the Scots army reached Carham. Murdoch, the Mormaer of Fife, led the vanguard and halted in the village whilst his scouts rode forward to reconnoitre the next part of the route. Minutes later they came galloping back on their sturdy mountain ponies to report that the enemy were massed between the woods and the Tweed just a mile ahead of them. Leaving his men to hold the village, Murdoch rode back to consult with Malcolm.

Eadwulf's army had been standing under the hot summer sun for nearly two hours by the time the scouts appeared and then hastily retreated. Aldred's advice about water had been heeded by all except the most stupid but, even so, standing under the hot sun was sapping the men's strength. Most had removed their helmets and those fortunate enough to possess byrnies were beginning to suffer from heat exhaustion because of the weight of the chainmail.

The appearance of the first of the Scots therefore came as something of a relief.

Aldred's seventy odd horsemen weren't bothered by the heat as they waited under the shade provided by the trees. It was an hour or so later, when the sun was at the highest point in the sky, that Malcolm's army disgorged onto the flood plain between Carham and the sweltering Bernician army.

Chapter Sixteen – The Battle

8th August 1018

Wulfgar was scared stiff. From boyhood his father had regaled him with stories about the bravery of his ancestors. He wasn't sure that he believed a word of it, but that didn't matter; what mattered was this was the tradition he was expected to live up to. Even his name, Wulfgar, meant fighter. It wasn't as if his father was anyone important; he was a tenant who farmed fifty acres near Norham a few miles west of Berwick.

In addition to paying rent to his landlord, a man called Coelfrith, and tithes to the Church, his father was obliged to provide two men to serve in the fyrd whenever needed. The times when this was thought necessary seemed to have come around more and more often in recent times. However, this time the Earl of Bernicia had called upon every able bodied male over the age of fifteen to answer the call to arms, not just those who were bound to do so. As he'd just turned fifteen he answered the call with his father and elder brother. However, instead of marching to the muster point, Coelfrith had led them to join Lord Aldred's small contingent.

He had no idea of what to expect when they had engaged the Britons led by Owain the Bald but that battle had opened his eyes to the chaos, noise, brutality and horror of war. Wulfgar wasn't certain how he'd survived it, but he had, and without anyone discovering how frightened he was, or so he fondly imagined. Of course many had realised he had been terrified, but they had been just as scared themselves. After that he was convinced that he never wanted to be in another fight, yet here he was again.

Unfortunately both his father and his brother had been killed by Owain's Britons. As his mother had died two years ago, that left him without any family and, as he had no one he could really call a friend, he was acutely aware how alone he was in the world.

He stood gripping his spear in white knuckled hands as the heat of an August day sapped his strength, praying for rain. Not only would it cool him down but it might wash away the smell of the urine which had trickled down his legs, soaking his woollen leggings.

From where Wulfgar stood at the rear of the fyrd, behind three ranks of taller men, he could see very little. The nobles and housecarls formed the shield wall and would face the enemy first. They all wore helmets and either chain mail byrnies or else leather tunics to which metal plates had been sewn. The fyrd formed the next three rows. The most experienced men were in the second rank, ready to take the place of those in the shield wall who fell. Like the housecarls, they were armed with swords, battle-axes and large round shields but few possessed armour, except for the odd helmet. His job was to add his puny weight behind the other three rows to stop them from being forced backwards.

Wulfgar was lucky in that he wore a stout leather gambeson bought for him by his father, but few of the peasants around him could afford such a protective garment and wore their normal clothes – a homespun tunic and leggings tied around the lower leg with ribbons.

Apart from his spear, the boy was fortunate enough to own a seax and a stout lime wood shield. Few members of the fyrd possessed much in the way of weapons. Many had spears, but others were only armed with woodsmen's axes, scythes or pitchforks whose wooden points had been hardened by fire. It wasn't much with which to take on a wild Scotsman armed with sword or axe and a targe – a small round shield with a thin pointed blade up to a foot long in lieu of a boss in the centre.

Wulfgar took heart from the fact that the Bishop of Durham had said mass and had given him the body of Christ himself. Aldhun now sat on his horse beside Earl Eadwulf and his bodyguards just behind Wulfgar. The banner of Durham – a gold cross on a blue field – and that of the earl – a black wolf's head on a yellow field, flapped languidly in what little breeze there was.

The Scots had appeared from the village of Carham in dribs and drabs and started to hurl insults at the opposing army, bending over and exposing their naked backsides to the Bernicians now and then. Earl Eadwulf's men stood and regarded the capering Scots impassively. Wulfgar couldn't see what was happening and had to rely on the taller men keeping up a running commentary.

After a while he became impatient and wished that someone would attack. However, he was astute enough to realise that was what the Scots were trying to achieve. A strong shield wall was difficult to break and Malcolm was inciting the Bernicians to attack first. Even Earl Eadwulf knew that it would be a disastrous mistake.

Wulfgar's eyes drifted over to the trees where he had seen Aldred's horsemen disappear some time ago. He imagined that they would carry out surprise flanking attacks from there, just as they had done before, but he was too insignificant to have been told what the battle plan was. He was just told to stand in line and keep the shield wall firm.

Just after midday the Scots army organised itself into some sort of formation just as clouds appeared in the sky to obscure the sun. The change in the weather came as something of a relief to the Bernicians, many of whom had mild sunburn on their exposed skin by then. Malcolm sent in the near naked Highlanders from Perthshire first. They came forward in a mass but what they lacked in terms of formation they made up for in bravery. Many of them leaped clean over the first ranks of housecarls and landed amongst the fyrd. Few of the Anglian peasants and artisans had encountered the fierce half-naked warriors before and they started to panic. It was only the fact that they were hemmed in by their fellows in the rear ranks that prevented some of them from fleeing. In the end the Highlanders were repulsed after suffering heavy losses, but they had wreaked havoc before they withdrew. The attack had weakened the resolve of the fyrd and Wulfgar wondered if they could resist another such attack.

Malcolm sent in his main body next. They screamed their war cries and capered like madmen as they raced towards the shield wall. Then, whilst they were still fifty or sixty yards short of their target, two things happened. The archers on the left flank sent volley after volley into their right and Aldred's horsemen charged at the enemy's left flank.

Wulfgar couldn't see what was going on but he gathered from the comments of those in front of him that the combined effect of the hail of arrows and the repeated charges by the horsemen had disrupted both enemy flanks and only their centre had reached the shield wall. Not that this made much difference to Wulfgar. He found himself being shoved back due to the pressure on the three ranks in front of him. He put his shield against the back of the man in front of him and pushed with all his might and the line seemed to steady as others did the same.

He saw to his horror that the housecarls in the front rank and then the men behind them were cut down. The men in front of Wulfgar stepped forward to stop the Scots breaking through. Then the man immediately to Wulfgar's front was killed and he found himself facing a fierce looking Scot with a bushy red beard. He thrust his spear at him, surreally conscious at the same time that he had now fouled his trousers and the stink of faeces combined with that of urine. The coppery tang of blood also assailed his nostrils, making him want to vomit. He was lucky and the point of his spear hit the warrior in the mouth, continuing up into his brain and he dropped out of sight. Wulfgar then promptly spewed all over the man's corpse.

Wulfgar scarcely had time to recover his spear before he was attacked again. By now the Scots were working in pairs: one attacked head on whilst a second, often a young boy, tried to disable their opponent by hacking at his legs below his shield with a dagger. Not for the first time, he thanked the Lord God that his father had bought him boots reinforced with metal strips. He blocked a blow from an axe with his shield, which jarred his arm quite badly, whilst kicking out at the head of the boy trying to cripple him.

There was no room to use his spear so he dropped it and pulled out his seax. Still fending off the axeman with his shield he stabbed down at the boy with his seax. Perhaps his kick had stunned the lad because he didn't try to roll away and Wulfgar felt the blade go into the lad's neck. The axeman uttered a sound that was partly a cry of fury and partly a wail of anguish; making Wulfgar think that the boy was probably his son. The man raised his axe high preparatory to bringing it down onto Wulfgar's damaged shield once more – too high because Wulfgar was able to stab him in the armpit with his seax before he could strike.

The man was only wounded but he had to drop his axe. Wulfgar swung his seax at his opponent's neck and he was surprised how resistant it was. He jarred his hand and the seax stopped a few inches into the neck. As the man fell away he was forced to let go of the seax. Now he was weaponless except for his dagger. Thankfully there was a lull for a few seconds and he managed to find a sword that someone had dropped.

The ground on which Wulfgar stood was getting slippery with mud and blood, which made keeping his position difficult, but the pile of bodies in front of him and his companions had started to impede the Scots' attack. He managed to stab one more man but he knew that he was tiring and was about to step back and hope that there was someone behind him to take his place when the Scots decided that they had had enough and withdrew just as suddenly as they had attacked.

Wulfgar drew in great lungfuls of air and drank greedily from his water skin. He had never known his throat to be so parched. He recovered his own weapons and threw the blunt and rusty sword away. He was still trying to recover when someone tapped him on the shoulder and he stepped back to allow another to take his place. He looked along the line as he did so and was dismayed to see that over half of the first rank in the Bernician army lay dead in front of the pile of Britons. They might have won the first encounter but it had been at a heavy cost.

Eadwulf reorganised his army into three ranks instead of four. Now Wulfgar was placed in the second rank, immediately behind a great brute of a housecarl armed with a double handled battleaxe. He hoped the housecarl would survive because he was exhausted and doubted if he could summon up the energy to fight off another attack like the last one.

ϮϮϮ

In the woods Aldred had been pleased with the effect his horsemen had on the right flank of the enemy. They had made two charges and each time they had slain perhaps fifty of the enemy or more; but that wasn't important. The Scots had been terrified of the armoured horsemen and had moved away from them, crowding into the centre and causing chaos. No doubt their fear had been infectious too.

'Lord, there are enemy making their way through the trees towards us,' Oxa told him.

Malcolm was obviously using the lull in the battle to try and eliminate the threat to his left flank.

'Thank you, Oxa. Tell the men to dismount and tie their mounts to a tree. We'll give these Scots something to remember us by.'

The seventy warriors, all dressed in armour and carrying shields and swords or seaxes, advanced in line through the trees. Their spears were too long for the close work required in such a confined space. They soon spotted the enemy who'd been sent to kill them. There were around three hundred of them but they were moving as individuals, not in formation. It was easy for Aldred's men to kill the first few that reached them, but as the housecarls advanced they were opposed by more and more foes.

The Scots worked in pairs once again, one pulling down the shield whilst the other tried to stab at the helmeted head of his opponent. However, the Northumbrians were well trained and, like Wulfgar, had metal strips sewn into the front of their boots. As they had practiced time and time again, when a Scot grabbed the top of the large round shield, his Northumbrian opponent either chopped off his hands or thrust his sword into the man's face. The natural reaction of the second man, discovering that he was unable to wound the legs under the shield, was to get to his feet and flee, but many were killed before they could do so.

The Scots realised that they were getting the worst of the encounter and fled, leaving behind over a hundred dead and wounded. The latter were quickly dispatched and Aldred led his men back to their horses. They hadn't escaped completely unscathed; ten of the additional horsemen sent to bolster their numbers had been killed or badly wounded. Thankfully, none of Aldred's own warriors had suffered more than the odd scratch.

They mounted again and waited for the next attack.

†††

Just as Eadwulf finished reorganising his men, Malcolm sent his archers forward. They were mainly equipped with self-bows, which were made from a single length of wood and which had a relatively short range. Only a few had war bows but those that did knew how pick their targets and were skilled in their use. The Scots started to fire over the heads of the front ranks, striking the unprotected fyrd in the rear. The hail of arrows from the sky started to unnerve the fyrd but their own archers were quick to respond.

As soon as the Scot's bowmen began to suffer significant casualties, they forgot about the fyrd and concentrated on the enemy archers away on the flank. It was a mistake. Because of their longer range the Bernician arrows could reach the Scots but most of the enemy's shafts fell short.

A horn blew and the Scots bowmen ran back out of range. However, once again they left a pile of bodies behind.

Next Malcolm sent his fighters forward once more to attack the shield wall. However, this time he placed his remaining archers behind his men so that they could shoot over their heads, not at the front rank, but at the unarmoured fyrd behind them. Wulfgar watched in horror as the man next to him fell to the ground with an arrow in his throat and he was on the point of running when the man next to him grabbed his shoulder and shouted 'have courage and faith,' in his ear. He nodded and gripped his spear and shield even tighter.

Then disaster struck. An arrow from a war bow flew over the rear rank and hit Bishop Aldhun in the left eye. It continued into his brain where it lodged. As he dropped soundlessly from his saddle a groan went up from those who had seen him killed and the tale of his death swept through the ranks of the army like wildfire.

This was the time when Eadwulf needed to steady his men and inspire them with strong words, but he was even more appalled by the bishop's death than they had been. Instead or rallying the army, he panicked and fled.

Aldred had launched yet another attack by his horsemen and a significant number of Scots had fled rather than face them. Panic was contagious and now several hundred more on that flank joined them in flight. The trickle became a flood when Aldred led yet another charge, this time not breaking off as soon as they had thrown their spears, but charging right into the mass of warriors, cutting them down in scores. The Scots' left wing was on the point of being routed when Earl Eadwulf fled the field.

†††

Aldred couldn't believe what had just happened. He'd been convinced that they were winning; certainly there were many more enemy bodies littering the ground than there were from his side and the Scot's left flank was routed. Then someone called out that the bishop had been killed. Aldred felt as if he'd been kicked in the guts when he heard about his grandfather, but he pushed his loss to the back of his mind. There would be time for mourning later.

He was about to order a fresh charge when he saw his uncle's banner disappearing to the east. Shortly afterwards the shield wall collapsed and he realised that the battle was lost. He cursed his uncle to Hell. There was no doubt in his mind that Eadwulf had panicked when Aldhun had been killed beside him and the lily-livered sod had deserted his army at the crucial moment. For that alone he deserved to die.

Aldred had sworn to kill him for his part in his father's death but he had held off because defending Lothian was more important. Well, that was no longer an obstacle to getting his revenge. However, his priority at the moment was to lead his men to safety.

†††

Wulfgar was unhurt, although he did have several arrows protruding from his damaged shield. When he saw those about him turning to flee he did likewise, throwing the shield away. But then, out of the corner of his eye, he saw his ealdorman, Iuwine, go down on one knee with an arrow in his calf. He pushed his way over to his lord, though he couldn't have said why he did so when his mind was screaming at him to run with the rest. He put his arm round the noble's waist and, giving him his spear to lean on, Iuwine and Wulfgar slowly made their way away from the battlefield.

As the fyrd fled, Malcolm sent everone forward to attack the remaining housecarls. They put up a stiff resistance and delayed the Scots long enough for many of the fyrd to make good their escape. The last of the Bernician army bravely held their ground until Ealdorman Gosric, the last remaining noble, was killed and then they surrendered.

†††

The arrow in Iuwine's calf had wedged in the muscle but hadn't done any serious damage. However, it had a barbed point and so Wulfgar had to cut off the feathered end cleanly and then push what was left through the leg muscle until he could pull it clear. It must have hurt like Hell but Iuwine bit down on the leather belt Wulfgar had given him and didn't utter a sound. Once it was out the boy did his best to clean out the strands of wool from Iuwine's leggings that had been driven into the wound. After that, he washed the wound thoroughly with water from a small stream before binding it with a strip of cloth torn from the ealdorman's fine linen under tunic. The entry and exit wounds really needed sewing up, but he had neither catgut nor needle on him.

It was obvious that Iuwine couldn't walk very far so Wulfgar decided that the best plan would be to hide him somewhere and make for Cornhill where he hoped to be able to borrow or steal a horse. There had been some pursuit of the beaten Bernician army but, as they had been drawn from all over Bernicia, from Lothian to Teesdale, they had scattered north and south of the Tweed and the Scots had soon given up and returned to the easier pickings on the battlefield.

Malcolm studied the bloody ground and the piles of bodies thinking morosely that he might have won the battle but he'd lost many more men that the Bernicians had; perhaps twice as many. He couldn't afford another victory like that.

☩☩☩

Wulfgar crept through the huts that constituted the hamlet called Cornhill but couldn't find a horse anywhere. He was challenged at one stage but the old man fled when Wulfgar drew his seax. The youth noted with surprise that he no longer felt afraid and, in fact, felt quite proud of himself.

Most of the inhabitants had evidently fled into the hills when they heard about the outcome of the battle. He had just about given up hope of finding a horse when he heard the sound of unshod hooves. He darted into a hovel and peered out through a crack in the shutters covering the unglazed window that faced the track running through the hamlet. Two riders came into view, both little more than boys. They were riding shaggy ponies and each carried a spear and a targe. They stopped near the hovel and started talking to each other in a language that Wulfgar didn't recognise.

One turned his pony as if to retrace their steps when his friend said something to him and slipped off his pony's back. Handing the reins to the other boy he started to walk over to the hovel where Wulfgar was hiding. He stood directly outside the window behind which Wulfgar lurked, but he was looking down. Then Wulfgar heard the sound of liquid splashing on the ground and he realised that the boy was relieving himself.

When he'd finished, he gave himself a shake then looked up and straight through the gap in the shutters into Wulfgar's eyes. The Scot made the mistake of putting his eye to the gap to see inside better and, before he could utter a sound, Wulfgar thrust his seax through the poorly made shutter and into the boy's eye. The point penetrated his brain and he slumped to the ground without making a sound.

Wulfgar glanced at the other Scot. He was looking across the river towards another settlement where he could just make out a party of Scots looting the village. He called out something to his friend and then turned his head when there was no reply. He looked at the damp patch of earth then around and about, but there was no sign of his companion. Wulfgar tried to stop panting so hard. He need to keep quiet so that the second Scot didn't hear him, but he was out of breath. Dragging the dead boy's body inside the hovel had been hard work.

The surviving boy spotted the splashes of blood on the shutters and the wall and, gripping his spear tightly, he jumped off his pony. He cautiously approached the hovel and kicked the door open. As he did so Wulfgar knocked his spear aside and thrust his seax into the boy's guts. He thought the blow would have killed him but the point skidded off a large, decorated bronze buckle that secured the boy's leather belt around his waist and merely succeeded in scoring a thin line along his abdomen.

The Scot took several steps backwards pointing his spear at Wulfgar and cursing him. He moved cautiously, watching his adversary through narrowed eyes. Because he was smaller, Wulfgar had thought that the boy must be younger than him but, as he studied him in turn, he concluded that he was probably a year or two older than he was. Wulfgar followed him as the Scot backed away from the hut.

Suddenly his opponent made a lunge towards Wulfgar. He had been expecting it and batted aside the spear with his seax. His own thrust in response missed anything vital but it did make another bloody gash along the boy's bare stomach as he turned aside.

The two circled each other more warily now. Suddenly the Scot dropped onto one knee and scoped up a handful of dry earth with his free hand. He flung this into his opponent's eyes, temporarily blinding him. Wulfgar threw himself to one side, narrowly avoiding the next spear thrust, but he let go of his seax as he fell. He scrambled to his feet and ran a few paces away, blinking furiously to clear his vision. As he moved again he tripped over something. Glancing down he saw blearily that he had stumbled over the targe belonging to the first boy. It had a wicked point some nine inches long protruding from the boss so he quickly scooped it up.

Now he was armed with just a shield, albeit a lethal one, against a boy with a spear. By now he could see a little more clearly, but he knew that his only chance was to get inside the reach of the spear. When the Scot thrust again, Wulfgar stepped forward, grabbed the haft and gave it a sharp tug. The Scot tottered towards him, caught off balance, and Wulfgar sunk the point of the targe's wicked blade into his enemy's stomach.

He was fatally wounded, but he wasn't dead. Wulfgar retrieved his seax and chopped down at the boy's throat until he was sure that he'd killed him.

It wasn't until the fight was over that Wulfgar started to shake uncontrollably and then vomit in reaction. He marvelled how the cowardly boy of that morning had changed into a cool and calculating fighter. He didn't understand it, but he was glad that he seemed to have slain his demons along with several of the enemy. When he had recovered sufficiently, he dragged the second body into the hovel and mounted one of the ponies. Leading the other, he cautiously made his way back to where he had left Ealdorman Iuwine.

Chapter Seventeen - The Peace Treaty

Mid August 1018

Already ravens, crows and even birds of prey were feasting on the corpses. The cries of the wounded were everywhere. They were just the wounded Scots, of course, who the monks, priests and other healers had yet to reach. There were no screams from the wounded Bernicians. Their wounded had been killed immediately after the battle and the bodies looted.

Malcolm now faced conflicting demands. As soon as his own dead were buried he had to consolidate his hold on Lothian, but he also needed to seize the throne of Strathclyde following the death of his cousin, Owain. Last but not least, he had a score to settle with Findlay of Moray. He vowed that both he and his son Macbeth would die, despite the fact that the boy was his own grandson.

He also worried about Cnut's reaction. Although he had bought off the Earl of Northumbria, Cnut might not accept the loss of part of his kingdom and Malcolm was in no position to fight him in order to retain Lothian after the loss of so many warriors.

He kicked his horse forward across the battlefield towards the Tweed. Both of them needed to cool off in its waters; however, the horse skittered away from the stench of urine, faeces blood and guts, made even worse by the hot sun which now beat down once more. He pulled back viciously on the reins until the horse calmed down, then he rode forward again until they reached the river bank.

A body lay face down in the water and so he walked his horse further upstream to where it was less likely to be polluted. As he dismounted to strip to his braies for a swim to cleanse the filth from his body and cool down he saw another horse lazily cropping grass a hundred yards away. A man in chainmail but no helmet sat on the river bank staring into the water. For a moment Malcolm didn't recognise him, but then he realised that it was Hacca, the Ealdorman of Edinburgh. One of the many tasks facing him was to reorganise the governance of Lothian. The Scots didn't have ealdormen; under the mormaers the next layer of government rested with the chieftains, who ruled over lands occupied by their clans, and thanes, who were landowners without specific tribal attachments. He had been meaning to see Hacca, but not quite so soon.

'Are you wounded?'

On hearing the king's voice, Hacca scrambled to his feet. His armour was covered in blood but none of it was his.

'Lord king, I'm sorry. I was deep in thought.'

'It can't have been easy, fighting against so many of your own race.'

He was referring to the fact that Hacca, like many from Lothian, was of Anglian descent – the same as most Bernicians.

'No, lord. But my allegiance is to you, now more than ever.'

'Good. That makes what I have to say easier. I need to reward the nobles and chieftains who follow me and many of them will receive vills confiscated from their former thanes. However, I need someone I can trust and who will be accepted by the population as their overlord. I have therefore decided to make you Mormaer of the whole of Lothian. It will be your task to oversee the transfer of lands and bring peace to the region.'

'I am honoured, lord king. Thank you for your faith in me. I will do my best to serve your interests and, at the same time, endeavour to ensure that the general population do not suffer more than necessary.'

He paused.

'There is something on your mind?'

'The title of mormaer won't go down well in Lothian. It is not a term people will understand and they'll regard it as alien.'

Malcolm was about to retort that the people would just have to damn well put up with it. Then he had a thought. In the original seven kingdoms that had made up Pictland the lesser kings were called ri and the one of their number elected by them to be the high king was called the ard ri. With the decline of Pictish culture and the rise of the Scots, ri had become mormaer, but it still meant minor king. Some mormaers, like Findlay of Moray, still regarded themselves as kings with Malcolm being no more than the high king. Thus he, and one or two others, acted more indecently than Malcolm would like. Perhaps the time had come for a break with the past?

'Would the title Earl of Lothian suit you better?'

'Yes, lord. It is a title that everyone in Lothian, and more widely in England, would understand.'

'Good,' thought Malcolm to himself. 'Perhaps in time the rest of the lords of the regions of Scotland could become earls instead of mormaers.'

ተተተ

'Lord, there are two riders ahead who are about to cross to the north bank of the Tweed,' the scout reported to Aldred.

'What do they look like?'

'They are dressed like us but they are riding those ponies the Scots use and one has a small shield on his back with a blade protruding from the boss.'

'Scots then?'

'If so they are not dressed like them. The one with the better byrnie has a wounded leg which has been patched up, but blood has stained the dressing.'

'Ceadda stay with the men,' Aldred ordered. 'I'm going to the ford near Norham to have a look for myself.'

Taking the scout and four mounted warriors with him, he cantered through the village to the ford to the east of the dwellings. The crossing was dominated by a high bluff but there was a strip of land leading to the shallows to the south of a small island in the middle of the river. From this islet a causeway had been built under the surface between it and the north bank.

By the time that Aldred arrived the pair had reached the islet and were about to cross the wider part of the river to the north bank.

'Hold, hold I say and identify yourselves!' he shouted.

Wulfgar stopped and looked fearfully behind him, but the man had called out in English. He and Iuwine rode back to the other side of the small island from where they could see the five riders more clearly.

'Lord Aldred,' Wulfgar muttered in relief, recognising the distinctive hauberk and the Norman helmet.

'Well met, Aldred,' his companion called across, no less relieved than Wulfgar.

'Lord Iuwine? The Good Lord be praised! I thought you were dead.'

'No, not quite,' he replied with a grimace.

'Where are you headed?'

'To Berwick. Perhaps we can hold the town against the Scots. It has a stout palisade.'

'But few men to man it,' Aldred pointed out. 'Nothing can stop Malcolm taking the whole of Lothian now.'

'But Berwick is close,' Iuwine objected, 'I'm wounded and that's the nearest place to get treatment.'

Aldred nodded. The ealdorman was still losing quite a lot of blood.

'Uuen can sew the wound up for now. Come with us to Alnwick, which we hope to reach before nightfall. They can look after you there and hopefully the Scots won't venture further south; at least not yet.'

'Very well,' Iuwine agreed reluctantly.

He dreaded the thought of riding all that way in pain and he was still worried about his wife and children in Berwick, but Aldred was right. He'd be trapped in Berwick and at Malcolm's mercy.

ƮƮƮ

Eadulf and Gunwald were riding behind Archbishop Wulfstan and Ealdorman Bjorn of Beverley as they made their way along the east coast. It had been a long and tiring journey north from York but, now that they were nearing the area where there might be fighting, both boys were getting excited.

They had crossed the River Tyne the day before and were now making their way from Morpeth to Alnwick. The two envoys felt frustrated because they had heard nothing about what was happening in Lothian since they had left the monastery at Jarrow. At that stage all they knew was that King Malcolm had invaded from the north and Owain of Strathclyde from the west. There was a rumour that Owain was being harassed on his way into Selkirkshire but nothing definite was known.

They rode into Alnwick to find the place devoid of men of fighting age; old men, women and small children rushed out of their huts to see if the newcomers had any news, but soon dispersed when the found out that they had had come from the south.

Eadulf and Gunwald were sitting on the steps of the hall playing knuckle bones when Fiske appeared with two goblets of watered mead. Instead of handing them the goblets, Fiske suddenly straightened up and stared at the gates. A moment later the compound had filled with armoured riders. As soon as Eadulf saw the hauberks and helmets worn by many of the new arrivals he knew they had to be his brother's men.

'Aldred, Aldred where are you?'

A man who had just dismounted and taken off his helmet turned at the sound and stared incredulously at the boy on the steps.

'Eadulf? What in the name of all that's Holy are you doing here?'

His brother ran to Aldred and hugged him.

'You're alive. I was so afraid you'd be killed. Did we win?'

'Would I be here if we had? We might well have beaten Malcolm if our coward of an uncle hadn't fled the field at the crucial moment.'

At that moment Wulfstan and Bjorn came out of the hall to see what was going on.

'Come inside and tell us what has happened, Aldred.'

'Archbishop? Yet another surprise! Yes, I will, of course, and you can tell me what you are doing here with my brother. Let me see to my men first though; and Ealdorman Iuwine needs urgent attention, he's been wounded in the leg.'

☦☦☦

When Aldred had finished his tale both Wulfstan and Bjorn looked grim. Both men were sad to hear that Aldhun had been killed in the fighting but Aldred had a suspicion that the archbishop was already thinking about who should replace his grandfather at Durham.

'It sounds as if Eadwulf's cowardice may have lost us Lothian. Cnut will have his head for this,' Bjorn said.

Wulfstan nodded, but sat lost in thought for a moment before speaking.

'I think you should continue on to Aycliffe with your men and then take ship to London. Lady Emma will want to hear about this first hand. As regent she might even have the power to depose your uncle and, if she has any sense, put you in his place. I'll give you a letter of recommendation.'

'What about Iuwine?'

'What about him? He can stay here until his wound heals,' Wulfstan said, looking puzzled.

'Yes.' Aldred resisted the temptation to add 'of course.' 'His family are in Berwick and I doubt that Malcolm will let him remain as ealdorman.'

'We need to find the Scots and get negotiations for peace underway as soon as possible; it's possible that Malcolm is now at Berwick and we'll head there tomorrow. If he's not there yet, I'll make sure that his family are escorted back here so that they can be re-united. I can do no more than that.'

'And if he is there already?'

'Then we'll negotiate their release as part of our mission,' the archbishop promised.

'Thank you, archbishop. If you'll excuse me, I need to wash the filth and blood off me and then get some rest.'

'Of course,'

'Will you not eat and drink something first?' a young female voice said from the shadows of the hall.

Aldred knew that the wife of Theomond, the Ealdorman of Alnwick, had died two years ago, leaving a daughter and young son. The daughter – Merewina – had been left in charge whilst Theomund had answered the muster. Aldred didn't know if he had survived the battle and he felt for the young girl, who can't have been more than thirteen. She must be worried sick about her father and now she had to cope with all these visitors on top of everything.

'You are very kind, Merewina. Please excuse my bad manners in not greeting you earlier. Yes, a bite to eat and a tankard of mead or ale would be most welcome; thank you.'

As she departed to find a servant he noticed the boy who'd been standing behind her. He looked to be about seven and Aldred wracked his brains trying to remember his name. He looked close to tears and suddenly ran from the hall in the wake of his sister. Aldred prayed silently that their father had survived. He thought about the route that Theomund would take to get back to Alnwick: probably down Glendale as far as Hedgeley Moor where he'd need to follow the track across the hills to his home. He got up and went to find Ceadda.

'Send two men, those who are least exhausted, with a spare horse across to Hedgeley Moor and then back up Glendale to see if they can find Ealdorman Theomund.'

Ceadda nodded and went to do as he was bid.

It was dusk before the two men returned bringing with them a wounded Theomund and a dozen of his men. Perhaps more would drift in over the next few days but sixty five had set out from the village with their lord and there would be many widows and orphans now. It would be the same in the other vills that made up Theomund's shire. Aldred suspected that it would be the same story throughout Bernicia. It was little consolation to know that the Scots' losses had been much higher.

Thankfully it wasn't a serious wound but Theomund's right forearm had received a blow from a sword which had cut through the flesh and broken the radius. Thankfully the other bone in the forearm – the ulna - seemed to be undamaged. Someone had bandaged it and splinted the broken bone to the ulna for support, but Aldred worried that infection might have set in.

His children had run to him as soon as he entered the hall and embraced him. However, Merewina wasn't the type to sit and weep, offering up thanks for her father's survival. She immediately set about cleaning the wound and extracting clothing and other detritus from it before washing it thoroughly. Uuen went and fetched his needle and catgut once more and stitched the cut together. It wasn't the easiest job as he had to avoid applying any pressure to the broken radius. In the meantime Merewina had sent her brother to find the priest, who had some knowledge of which herbs to use to prevent the wound from becoming septic.

She kept up enough pressure on the wound using a pad to minimise the bleeding, though she couldn't press as much as she would have liked because of the pain from the fracture. When the priest arrived Aldred left them to it. He thanked the men who'd found Theomund and then lay down wrapped in his cloak in the barn in which his men were sleeping.

ϮϮϮ

Hilda, Iuwine's wife, stared down from the walkway above the gates of Berwick at a long column of Scots as they appeared around the bend in the River Tweed. She already knew that Malcolm had won but no one had any news of her husband. Perhaps two hundred men had made their way back to Berwick ahead of the

Scots. Not all were Berwickers; many came from elsewhere in Lothian but had taken refuge there.

Nevertheless there weren't enough to defend the palisade, even if supplemented by those boys and women of the town who wanted to fight. She sighed; she had already decided that she had no option other than to surrender.

She was still looking at the Scots when a girl standing beside tugged at her arm and pointed to the east. A small birlinn was rounding the headland. As she watched, it entered the estuary and fifteen minutes later it had tied up at the jetty. Several men disembarked and made their way into the town through the sea gate.

Shortly after the Scots had encircled the town a few horsemen left their army and rode up the steep slope leading from the north bank of the Tweed to the town's north gate.

Malcolm reined in his horse a hundred yards from the gates and was about to demand the surrender of the town when he saw that there was a man carrying a crozier and dressed in ecclesiastical robes staring down at him. He was standing next to a woman dressed in an expensive red woollen dress. A second later a man in an expensive blue tunic embroidered around the edges in gold appeared at her other side.

'Malcolm, King of Scots, I am Archbishop Wulfstan of York and this is Ealdorman Bjorn of Beverley. We are members of the council of Cnut, King of England, Denmark and Norway. We have been sent by Queen Emma, regent during her husband's absence overseas, to negotiate peace with you. Will you receive us?'

Malcolm was incredulous. How had an embassy reached Berwick only three days after the Battle of Carham? He was totally unprepared for this and he needed time to think. He would also have to consult his own council as to the terms he should insist on. He knew what he wanted – undisputed and unconditional title to Lothian – but there would be trouble if he didn't listen to their views first.

'Very well, I agree to a meeting. I will send you one of my nobles to discuss where and when if you will send me a hostage whilst my representative is with you.'

Wulfstan looked at Bjorn who suggested that they send his foster son, Gunwald.

'We agree. Send your man to the gates and we will send out King Cnut's son, Gunwald.'

Malcolm looked surprised. He didn't know that Cnut had a son, let alone one of that name. He suspected a trick.

'Who is this Gunwald?' he called back.

'Cnut's bastard and my foster son,' Bjorn called back. 'We are not trying to deceive you, lord king. However, if he is not acceptable, will you settle for Eadulf, the eleven year old son of the late Earl Uhtred of Northumbria?'

Malcolm thought grimly that he would rather have the boy's elder brother. He would gladly have cut his throat in retaliation for the defeat of the Strathclyde army and let his own negotiator take his chances. He wondered what the boy was doing with the emissaries, but such speculation was irrelevant.

'Very well, send the boy to the gates.'

Eadulf was nervous about going alone into the camp of the barbarian Scots, as he thought of them. However, he squared his shoulders and put on a brave face, determined not to let anyone see how scared he was. The right hand gate opened a fraction and he walked through it to wait for the Scot's envoy to appear.

Hacca, now confirmed by the king's council as Earl of Lothian, walked steadily towards the young boy standing staring at him and then halted just out of range of the few archers on the walls of Berwick.

'Walk towards me, Eadulf, and don't be afraid. This is just a formality,' Hacca called across to him.

'I'm not afraid, especially not of a traitor and turncoat like you,' the boy called back.

Eadulf knew very well who Hacca was. The man was an Anglian who had been given his shire by his father, Uhtred.

Hacca flushed.

'Watch your tongue boy or I'll cut it out of your mouth myself.'

The archbishop and Bjorn listened to the exchange in puzzlement until Hilda explained who Hacca was.

'No wonder Malcolm wanted a hostage to ensure that bloody man's safety,' Bjorn muttered in disgust.

'Don't be so quick to judge, Bjorn,' Wulfstan said reasonably. 'What would you have done in Hacca's place? We mustn't allow personal animosity to influence us in our discussions. Lothian is lost to us, at least for now; this is an exercise in damage limitation and we need to confine our thoughts to that single aim.'

'I'm sorry, Wulfstan. Of course you are correct,' he replied but his face told a different story. He'd have gladly sunk a dagger into Hacca's heart if he could have got away with it.

Eadulf was introduced to Malcolm but he didn't bend the knee when told to do so.

'Why should I? You're not my king,' he said defiantly.

'I may not be your king for now, whelp, but I will be when I conquer the rest of Bernicia.'

'Does that mean that you have no intention of keeping this treaty you are about to negotiate?' Eadulf asked with a sweet smile. 'I'm sure that Archbishop Wulfstan and Ealdorman Bjorn will be interested to hear that.'

Malcolm cursed. The boy had provoked him into saying more than was wise. He would have liked to have beaten Eadulf for his insolence but he had granted him safe conduct.

'Get this little brat out of my sight before I do something I might regret. He is to be tied up and kept secure.'

†††

Synne waited demurely on the steps of the hall as Aldred dismounted and walked towards her. His desire was to rush to her and sweep her off her feet, covering her mouth and face with kisses, but that was not how a lord and lady behaved in public. Their celebration of his safe return would have to wait until they were alone. He could hardly wait.

The next day was wet and miserable but, much as he would've liked to, he couldn't spend the day in bed with Synne. He needed to show his face in all the vills he now owned and check on their respective reeves to ensure that they were being run properly, not that he knew much about running estates. Thankfully the steward that Synne had engaged seemed to know what he was talking about. His wife might be a good lover but she hadn't been brought up to run a hall, let alone a large estate. She had, however, been endowed with the ability to judge people's worth.

Aldred hadn't realised before how generous his grandfather had been. Apart from Aycliffe itself, there were five other vills situated between it and a sizeable settlement called Stockton on high ground close to the northern bank of the River Tees. Compared to the three previous vills he had owned in Lothian, the soil was much better for growing crops and vegetables and the pasture was much lusher.

The local ealdorman was Leofwine of Durham, though no one knew whether he had survived the battle or not. He remembered that the man's younger son and heir had also been at Carham, even though he was only thirteen. If both had died then Beda would be the obvious successor.

He was now seventeen and one of Aldred's mounted warriors. Beda hadn't been at Carham because he was one of those who had escorted Synne and Macbeth to Aycliffe. Aldred had thought it best at the time to send him away from the camp in case his father saw him. The man didn't know that Beda had left Durham Monastery and it was best if it stayed that way.

If Leofwine was indeed dead then Aldred needed to persuade Queen Emma to appoint a successor or Durham would be without a lord as well as a bishop. He should really set out by sea from Stockton for London as soon as possible; he needed to tell Emma of Eadwulf's disgraceful conduct before anyone told her a different version of events. Eadwulf wasn't without friends in London. He could also raise the question of the new ealdorman with the queen at the same time. However, he needed to know Leofwine's fate first.

The next day Aldred set out for Monkwearmouth to see Leofwine's wife and ask if she had any news of her husband and son. He was tempted to take Beda with him, just to see her face, but he decided that taking the offspring of Leofwine's first wife might satisfy his sense of mischief, but it wasn't the most sensible idea he'd ever had.

Before going to the hall he'd asked around for news. Several of the men who had just managed to return to Jarrow said that Leofwine had been wounded. He might still be alive but, if so, he could well be a prisoner of the Scots. However, they were certain that his son had been killed. He rode up to the hall with a heavy heart.

He had expected to dislike Kendra just because she had been responsible for turning Leofwine against his eldest son. However, when he met her he realised how unfair he'd been. As Synne commented later, it was natural for a mother to want to advance the interests of her own child over that of her step-son.

Aldred told her what he'd heard and she did her best not to break down in front of him. He felt sorry for her but he was at a loss to know what words of comfort he could offer. Instead, after a decent pause to allow her to collect herself, he explained the reason he'd come to see her.

Until Leofwine's fate was known Kendra was acting in his stead and so Aldred showed her the deeds to his six vills to confirm his title. She handed the documents to her steward who formally recorded the transfer in the shire's records. He stayed making idle conversation for politeness' sake, but he knew she wanted to be alone to grieve and he took his leave as soon as he could without appearing to be rude.

He hadn't gone more than five miles before he and his escort encountered a group of men returning to their homes. Several were wounded, not seriously but badly enough to explain why it had taken the group so long to get back. Aldred questioned them and most of what they said merely confirmed what he already knew. However, two of them were certain that Leofwine had been badly wounded and had died of his injuries well before the end of the battle.

Aldred thanked them for their testimony and asked them to let the Abbot of Monwearmouth and Jarrow Monastery – a joint establishment – know of Leofwine's death. He would be best placed to break the news to the Lady Kendra.

Now he that he knew that Leofwine was dead he could set sail without further delay.

ϮϮϮ

It was the eighteenth of August before Aldred's ship docked in London. He had left Synne in charge, assisted by the steward, and had taken Ceadda, Beda and a dozen warriors in case they encountered pirates. He had also brought Macbeth along because he had a feeling that the further away from Malcolm he was the safer he would be.

The voyage had been incident free, apart from a minor gale as they passed the Norfolk coast, during which Macbeth had been extremely seasick. Even his bright red hair seemed to have lost some of its lustre. He was feeling a little better by the time that they entered the Thames Estuary and when they disembarked he looked more like his usual self.

It was raining as they made their way to the west of the city on hired horses. The downpour muted some of the stench but it had turned the streets into a sea of mud. Even though they were riding well above the muck, they still managed to get splattered by wet filth by the time that they reached the church known as the West Minster and the adjacent palace.

They had to wait some time to see the queen, which gave the mud a chance to dry so that most of it could be shaken or rubbed off by the time that they were summoned. Emma wasn't interested in most of the details of the battle, for which Aldred was thankful, but she did want to hear about Bishop Aldhun's death and Eadwulf's precipitate flight.

When Aldred said that, in his opinion, his uncle's cowardice had lost the battle her eyes narrowed but she said nothing. He presented Macbeth to her and described the background to his current situation and then went on to introduce Beda. He explained that his father had been the Ealdorman of Durham before he'd been killed. The queen offered her sympathy, but when Aldred recommended him as his father's replacement she made no comment.

'You have given me much to think about, Aldred. I'm grateful to you for what you have told me and also for confirmation that my emissaries reached Bernicia safely. Hopefully they will be able to give me a clearer picture of the current situation when they return. I fully expect that Durham isn't the only shire without an ealdorman.

'I would be grateful if you would come and see me tomorrow at the same time, but this time come alone. There are private matters I need to discuss with you. Now, no doubt you would like to talk to your step-mother before you depart. I know she would appreciate news of her other stepson.'

Ælfgifu had been standing behind the queen and now she followed Aldred when he and his companions took their leave. They chatted for half an hour and he paid a brief visit to the nursery to see his half-sisters, Ealdgyth and Ælfflead, but he was totally at a loss how to engage with such young children. Macbeth, on the other hand, played with them while the adults were talking and proved to be a great hit with both girls; so much so that they cried when he had to leave.

Aldred left the palace feeling frustrated. It had all been waste of time as far as he could see. She hadn't condemned Eadwulf for his cowardice, let alone confiscate his earldom, and she hadn't agreed to Beda replacing his father. Perhaps Emma might be more forthcoming when he returned on the morrow, but he doubted it.

On the other hand he wondered why she wanted to see him privately. Was it to give him more bad news?

ᛏᛏᛏ

It was with some relief that Eadulf left Malcolm's custody and walked passed Hacca outside the gates of Berwick. He was tempted to spit at him, but decided that he shouldn't lower himself to that level. Instead he ignored the man and kept his eyes on the partially open gate.

The next morning the two envoys and four guards crossed on the ferry to the south bank where Malcolm, Hacca and four of the king's bodyguards waited having crossed the Tweed earlier in the morning at Norham.

Eadulf had told Wulfstan and Bjorn what Malcolm had said and so they were well aware that the King of Scots might play them false. Wulfstan was also troubled about what Malcolm had said to the boy.

'The information is helpful, Eadulf, and we are grateful for that. However, it is never a good idea to antagonise powerful men unless it is necessary. You have made an enemy of Malcolm and that was foolish,' the archbishop told him.

Eadulf looked at the ground and nodded.

'Yes, I understand, lord archbishop. I am sorry.'

'Don't be; as I said the insight into Malcolm's mind is useful. Just learn the lesson and don't make the same mistake again.'

The spell of hot weather had come to an end and the sky was overcast. It might have been humid were it not for the strong breeze from the north-east. The Scots had erected an awning just in case it rained and this now flapped and crackled as if it were trying to escape from the clutches of the guy ropes. It also made it difficult to hear and so the four men moved away from the awning and sat facing each other on four chairs a hundred yards away.

'I hope you don't expect me to give back Lothian,' Malcolm began. 'It was ceded to my ancestor, King Kenneth the Second, by

King Edgar and should have remained as part of my kingdom. My campaign was merely to take back what is rightfully mine.'

The two English envoys thought that such a defensive statement boded well for their mission but kept their faces impassive.

'King Edgar ceded Lothian to King Kenneth some sixty years ago on the proviso that Kenneth pledged fealty to Edgar as his vassal. His successor repudiated Edgar's supremacy and therefore lost his title to Lothian.' Wulfstan pointed out.

'I am an independent monarch who recognises no superior, save God himself.'

'In that case you cannot cite King Edgar's treaty with the King of Scots as you have also repudiated the vital condition on which the treaty rested.'

Malcolm was well aware of the archbishop's reputation as a law maker and quickly recognised that he was going to get nowhere with that line of argument.

'The northern part of Lothian has been part of my kingdom for some time now. The lack of a clear border between us is in no one's interest. The Tweed is a much more sensible boundary; one that we can both recognise and accept.'

'Even if that were true, which we don't concede, Lothian is not bounded in the south by the Tweed. The present extent of Lothian is unclear as the border between it and the rest of Bernicia heads due south just to the west of Carham until it reaches the Cheviot Hills. Then it runs south west through the hills until it meets the border with Cumbria, currently part of Strathclyde. There are no markers, nor indeed is there anyway of precisely delineating what lies within Lothian.

'That doesn't matter at the moment as both are part of Bernicia,' Wulfstan continued. 'Were it to become a boundary between two kingdoms then it would matter a great deal. Therefore King Cnut can never accept that Lothian is part of your territory. It would be much more satisfactory for all concerned if the border lay along the Firth of Forth and the River Forth.'

'You can't seriously suggest that I should give up all that I've gained? No, Lothian is Scottish and will remain so,' Malcolm said with finality.

'Are you willing to risk war with Cnut,' Bjorn asked, speaking for the first time.

He exchanged looks with Wulfstan, who nodded to indicate that he should continue.

'You're weak after your losses at Carham. We destroyed the Strathclyde army and Moray has deserted you. His son is safe in England so you have no hold over Findlay. We know you bribed Earl Erik. Because he is close to Cnut he may be allowed to keep his earldom, but only if he takes the field against you. You are hardly negotiating from a position of strength, are you lord king?'

'You didn't kill Owain and defeat his army, Uhtred's son did, God curse him. As for Findlay, he won't be Mormaer of Moray for much longer and Macbeth won't succeed; a man loyal to me will, then I will have the strength to keep what is mine. Cnut has three kingdoms to try and hold onto. He can't afford the luxury of going to war over Lothian, or over Bernicia come to that.'

'You may tell yourself that, but our king tends to hold onto what is his with ruthless tenacity, as you will find out unless we can reach an accord. The choice is yours.'

So saying Bjorn got to his feet, as did the archbishop, and made as if to leave.

'Wait,' Malcolm barked at them. 'Sit down, I haven't finished.'

'No, but we have,' Wulfstan said, 'unless you are prepared to be reasonable.'

Malcolm thought for several minutes whilst the two envoys continued to stand.

'Very well, I agree to leave the border on the Tweed and I won't take the rest of Lothian south of the river. Will that satisfy you?'

'Partially, provided you agree to our other conditions.'

'Other conditions? Don't try my patience too far.'

'We understand that you have plans to take the whole of Bernicia and settle your border on the Tees, perhaps not now, but as soon as you are strong enough for a new campaign.'

Malcolm knew that Eadulf would have told them what he'd said in the heat of the moment so there was no point in denying it. Instead he said nothing and an uncomfortable silence grew. He waited for one of the two envoys to say something further, but they were too experienced to fall into that trap. Whoever spoke next would be at a disadvantage.

'Perhaps there is some merit in giving your oath not to cross the Tweed for, say, the next five years,' Hacca eventually suggested.

Malcolm gave him a furious look but the damage had been done.

'Make it ten years and I think we have a proposal that we can put to Queen Emma,' Wulfstan said smoothly. 'You will need to swear an oath on Holy relics to abide by the treaty, of course.'

Malcolm was on the point of refusing when common sense prevailed. He'd managed to push his border south to the Tweed and, once the treaty was sealed, he wouldn't have to worry about reprisals when Cnut returned. That would leave him free to take over Strathclyde and combine the two kingdoms, and then deal with Findlay of Moray at his leisure.

'I think we are in agreement, my lords. Have your clerks draw up the appropriate wording with mine and get Queen Emma's approval. I suggest we meet here again in one month's time to formally ratify it.'

The four men got to their feet and Wulfstan turned to leave. However, Bjorn turned back to Malcolm.

'There is one other thing, lord king. When we depart we will be escorting the Ealdorman of Berwick's family south so that they can be reunited with him.'

Malcolm just shrugged.

†††

Aldred returned to the palace the next morning with mixed emotions: curiosity tinged with a little anxiety.

'I'm sorry that I couldn't say anything constructive yesterday, Aldred,' the queen began. 'I will write to my husband to acquaint him with what you've told me, but I feel that I have already overstepped the boundaries he set for my regency by sending peace envoys north to treat with King Malcolm. If I make any more decisions without consulting him he is likely to overturn them just to teach me my place. It goes without saying that I've explained this to you in strictest confidence.'

'I understand, lady. I'm grateful to you for doing so and you have my word that none of this shall pass my lips. I shall merely tell Beda that you are consulting the king.'

He left thinking what a careful path the queen had to tread. Cnut had already divorced one wife and he could easily do the same with Emma, if she gave him cause. He didn't envy her.

Chapter Eighteen – Aftermath

May 1020

Cnut was in a good mood as he stood on the prow of his longship, the rain and wind in his face, as he entered the Thames Estuary. His wife had given birth to a son who Emma had christened Harthacnut, or Cnut the Tough, towards the end of 1018. Much to everyone's surprise, Cnut had sent for his son when he was eighteen months old and had had taken the unusual step of declaring the boy his heir to the Kingdom of Denmark. He had left him in the care of one of his brothers-in-law, Jarl Ulf, as regent.

Emma had hated being parted from her son at such a tender age, but she was enough of a pragmatist to understand that it meant that his future was now secure. Harold, Cnut's son by his first wife, Ælfgifu of Northampton, was two years older than Harthacnut and he would have probably found a way of disposing of his half-brother had he seen him as a rival for the crown of England when they were both older.

Through Emma's letters Cnut had learned of the loss of most of Lothian and Erik Håkonsson's lack of action to defend Bernicia. He wasn't very happy about either but he was constrained not to attack Scotland for another eight years under the terms of the treaty. To have repudiated it would have meant undermining his queen and that would have weakened his position as well, so he was stuck with the situation. Erik had powerful connections and Cnut still needed his support, so he'd have to ignore Erik's treachery, at least for now.

However, he did need a strong man in the North. Eadwulf of Bebbanburg had shown himself to be a coward and he was directly responsible for Malcolm's victory as far as Cnut was concerned. He'd have to be deposed and he thought that perhaps the man's nephew might be the ideal replacement. However, he needed to discuss the matter with Emma and with the man who'd been the power behind the throne in his absence – Archbishop Wulfstan.

There was another, more minor matter, which he needed to talk to Wulfstan about and that was the replacement of the unfortunate Aldhun as Bishop of Durham. Wulfstan had proposed his chaplain for the post but the monks of Durham were being difficult and insisting on the appointment of Edmund, their present Prior. To add to his problems, Archbishop Lyfing of Canterbury had just died and the Pope wanted to appoint someone who both Wulfstan and Emma thought totally unsuitable.

He sighed. Of all the matters needing his attention on his return, reconciling opposing factions in the Church was likely to be the most problematic.

†††

It was a bright summer's day in July 1020 when Máel Coluim mac Máel Brigti and his brother Gillecomgan walked into Findlay's hall in Elgin on the Moray Firth. The Mormaer of Moray was relaxed. King Malcolm hadn't yet carried out his threat to make him pay for deserting him on the eve of the Battle of Carham, nor was an attack likely in the near future. The king had other problems to worry about: he was still busy securing Strathclyde; the people of Galloway had risen in revolt last year; and now the Norsemen in Cumbria were refusing to pay him the taxes they owed him.

With Malcolm preoccupied in the south of the kingdom, Findlay felt safe for now. However, he was certain that Malcolm would seek a reckoning with him eventually and so he had reluctantly decided to leave his son at Cnut's court in London for now. He missed him and his wife kept nagging him to send for her son, but he felt better knowing that the boy was safe.

He was in the middle of hearing a dispute over land between two thanes when his two nephews arrived. As was customary, they left their weapons on the table beside the door and went towards

Findlay. They waited patiently until Findlay made his judgement and then, before the next case could be called, Máel Coluim stepped forward.

'Uncle, we have received a letter from King Malcolm for you,' he said loudly.

'A letter from Malcolm? What does that man want, and why wasn't it sent directly to me?' he asked angrily.

'May we approach?'

When their uncle nodded the two brothers stepped forward onto the dais on which Findlay sat. Two guards stood on duty behind him but they were bored and not paying much attention to what was going on.

Findlay read the document which Máel Coluim handed him and his face paled.

'What does this mean?' he asked puzzled.

'I'd have thought it was pretty clear, uncle. It's your death warrant.'

'Huh, and how's Malcolm going to carry it out?' Findlay asked in derision.

'Like this,' Gillecomgan said, producing a dagger he had hidden up the left sleeve of his tunic.

He thrust it into Findlay's chest. The point found his heart and he died without uttering another sound. The two guards lowered their spears in alarm but Máel Coluim waved the document at them yelling that not only was it the king's order for the death of Findlay but also his appointment as the new mormaer. They hesitated.

'Lay down your weapons now,' Gillecomgan told them quietly. 'To do otherwise is to commit treason.'

The people who had crowded into the hall for the monthly hearing of complaints and law suits were stunned by what had just happened and looked on with horror at the body of their lord lying dead on the dais. There was little blood as his heart had stopped beating the second it was penetrated by Gillecomgan's dagger.

Just as pandemonium was about to break out, the assassin raised his brother's hand, still holding the king's warrant in his hand and cried out 'all hail Máel Coluim mac Máel Brigti, Mormaer of Moray by God's grace and the will of King Malcolm.'

There were some who didn't accept the new mormaer and spoke against him for his involvement in the killing of Findlay, but they mysteriously disappeared the following night or else fled. A month later Máel Coluim had undisputed control over Moray and he rewarded his brother by giving him Glamis and half a dozen other estates. All of them had been Findlay's personal property and not owned by him as Mormaer. Therefore they should have been inherited by Findlay's son.

Macbeth grieved deeply for his father when he heard and vowed to kill his two cousins. There was a rumour that Duncan, Malcolm's designated heir, was involved and Macbeth swore that he too would pay dearly. However, it wasn't the only blood feud that was to dominate the north of Britain in the coming decades.

†††

Aldred received his second summons to London with some astonishment. It seemed that the king wanted to see him, but the letter didn't say why. He had been kept busy for the past two years and, whilst he had lost none of his determination to kill both Eadwulf and Thurbrand the Hold in revenge for the death of his father at their hands, the opportunity to do so hadn't arisen.

Synne had given birth to a daughter, Edith, the previous year and now she was expecting their second child. That, and the need to manage his new estates after years of neglect, had kept him busy. Now, just when he had started to think how he could take his revenge on his uncle and Thurbrand, he'd been summoned south to see Cnut.

As Thane of Aycliffe and his other vills he was becoming a wealthy man; wealthy enough to maintain forty mounted housecarls. These were Norman knights in all but name and he also had a dozen boys in training to join them. A year ago he had bought two knarrs for trading out of the natural harbour at Hartlepool, near the mouth of the Tees. The town had grown up around Hartlepool Monastery, but had declined when Vikings had destroyed the monastery a century and a half ago. However, in recent decades it had seen something of revival as a port.

He had also had a large birlinn constructed to escort his knarrs across the sea to the continent. The main danger was from Flemish and Danish pirates but they tended to steer clear of merchant ships escorted by a warship; there were easier prey to be had.

Aldred decided that it would be quicker to wait for the return of his ships and sail down to London than to undertake the journey on horseback. Synne was desperate to go with him to visit London but, given her advanced state of pregnancy, Aldred persuaded her to stay at Aycliffe.

Beda asked to accompany him as soon as he heard about Aldred's summons to court. Cnut had agreed to appoint him as Ealdorman of Durham some time ago, but now he was concerned that the diocese was still without a bishop after Aldhun's death two years previously. The vills in Lothian owned by the Bishopric of Durham, including Duns, had been seized by Malcolm and given to his followers as a reward for their support during his campaign. Without a bishop in post to argue that they were Church lands, they had been lost without a protest. Fortunately Norham and Carham were on the south side of the Tweed and so had remained the diocese's property.

Wulfstan still spent most of his time in London and his visits to his archdiocese were less frequent than ever as he got older and more frail. He had given up the See of Worcester, which he had also held, in 1016 to lighten his load but now, four years later, the distance to York was too long a journey for him to manage. That meant that effectively there was no one to lead the Church in Northumbria. The abbots of Durham, Jarrow and Ripon had their monasteries to manage and seemed little bothered about the religious care of the people. The priests who had died in the archbishopric in the last two years were not replaced and it was almost as if an interdict lay upon the land. Earl Eric didn't seem to be much troubled at this state of affairs and Eadwulf of Bebbanburg positively welcomed the lack of censure for his dissolute behaviour. Eric might not be concerned, but Beda was.

Aldred was well aware that he risked an encounter with Thurband's pirates off Holderness and he half-hoped that Thurbrand himself might come out to attack him. However, they sailed past the mouth of the Humber without seeing anything more threatening than the odd fishing vessel. Perhaps Thurbrand the Hold was casting his net a little further from home these days?

☨☨☨

Macbeth greeted Aldred warmly. The boy was now fifteen and had the beginnings of a beard. It was a darker red than his hair which gave him an even more striking appearance.

'I was sorry to hear about your father,' Aldred said after the initial greetings.

'Máel Coluim and Gillecomgan will pay for murdering him,' Macbeth replied with a dangerous glint in his eye, 'so will Malcolm and my cousin Duncan who, I'm told, urged Malcolm to agree to it. I may have to wait as long as you have for revenge, but my time will come.'

Aldred looked at him sharply. There was no doubt that Macbeth meant what he'd said. It had been four years since his own father had been slain but Ceadda had once said to him that revenge was a dish best served cold. He had to admit that he was now impatient for vengeance against Uhtred's killers. However, something in the boy's tone made him think that there was something he wasn't saying.

'Is there something you know?'

'Yes, but I'm sure that the king will want to tell you himself.'

As he followed a servant to the queen's private chambers he encountered one of Cnut's housecarls. For a moment he didn't recognise him but he knew that his face was familiar. The man avoided eye contact and suddenly Aldred remembered who he was – Regnwald - the man who'd sent assassins to kill him in revenge for making him look a fool when Emma of Normandy had landed to marry Cnut.

He stepped in front of the housecarl, forcing him to stop.

'Remember me, Regnwald? Ever wonder what happened to the dozen men you sent to kill me? Tread carefully or you might disappear just as they did.'

'I don't know what...' he started to reply, but realised he was wasting his breath.

He nodded and Aldred stepped out of his way. Feeling pleased with himself Aldred continued on his way, little realising that confronting Regnwald had been both stupid and unnecessary. For all he knew the king's housecarl might have thought that the killers he had hired had just taken his money and disappeared. Now he knew that Aldred and his men had killed them and disposed of the bodies. If Aldred had seen the vengeful look that Regnwald had given his departing back he might not have been so cheerful.

A few minutes later he was shown into a chamber where his stepmother sat talking to Eadulf and two young girls. He greeted Ælfgifu dutifully and then turned to his half-brother. Eadulf had turned into a tall but gangling thirteen year old since Aldred had last seen him. He stood there diffidently, uncertain how to greet his elder brother until Aldred threw his arms about him and nearly hugged the life out of him.

'It's good to see you brother,' Aldred said, grinning at him. 'You look nearly ready to start your warrior training.'

He would have said more but Ælfgifu told him that he should also greet his sisters. Aldred hadn't recognised them. Ealdgyth was nearly five and Ælfflaed was three. He wondered what to say to them and then he had an idea.

'Do you know that you have a niece who is sixteen months old and who can now walk without falling over?'

The two little girls giggled and then started to ask questions about Edith. They seemed to find it odd that they now had a niece who was nearly as old as they were. Once the ice was broken they didn't stop chattering and asking questions. Eventually they had to stop when a servant appeared and asked Aldred to follow him. To his surprise Eadulf accompanied him.

'You know what this is about then?'

His brother nodded but said nothing.

Aldred had expected to be shown into the main hall where Cnut heard petitions and carried out the business of governing England. Instead the man led them to a small side chamber which evidently served as the king's office. They passed through an outer room where half a dozen clerks were busily copying documents and into the inner sanctum.

Like the rest of the palace, the walls had been constructed using a frame of seasoned oak into which thin strips of wood, usually hazel, were woven before the spaces were packed with daub - a mixture of wet soil, clay, sand, animal dung and straw. Sometimes the shields were hung on the inside walls but often they were left bare. However, the walls of Cnut's office were hung with two large embroidered panels, one depicting several saints and the other a hunting scene.

Aldred had seen such embroideries before, but only in cathedrals such as Durham. These two surpassed anything he'd seen hitherto. Both included gold and silver wire, and even precious stones, woven into the heavy woollen panels.

Aldred tore his eyes away from the breath-taking pictures and bowed the knee to the king. He was sitting behind a carved table on which lay several scrolls and an illuminated bible. Queen Emma sat on a lower chair to one side of the table and a monk stood at the other side.

'Rise Aldred; I see you admire these embroideries. Unfortunately our Danish craftsmen can't produce such fine works of art. These were commissioned by King Æthelred, or so I'm told.'

Aldred got to his feet and bowed to Emma, who smiled back at him.

'I understand that my brother's armour and training came in useful. It is a pity that it was all for nothing,' she said.

'Do you think that the battle could have been won?' Cnut asked Aldred.

'Yes, the Scots were losing many more men than we were and the combined attacks by the archers on one flank and my horsemen on the other were bunching them in the centre. They were on the point of breaking before my grandfather was killed and that certainly shook our men. However, I believe that they would have held firm given the right leadership. Instead, the earl fled and unsurprisingly the fyrd followed his example' leaving the nobles and housecarls to fight the Scots on their own. '

'Thank you. That corresponds with the reports from those ealdormen who survived.'

The king turned to the monk who handed him two scrolls.

'This is the order depriving Eadwulf of his earldom and his lands. It also exiles him for life on pain of death if he returns. The other is your appointment as Earl of Bernicia. You are also to receive your uncle's lands, including Bebbanburg. I rely on you to watch my northern border and ensure that Malcolm stays behind the Tweed. When I'm able to spare the time and the resources I intend to come north and teach him a lesson he won't forget.'

'Thank you, lord king. I am most grateful.'

'I sense a 'but' coming.'

'Two really. The treaty is due to last until 1028. That's when I would expect Malcolm to invade again; after all, he's said more than once that he wants to extend his southern border to the Tees.'

'Perhaps. I'll give it some thought. And the second point?'

'Eadwulf will not give up Bebbanburg easily and it is an impregnable fortress.'

'That's your problem, Earl Aldred. Starve him out if you must but I cannot give you any men, other than those obliged to answer the muster in Bernicia.'

'Of course, is there anything else?'

'One thing,' Emma said. 'I have discussed your brother's future with the Lady Ælfgifu and we are agreed that it is time that Eadulf started training as a warrior, although he is still six months shy of his fourteenth birthday. He is bored here and he and my stepson, Gunwald, keep getting into trouble. We would like you to take both boys and arrange their military training.'

'When my son is sixteen and has completed his training,' Cnut added, 'I propose to grant Gunwald an estate of his own. At that juncture you will have to find land or some occupation for Eadulf yourself, of course. I take it you are agreeable to taking the two boys with you?'

'Yes, lord king. I have recently adopted the Norman system of appointing boys of noble birth to serve my mounted housecarls, who train them in turn to join them when they are old enough. The concept was developed by the Franks who called them earmigers. I have already have half a dozen, all the younger sons of thanes, so Eadulf and Gunwald can join their ranks.'

Aldred wasn't being completely truthful. He was also training boys of lower birth like Oeric who showed potential as mounted warriors. In Oeric's case, he was very young at twelve, but he was an excellent rider and Aldred had high hopes for him. Wulfgar had also been an armiger before he had turned seventeen and became one of Aldred's mounted housecarls.

'Excellent,' Cnut said, sceptically. 'I'm not convinced of the value of fighting on horseback, but perhaps you can prove me wrong.'

†††

Aldred stood on the hill a mile away from Bebbanburg studying the fortress across the valley. Ceadda stood by his side whilst Gunwald and Eadulf, now their respective armigers, held their horses on the reverse slope.

'Our best chance of capturing him is to wait until he goes hunting,' Cetta suggested.

'Except that he never does. He knows now that I am his replacement and that I govern all of Bernicia, except for Bebbanburg. Perhaps our best hope is to starve him out?'

'For that you will need a strong force to besiege him, and its harvest time. Even we shouldn't be here. The men are needed back in Teesdale to help to get in the crops.'

Just at that moment the main gates at the south end of the stronghold opened and half a dozen riders came out. The two men watched as they rode down into the village and entered the compound around the local thane's hall.

'Come on we need to speak to those men.'

Without waiting for a reply Aldred ran down the hill and mounted his horse. Ignoring Ceadda's cries to wait he cantered down the other side of the hill towards the village which lay in the shadow of the great rock on which the fortress was built. Muttering curses Ceadda followed with the two boys bringing up the rear.

The ten warriors and four other armigers who had been resting in the shade of a few trees further down the hill, seeing both their lord and their captain disappearing over the crest, hastily mounted and galloped after them.

The sentry at the gate of the thane's compound was half dozing, enjoying the late summer sunshine on his face, when he was startled into full wakefulness by four horsemen riding through the village, scattering squawking chickens and young children playing in the dust, as they passed. They rode towards him slowing to a trot as they neared the palisade. The housecarl lowered his spear in what he hoped was a threatening manner.

'Who are you and what do you want,' He called out in a somewhat shaky voice as he saw a dozen or more riders chasing after the first group.

Aldred slowed his horse to a walk as he replied.

'Aldred, Earl of Bernicia, now get out of my way.'

'But-t-t, Lord Eadwulf is-s the e-earl,' he stammered uncertainly.

'Not any more, by decree of King Cnut, Eadwulf is declared outlaw,' Aldred said riding past the sentry and into the compound.

The other three followed him closely, followed by the rest of the armed riders, kicking up enough dust to make the housecarl cough. A stable boy came running as he heard the sound of hooves on the hard baked ground. It was the second time that morning and he had only just finished taking the first half a dozen horses to the stables. Now he stood open mouthed as he was confronted by eighteen more.

'Don't worry, lad,' Eadulf called to him as he dismounted. 'We'll look after these.'

Whilst Eadulf, Gunwald and the other armigers held the horses Aldred and his housecarls made their way towards the hall. Three men dressed in rusty byrnies had been standing outside the door drinking ale brought to them by a serving girl when Aldred and his men arrived. Aldred correctly assumed that they were members of Eadwulf's garrison and not the thane's housecarls. The three put down their flagons and nervously fingered the hilts of their swords.

'I wouldn't if I were you,' Ceadda told them with a grin, 'not if you want to live. Kjetil, Hakon, disarm them.'

Aldred opened the door very slightly, so as not to alert those inside, and let his eyes adjust to the gloomy interior. The other three warriors from Bebbanburg had surrounded the thane, a man called Durwin, and were arguing with him. A middle aged woman and two small children cowered in a corner of the hall, which was a simple affair with no separate chamber for them to retreat to. Four servants – two women, a boy and an elderly man stood helplessly beside them.

'You will do as you are told, Lord Durwin. The earl required you to empty your stores, and those of every villager, and bring the contents up to the fortress.'

'But everyone is busy gathering in the harvest whilst the good weather lasts; besides we need what we have to survive the winter.'

'You won't survive the hour, nor will your family, unless you do what I tell you,' the man said nastily.

Aldred opened the door wide allowing the sunlight to spill across the dirt floor. The occupants of the hall looked up and the three men in byrnies went to draw their swords.

'Who is this earl who demands all that the villagers have?' Aldred asked quietly as he walked towards the thane and the men around him. As he did so he nearly tripped over a body he hadn't seen. He glanced down at the elderly housecarl. Someone had ripped his throat out with a dagger.

He stepped over the body and waited for an answer as the rest of his men entered the hall and stood behind him.

'Why, Earl Eadwulf of course.'

'The king has deprived Eadwulf of his earldom and his property. He is to be declared an outlaw if he doesn't leave the kingdom immediately.'

'Who says so?'

'I do, Earl Aldred of Bernicia. Now, take these documents and return to the fortress. Spread the word that, unless the garrison surrenders by noon tomorrow, they and their families will also be declared outlaw.'

'What are the documents?'

'Copies certified by the Archbishop of York of my appointment as your earl and the king's order dispossessing my uncle of his lands and exiling him.'

'I beg pardon lord, I didn't know. Unfortunately I can't read, nor can any of my men.'

'In that case I'll send for the priest and he can read them to you.'

The man looked uncomfortable.

'Earl… I mean Eadwulf expelled the village priest some time ago because he criticized him for losing the Battle of Carham.'

'He means that Father Edric preached against Eadwulf's cowardice and was whipped from here for doing so. He was found dead with his throat cut not five miles away,' Durwin explained.

'So it seems that I can add another murder to my uncle's list of crimes,'

'Another, lord?'

'Yes, he was involved in the assassination of my father, Uhtred, and the slaughter of his housecarls.'

Silence greeted this statement. He couldn't be sure whether it was news to Eadwulf's men or not but it certainly was to Durwin.

'Give me the documents lord. I'll take them to Eadwulf and insist that he reads them out to us,' the leader of the Bebbanburg housecarls said unctuously.

Aldred did so, not because he trusted the man; indeed he would stand trial later for the murder of Durwin's housecarl; but because he was fairly certain that he would go straight to Eadwulf.

After Eadwulf's six men had left, Aldred sent a man to fetch the remainder of his housecarls. They were waiting out of sight in a wood five miles away. He hadn't wanted to arrive in the vicinity with a hundred men for fear of alerting his uncle to their presence. He was now gambling that, once he heard that Aldred had so few men with him, Eadwulf would sally forth with his whole garrison to kill him, and so it proved.

As some seventy men issued forth and came running down the hill towards the village, Aldred ordered the gates shut and his men manned the fighting platform around the palisade. He had chosen men who were adept with the bow as well as being good with spear and sword. He calculated that it would take about half an hour for the messenger to reach the camp and another thirty minutes for them to reach the village. His small force should be able to hold out that long, protected as they were by the palisade.

A lot of what had happened was unplanned. That morning Aldred and his small escort had set out from their campsite with the intention of carrying out a reconnaissance. It was purely fortuitous that the six men had left the fortress.

Most of the villagers were out in the fields getting in the harvest and so they had no idea what was going on. The village of Bebbanburg was a sizeable settlement with some eight hundred residents – almost a small town. Many of these were slaves, women and children, of course, but there were nearly two hundred freemen who formed the fyrd. Leaving the rest working, they raced back to the village in the belief that for some reason Eadwulf and his bunch of thugs were attacking their homes.

The thane's hall lay on top of a low hill to the south west of the fortress. Eadwulf's route took him round the outskirts which allowed the villagers to reach their homes and gather their weapons. Relieved that the village itself wasn't in danger, it soon became apparent to them that the target was the thane's hall. With a cry of rage, the reeve led them in that direction.

There wasn't much clear ground between the villager's nearest huts and the palisade but, as soon as the attackers started to run across the open space they were met by a dozen arrows followed by two more dozen in quick succession. Some ten of Eadwulf's men were killed or wounded during that first assault and they hesitated, arguing amongst themselves how best to scale the palisade. Eadwulf should have taken change but he was bereft of ideas. It wasn't a problem he had encountered before.

'We need ladders,' someone shouted and Eadwulf's men split into small groups to look for them.

Just at that moment the villagers arrived and attacked the isolated groups of warriors as they searched the village for anything that they could use to scale the palisade.

Compared to Eadwulf's housecarls, the villagers were poorly armed and trained and most lacked any form of armour. However, they outnumbered his warriors and what they lacked in equipment they made up for in courage and a burning hatred of their evil and craven earl.

When Aldred saw the villagers attacking his uncle's men he cursed. He could have easily held the palisade against Eadwulf until his other warriors arrived, but now he saw good men being killed needlessly.

'Open the gates, we need to go to their aid,' he yelled, running down from the walkway and heading for the gates as two of his men tugged them open.

With Ceadda at one shoulder and Durwin at the other he charged out and started attacking the enemy. His dozen men were right behind him and between them they drove the garrison of Bebbanburg back. The villagers swarmed into the narrow lanes leading to the hall and drove the men of the garrison towards Aldred. Eadwulf's housecarls were encircled and being forced into a smaller and smaller area every minute. Only those at the edge had room to wield their weapons effectively.

Eadwulf had stayed on his horse at the rear and quickly realised that his men were losing the fight. Kicking his heels into its side, he forced his horse through his own men and then through the villagers, wildly striking about him with his sword.

Aldred saw him break free and head back towards the fortress. He screamed in frustration but then he heard the pounding of hooves above the clash of weapons. He stood there, his mouth agape, as Eadulf and Gunwald led the rest of the armigers out of the compound and around the area of combat. They set off after Eadwulf and Aldred groaned.

'You fools,' he yelled impotently, 'you'll get yourselves killed.'

In keeping with the tradition on the Continent, armigers were non-combatants and only carried a dagger. The boys wore padded leather gambesons to protect them but no helmets. Then he saw that each armiger carried a spear which they had found somewhere and he breathed a sigh of relief. At least they now stood a chance against a fully armoured and armed man.

Eadulf and Gunwald raced to be the first to reach the former earl. Their mounts were tiring as they pounded up the slope towards the gates but Eadwulf's horse was carrying a much heavier rider wearing seventy pounds of chainmail and helmet. Slowly they gained on him but it was going to be a close run thing.

Eadwulf galloped through the open gates but there was no one there to close them behind him. The six armigers pounded up the cobbled road leading through the second gate and up onto the level ground on which the earl's hall stood.

Eadwulf realised that he was cornered and turned like a stag at bay. He drew his sword, settled his shield in place and kicked his horse into motion again. It had been years since he'd seen Eadulf but he bore a remarkable resemblance to his detested father, Uhtred. With a roar of rage he charged at his nephew, swinging his sword towards the boy's head.

Suddenly his horse stopped in its tracks, Gunwald's spear stuck in its chest. It reared up in agony and threw its rider over its rear end to land heavily on the ground. Eadwulf lay there painfully winded and unable to move. Eadulf dismounted and handed his horse's reins to Gunwald as the other armigers rode up to join him.

He walked slowly towards Eadwulf and knelt beside him.

'Goodbye, dearest uncle,' the boy said with a grim smile as he drew his dagger across the man's neck. He only managed to nick the left hand carotid artery but it was enough for the heart to pump out spurt after spurt of blood from the small hole. Eadulf stood up, his leather gambeson and face covered in bright arterial blood, and watched as his uncle slowly died.

He didn't hear the horse's hooves as they clattered over the cobbled roadway then ceased as Aldred reached the grass sward.

'You've cheated me of killing the gutless bastard,' he accused his brother angrily.

'Uhtred was my father as well as yours, Aldred,' Eadulf replied calmly, wiping his dagger clean on the hem of the dead man's tunic.

Aldred shook with rage. He had so wanted to be the man who killed both of the men responsible for their father's death. Now his brother had robbed him of his revenge on one of them. He took deep breaths until he calmed down. He reluctantly accepted that Eadulf also had a right to vengeance.

'Yes, he was, you're right. I'm sorry.'

He looked about him at the mighty stronghold in which he'd been brought up and suddenly he smiled.

'Welcome home, Eadulf.'

ALDRED AND EADULF WILL RETURN IN THE THIRD BOOK IN THE SERIES:

BLOODFEUD

Due Out in Summer 2019

Historical Note

The long but ultimately weak reign of Æthelred the Ill-advised - often mistakenly called Ethelred the Unready in the history books - led to a return of the invading Danes who Alfred the Great had fought a long and bitter war against in the ninth century. As a result the Danes, led by their king, Sweyn Forkbeard, and his son Cnut (or Canute), were more successful, eventually driving out Æthelred's family and taking the throne.

After his father's death a mere five months after been crowned King of England, Cnut was initially driven out and returned to Denmark where he raised a fresh army. He returned to England in August 1015 and over the next few months he pillaged most of the kingdom. In early 1016 Uhtred, the Earl of Northumbria, campaigned with Æthelred's eldest son, Edmund Ironside, in Cheshire and the surrounding shires. When he heard that Cnut was about to invade Northumbria, Uhtred returned to his earldom but he quickly realised that further opposition was futile and he agreed to submit.

Cnut summoned Uhtred to a meeting, possibly to get him to swear an oath in person. On his way there Uhtred and his escort of forty warriors were ambushed and killed by a Dane called Thurbrand. It's unclear whether he was acting on instructions from Cnut or not.

When Æthelred died on 23 April 1016 his son, Edmund Ironside, succeeded him. It was not until the summer of 1016 that any serious fighting took place. Edmund fought five battles against the Danes, culminating in his defeat on 18 October 1016 at the Battle of Assandun. Edmund and Cnut agreed to divide the kingdom, Edmund taking Wessex and Cnut the rest of the country, but Edmund died shortly afterwards. The cause of death may have been due to wounds received in battle or disease, but it is certainly a possibility that he was murdered.

Intent on keeping his succession secure, Cnut sent Edmund Ironside's two infant sons to his brother in Sweden with orders that they were to be quietly murdered. Instead, the princes were spared and sent to safety in the Kingdom of Hungary. Other members of Æthelred's family, including his son Edward - later to become King Edward the Confessor - fled to Normandy. With the last of the House of Wessex in exile, Cnut was now the undisputed ruler of all England and set about ruthlessly supressing any remaining pockets of opposition.

Uhtred was succeeded in Bernicia by his brother Eadwulf Cudel. Cnut made the Norwegian, Erik of Hlathir, Earl of York, thus balancing power in the north. By so doing he might have negated any opposition to his rule amongst the traditionally independently minded Northumbrians, but lack of cohesive government made the North much more vulnerable to attack by the Scots.

In the ninth century the Scots of Dalriada and the Picts had been united into one kingdom, initially called Alba and later Scotland. However, Strathclyde remained a separate kingdom, sometimes acknowledging Scottish dominion and sometimes not, until sometime between 1018 and 1054 when it was finally incorporated into Scotland. At the time of the Battle of Carham their King, Owain the Bald, was either a vassal of the Scots' king, Malcolm II, or his close ally.

Malcolm had managed to subdue internal resistance to his rule by the time of the battle but Caithness and Sutherland in the north, the Orkneys, the Shetlands and many of the Hebridean islands were occupied by Norsemen and were effectively either part of the Kingdom of Norway or independent jarldoms.

Little is known about the Battle of Carham itself. It probably took place nearer to the present village of Wark than it did to Carham; even the year is disputed. For a long time it was thought that it took place in 1016 and that the Northumbrian army was led by Earl Uhtred. However, other accounts state that he was killed in the first half of 1016 in an ambush whilst on his way to see King

Cnut, possible near Gainsborough in Lincolnshire or else at Wiheal in Yorkshire.

Many now believe that the year that the battle took place was 1018, two years after Uhtred's death. The evidence of the comet seen all over the known world in that year supports that date. If so the Northumbrians would have most probably been led by his younger brother, Eadwulf, who succeeded him as Earl of Bernicia: the northern part of Northumbria.

According to Symeon of Durham, who described Eadwulf as a very lazy and cowardly man, he ceded Lothian, the northern part of Bernicia, to the Scots after the battle. Eadwulf died sometime between 1020 and 1025 and I have chosen to use the earlier date.

He was succeeded as Earl of Bernicia by Uhtred's eldest son, Ealdred (called Aldred in the book as so many Anglo-Saxon names begin Ea). Ealdred's grandfather, Aldhun, Bishop of Durham, died in 1018 or 1019 when he would have been in his late fifties, or perhaps older. The myth is that he died of heartbreak following the defeat of the Northumbrians at Carham. It seems possible that, as the only bishop in Bernicia, he may have been present at the battle and, given the date of his death, might even have been killed, or died of wounds sustained there.

The death of Owain the Bold before the Battle of Carham is pure invention on my part. He is thought to have died during the battle, or possibly of the wounds afterwards. All that is (fairly) certain is that he was dead by 1030 and that Malcolm II – the King Malcolm in the story – merged Strathclyde with the rest of Scotland under his rule.

Finally, I need to say something about Findlay of Moray and his son, Macbeth. Little is known about Macbeth's early life. He was born around 1005, making him thirteen at the time of Carham. He was the son of Findlay of Moray and may have been a grandson of Malcolm II. He became Mormaer of Moray in 1032, and was probably responsible for the death of the previous mormaer, Gille Coemgáin. He subsequently married Gille Coemgáin's widow, Gruoch – Shakespeare's infamous Lady Macbeth.

According to the Annals of Ulster, Findlay was killed by his own people and the Annals of Tigernach say that the sons of Máel Brigte were responsible. The only sons we know of are Máel Coluim and Gille Coemgáin, both of whom evidently benefited from the killing as both succeeded him in turn as Mormaer.

Novels by H A Culley

The Normans Series
The Bastard's Crown
Death in the Forest
England in Anarchy
Caging the Lyon
Seeking Jerusalem

Robert the Bruce Trilogy
The Path to the Throne
The Winter King
After Bannockburn

Constantine Trilogy
Constantine – The Battle for Rome
Crispus Ascending
Death of the Innocent

Macedon Trilogy
The Strategos
The Sacred War
Alexander

The Rise of the Tudors Quartet
March Bravely into Hell

THE KINGS OF NORTHUMBRIA SERIES

Whiteblade
616 to 634 AD

Warriors of the North
634 to 642 AD

Bretwalda
642 to 656 AD

The Power and the Glory
656 to 670 AD

The Fall of the House of Æthelfrith
670 to 730 AD

Treasons, Stratagems and Spoils
737 to 796 AD

The Wolf and the Raven
821 to 862 AD

The Sons of the Raven
865 to 927 AD

EARLS OF NORTHUMBRIA SERIES

Uhtred the Bold
985 to 1016 AD

The Battle of Carham
1017-1018 AD

Made in the USA
Monee, IL
12 February 2020